Here are ... ad for enjoyme...

"This book is the perfect mix of mystery, humor, a sense of wonder, old-fashioned romance and good manners, science, history, and a great whodunit! Couldn't put it down!"
—Victoria Kashé

"It dances on the edge between fiction and non-fiction. Once you start reading this fascinating narrative you will find it difficult to put down. You will become friends with the good guys and distrust the bad guys. As you finish this story, you will want to know what happens next in the lives of both the aliens and earthlings. Perhaps this will remain a mystery, or they may emerge later. Stay tuned."
—Robert Gaylon Ross, Sr.

"A murder mystery, a love story, science fiction, women's liberation, all blended into one of the most interesting novels today. Like a great Russian novel, the reader becomes more involved, and fascination grows, with each page. At its ending we are both sad that it's over and satisfied with the reading, but want to know more about the Ezekiens and their motives for choosing the planet Earth for their colony. Something to think about, and make you reread it again later."
—Bill Ross

"I loved this story. It combines adventure, science, and an old-fashioned love story. I hope it becomes a movie."
—Louise Pepper

"Echo my wife's remarks above—plus, I'm not really a sci-fi reader, but got *so* into this story. Loved it."
—A.J. Pepper

FRIENDS OF THE EZEKIENS

A Sci-Fi Novel

Cecil Ross

Published by

RIE
1700-A R.R. 12, Suite 325
San Marcos, Texas 78666

Other Books By The Author:

Logical Physics
or
The Uncertainty Principle Is A Cop-Out

Copyright © 1997 by Cecil Ross
First printing January 1998

ISBN No. 0-9649888-2-8

All Rights Reserved,
including those to reproduce this book or parts
thereof in any form for use by anyone other than
the original purchaser.
Printed in the United States of America

For Kerry,
with a father's love.

And for my favorite niece.
I love you, Melinda,

Uncle Jack

PROLOGUE

January 1941

    Leona Graham huddled in darkness against a wall of a London subway. All about her were moans, cries, and screaming hysteria. An old woman beside her spoke aloud the words of the 23rd Psalm: '. . . Thy rod and Thy staff, they comfort me. . . .' Leona felt jarring thuds in the floor and the wall behind her, followed by showers of small debris and dust from the ceiling. She cringed, and clamped her eyelids tightly closed.

    This same experience had happened to her almost every night. It was the height of the famous London Blitz of World War II. Reich Marshal Hermann Goering had ordered the night air assaults to begin four months previously, after the Royal Air Force had coerced the Germans to give up daylight attacks.

    Leona recalled an event only six months ago: It was mid-afternoon, and she was sitting at her desk in school. She remembered having a mental vision of many Luftwaffe bombers approaching across the channel, and she clearly heard German voices above the sound of the engines. It was not her first vision, for she had heard the voices of people's minds as far back as she could remember, but this was different. Her mother and father were having tea at home, only a few blocks away. She suddenly stood up and screamed, startling her classmates. "Run, run! Go to the shelters!", she shouted, hoping that her parents would hear her warning. A moment later, air raid sirens began wailing the command to take shelter. She remembered their hurried march out of the building; how she had wanted to run home to see her parents before they died. She remembered her grief after the loss of her parents, and her shameful searching and begging for food, clothing, and clean water.

Another rain of bombs jarred her mind back to the present. Now, the people around her were almost quiet. They were thinking of their homes, or the last place they had slept; wondering if they had a place to live. German bombs would destroy or damage seven of every nine houses in London before the raids ended.

It seemed only a short while before she heard the all-clear signals. Some of the people lit emergency lamps, and began to leave. Many remained, including Leona. They knew that they had no place to go.

She slept for a while, and dreamed, but the cold, hard floor awakened her. By then, the subway was again brightly illuminated. She stood up, and looked around at other people trying to sleep. Something else had also caused her to awaken: a compelling need to go to the bridge.

Outside was pandemonium. Fires from burning buildings brightened the night. Volunteer firemen, already worn out from the night before, were doing their best to keep the fires from spreading. Leona began walking, unmindful of emergency volunteers telling her to go to a shelter. The fires were everywhere. She had to make detours many times, but always returned to the course that drew her. Somewhere ahead lay the bridge.

She thought again of her parents and her school friends, whom she would never see again, and the fires, and the war, and the hunger; they would all be gone.

The bridge loomed before her. She stepped aside to avoid a rushing ambulance, then stood beside a guard rail to wait. All became quiet. Suddenly, an intensely bright beam of blue light shone down on her. Her heart pounded, and

her breath exploded as she was drawn upward to the source of light.
    Leona Graham was then nine years old.

CHAPTER 1

May 1986

Eileen Two Bears had been murdered, and Ben now felt his lovely wife's presence replaced by a deep ache in his chest and a choking constriction in his throat. The murder made no sense at all to Ben, but he did not want to think about that yet. The depressing ritual of Eileen's funeral was over. Now he wanted to be alone with Trudy—to absorb his daughter's grief the way he had wanted to absorb her childhood aches and pains.

Trudy stood beside him waving good-bye to their guests as a white sedan turned into the paved driveway. They waited while the car stopped, and two neatly dressed people, a tall man and a woman, each carrying a briefcase, got out and approached them.

"Mr. Two Bears? Miss Two Bears?" The tall man spoke while they both reached into their jackets to produce wallets.

Ben nodded. "You must be Mr. Drake."

"Yes, sir. I'm Agent Drake and this is Agent Miller." They offered their wallets, displaying F.B.I. credentials. "We apologize for disturbing you at this time, but it's important that we talk to you while certain valuable information is fresh in your memory."

Ben understood such logic, but was forced to suppress a feeling of resentment because of the untimely interference. "Of course," he answered. "We understand. Will you come in?"

Ben and Trudy led the way into the living room as Trudy asked, "May I get you a cup of coffee?"

Agent Drake replied, "Yes, ma'am, thank you. We both drink it black." Agent Miller had not yet spoken a word.

When Trudy returned with the coffee, Agent Miller opened her briefcase, placed a tape recorder on the coffee table, and looked briefly at both of them as she spoke.

"I am required to inform you that this conversation will be recorded. May we have your permission to do so?"

Ben and Trudy nodded, then voiced their assent as Agent Miller stated the date and relevant case information, then turned to Agent Drake.

Agent Drake quickly scanned through several sheets of forms before speaking. "Mr. Two Bears, we know that you and your daughter have already been informed that your wife's death was not a result of natural causes." Trudy gasped. "I'm sorry, ma'am. Miss Two Bears, our records show that you live and work in Washington, D.C.. You share an apartment with Miss Kyoko Yamada. How long have you known Miss Yamada?"

"Kitty and I—that's her nickname—went to college together. We were members of the same sorority. I guess it's been about nine years. She graduated a year before I did, and went to Washington to work. I moved in with her shortly after I got a job there."

"What kind of work do you do?"

"I work for Ball Labs as a physicist. The nature of my work is classified because of the highly confidential government contracts."

"You're frequently seen with congressman Darrin Snell. What is your association with Congressman Snell?"

"Darrin and I have been dating for about two years. We're engaged to be married next April."

"Congressman Snell did not attend your mother's funeral. May I ask why?"

"He couldn't get away. There was an important vote. . . ." Trudy lowered her eyes and frowned, and wondered why she felt embarrassed to make such excuses for Darrin.

Agent drake continued, "Mrs. Two Bears spent several days in Washington just before her death. Did you spend much time together?"

"Oh, of course. She stayed with me in our apartment. We spent a lot of time together."

"Did she speak to you about her business in Washington?" About her associates?"

"No, not much. Mom and I don't . . . didn't agree in our views about women's rights. I understand her point of view, but the situation is changing—things are different now. She seemed very tired, and more upset about her work than usual. She said something one night that I didn't understand. She'd been very quiet for a while, then she said, as if speaking to herself, 'that woman is crazy—absolutely deranged!'. I asked her who she was talking about, but she refused to say more about it. Then she perked up, and everything was okay after that."

"Did she mention what she had done that day? Who she was with?"

"No, she didn't. But earlier, before I left for work, she said something about a luncheon meeting, and another important meeting in the afternoon. I wish she'd talked with me about it, but she said that she didn't want me involved in that 'mess'."

"What day was that?" Agent Drake asked. "Do you remember?"

"It was Wednesday. Last Wednesday."

"What about her last day? That would have been the following day, on Thursday. Can you think of anything that might have led to her death? Please excuse my abruptness;

this is very important."

Trudy did not speak for a full minute, while she hid her face in a handkerchief until the tightness in her chest subsided. Finally, she spoke in a choked voice. "Oh, I don't know . . . I just don't know. She said she was going home that night; that she wouldn't have time to see me before she left. She told me not to bother; that she'd get to the airport okay. We said good-bye. . . ." Trudy could not hold back any longer, and choked with convulsing sobs as her father held her in his arms.

Agent Drake looked downcast. "I'm very sorry, Miss Two Bears. Perhaps you'd like to leave the room for a while. Thank you for your cooperation."

Trudy quickly replied in a choked voice, "No, no, I'll stay. Please give me a moment to control myself. I'm sorry I've been such a baby."

Ben kissed her hand. "You've done just fine, honey. I hope I do as well."

Her crying ended in a few minutes, then she excused herself to bring in more coffee.

Agent Drake continued. "Mr. Two Bears, your wife was a well-known outspoken critic of the women's liberation movement. She must have received a lot of crank telephone calls before you had your number unlisted. Did she speak of any threats to her life, or did she receive any threatening letters?"

Ben looked directly into the agent's eyes while he spoke. "Well, she received quite a number of crank calls, and she did mention a couple that were threatening. I answered a few of those calls myself, some late at night, but she refused to let them bother her. I think I was more concerned about it than she was. Of course, the 'cranks' never gave a name, and they were too smart to call from a number where they could be traced. As for letters, I never read her mail. We can check her files though, if you think it might help."

"Yes, sir. It might be very helpful. We can do that later. Mrs. Two Bears made several calls to you while she was in Washington. Did she mention anything at all that we might connect with her death?"

"Eileen didn't talk much about her work, except to tell me that she'd found someone to take over a lot of the responsibility. She mentioned the lady's name—Marcella, I believe. She'd mentioned the name several times before, so I'm sure they'd worked together for some time. Another thing: she called me from the airport about thirty minutes before departure to let me know when to meet her. She sounded very tired. I asked what was wrong, and she said that it was no problem. '*India* has been giving me a lot of trouble,' she said. I asked when she'd gone to India, and she laughed—said she'd tell me all about it when she got home. I thought she talked very strangely, and I think there was something wrong with her then, but who would've thought. . . . If only I'd acted upon my hunch. I should've called airport security in Washington. I drove to the airport a little early to meet her. Don't ask me how, but I knew something dreadful had happened to her."

Trudy interrupted. "Oh, Pop, I felt it, too! But it was like a sketchy dream: so horrible that I forced it out of my mind." She hid her face again, but managed to keep from crying.

Ben nodded, and took her hand, then continued: "When the airport security and police officers boarded the plane, I asked one of the officials about my wife, and told him who I was. Then they took me into a private room, and explained what it was about. I remember very little of what happened after that."

"Thank you, sir", Drake said. "Now if you'll allow us to see your wife's files. . . ."

"Wait a minute," Ben replied. "Don't leave us hanging. We need some information, too."

"All right, sir, what would you like to know? We

have very little factual information at this time."

"Well, we want to know whatever you can tell us. All we know is that Eileen was murdered. How? Why? Who did it?"

Drake referred to his notes. "Mrs. Two Bears boarded a commercial aircraft in Washington, D.C. last Thursday night at 9:05 p.m., bound for Springwater, New Mexico. The aircraft made one brief, scheduled landing in Dallas before continuing to Springwater. The autopsy report indicates that Mrs. Two Bears died after the aircraft departed from Dallas. This was substantiated by a statement from the flight attendant, who observed that Mrs. Two Bears was breathing deeply, and was asleep while the aircraft was on the ground in Dallas. She was sitting in a window seat on the left side, in the smoking section at the rear of the aircraft."

"But Mom didn't smoke," Trudy interrupted. "Why would she be sitting in the smoking section?"

"Mrs. Two Bears' ticket and seat were reserved on the day before the flight, and she was able to get a reservation only because of a cancellation shortly before that. It was the only seat available, and there were no other cancellations."

Ben was exasperated. "But how could anyone be murdered on an airplane?" he asked. "People are crowded close together. Flight attendants continually walk up and down the aisle. And what about seat assignments? Surely the murderer was assigned the seat next to my wife's. Wouldn't someone remember who had that seat? Doesn't the airline keep records of those things?"

Agent Drake responded carefully, "We have a few good leads, and we're trying to investigate every person on that flight, but there are few records kept on people who pay cash for tickets purchased at the airport ticket counters. Names are easily falsified. Our agents have questioned a young man who sold his ticket to a woman at the boarding gate for five hundred dollars. He was happy to get the money, and asked no questions. His reserved seat was in the smoking section, but not the seat next to your wife. That seat was reserved by an elderly man who traded seats with a kindly woman asking to sit beside her sick friend.

"The description given by the elderly man was very vague, but the young man and the flight attendant gave us an accurate description of the same woman. She had a rather plain face; no make-up; short, straight blonde hair; about five feet ten inches tall; stout, very muscular build, and about forty years of age. She was described as being very calm and polite.

"It appears that the woman is totally fearless, and extremely dangerous. It is highly unlikely that someone would premeditate to commit murder on a crowded aircraft, simply because of the fear of being caught."

"I hate to ask this question," Trudy said, "but I have to know! How was my mother murdered? Did she have a horrible, painful death?"

"I believe you can rest assured that your mother felt no pain, although she did not die suddenly. The autopsy report states that she had ingested a slow-acting, but strong, sleep-inducing drug—probably before arriving at the airport, which might explain her strange telephone conversation with your father. She was in a state of deep sleep while the aircraft was on the ground at Dallas. Her death was caused by an extremely lethal poison that could only have been obtained from a highly sophisticated military arsenal. In this case, the reaction time was slowed because the poison was absorbed through the skin from a round adhesive patch applied to the inward side of Mrs. Two Bears' forearm. It was probably applied while passengers were departing.

"We now know that the suspect left the aircraft in Dallas. She informed the flight attendant, very pleasantly, that Mrs. Two Bears was then sleeping comfortably, and would probably feel much better when the aircraft arrived in

Springwater.

"Please understand that the information I've given you must remain confidential until this case is solved. We seldom divulge such evidence. In this case, however, we may need further cooperation from you. I must stress, especially to you, Miss Two Bears, that the people we're looking for are very dangerous and well organized."

"But you said 'people', which sounds to me as if more than one person is involved. What do you mean? And why especially me? That sounds distressing!"

"Yes, ma'am. We believe there are many more people involved. Your mother was not the first to die in this manner. Perhaps I can tell you more later, but not at this time. I must ask you to let me know when you expect to return to Washington."

"Now, hold on here!" Ben interrupted. "If my daughter is in danger, I want to know about it."

"I'm sorry, Sir. I certainly didn't mean to alarm you or Miss Two Bears. Your daughter is a very intelligent young woman. The fact that she is in sympathy with the women's liberation movement probably is in her favor, in this case."

Ben asked, "Are you saying that the women's lib movement is responsible for my wife's death?"

"No, sir. Not directly, that is. There are many good, well-meaning, dedicated women involved in their cause. We suspect, however, that another group of not-so-well-meaning fanatics are using the women's liberation movement as a shield. I'm afraid I can't tell you any more than that.

"Miss Two Bears is in an unfortunate position at this time. She lives in Washington, D.C., her famous mother was recently murdered, she is engaged to a U. S. congressman, she is sympathetic to the women's liberation movement—in opposition to her mother, and she works for a corporation that's heavily concerned with secret military contracts. Do you understand what that could mean? At the very least, both of you can expect to be bothered a great deal by news reporters."

Ben and Trudy looked incredulously at each other. It was a chilling thought, and each of them was concerned about the other.

With Ben's help, Agents Drake and Miller carefully examined Eileen's files. "Mr. Two Bears," Drake said, "We've found several letters and pages of notes that we'd like to examine further. Do you mind if we keep them for a while?"

"Not at all," Ben replied. "Keep them as long as you like. Would you like to examine the files in my office? It's upstairs."

"I think this will be enough, for now. We've bothered you enough. By the way, Mrs. Two Bears had no carry-on items with her on the aircraft. Did she normally carry an attache case when she traveled?"

"Why, yes, come to think of it, she always traveled with a briefcase. It was a simple, dark-brown leather case—quite worn, in fact—I intended to buy her a new one."

"I'm sure she must have had it with her," Trudy said. "She didn't leave it at my apartment. Do you think it was stolen by the . . . murderer?"

"Yes, ma'am, quite possibly."

CHAPTER 2

After the agents left, Ben and Trudy walked together as far as the den, then Trudy excused herself to fix their lunch. Ben sat in his recliner, looking around the large room. It was a comfortable house. He and Eileen had lived there for the last six years of her life. She had spent a lot of her spare time in the flower gardens beside the patio. Ben realized, almost with a shock, that her beautiful flowers would never receive such loving care again.

It occurred to him, now that he thought about it, that he could not remember a time that he had not known Eileen. They had grown up as next-door neighbors, and had literally been best friends for their entire lives. He remembered their confessions to each other—that they could not define a time when they had not been 'in love'; yet, they both had realized, for the first time, that they *were* in love when they were separated by the Korean war. Could it be possible to live without her again?

Ben had completed only two years of college when the United Nations asked its member countries to 'police' the conflict between North and South Korea. He enlisted in the Air Force, and was, immediately after advanced tactical training, sent to a combat squadron to fly the F-86 Sabre jet fighter. The war took its toll, and several of Ben's close friends were lost in combat; most of them had been shot down by Communist antiaircraft guns because UN planes had not been permitted to follow the Russian-built aircraft to their home bases across the Yalu River, which was the border between Korea and China. In spite of such stupid political strategy, fighter pilots instinctively followed the unwritten rule to 'Be tigers—bold if you must—just don't get caught!'. Ben had three MiG-15 kills when the truce agreement was signed in 1953.

He and Eileen were married soon after his arrival back home. Then, after six years of service, he decided to leave the Air Force, and to finish his education as an electronics engineer. It took two more years, and Eileen had worked hard for their support, but better times followed when Ben found a good job designing computers in California.

They had been married five years when Trudy was born. Trudy was a delightful child, who brought great pleasure to their happy marriage. Eileen could not bear to leave her baby in someone else's care, so she quit her promising career to be a full-time mother and housewife. It was a decision that she never regretted.

When Trudy was two years old, Ben had been offered a partnership in a small computer manufacturing company in Springwater, New Mexico. He accepted the offer, and helped turn the company into a large, successful corporation; later, becoming its president and general manager. Eileen was always the inspiration for his success. She picked up the pieces when he failed, encouraged him when he felt like quitting, and congratulated him when he succeeded. She was always there when he needed her.

In later years, Eileen had found herself with a lot of idle time, so she became interested in politics; not as a candidate, but as a working observer and critic. The women's liberation movement became her favorite target. Their doctrine of equal rights and pay, etc., was good, and as it should be, she thought, but they had become too fanatic and 'picky' about insignificant discrepancies. They were demeaning women who enjoyed a more traditional homemaker's role. Their campaign to legislate absolute equality for women, without considering the natural physical and emotional differences between men and women, was 'the last straw', in her opinion, and Eileen worked vigorously to organize opposition to the movement. Somehow, her political interests got out of hand, and she was away from home far more than she liked. Television talk shows, congressional hearings, club meetings, political endorsements, and many other commitments required her time.

Before her fatal trip to Washington (the last time that Ben had seen her alive), she had promised him that she would find someone else to carry-on the routine organizational and bureaucratic portions of the work for her. Now it was too late. Eileen was dead, and they had buried her body only yesterday.

When the grief became overwhelming, Ben walked outside to look at the scene beyond his home. He and Eileen had chosen the site on the ridge because of the beautiful panoramic view it provided. The patio faced to the south, toward a long, gradually descending slope of pine forest that ended abruptly at the base of a tremendous red cliff. The forest continued briefly above the cliff until it disappeared beyond another ridge. The canyon below rose upward to the west, narrowing until it blended into the side of a towering, multi-peaked mountain. To the east spread the desert, and the city of Springwater.

Later, just before sundown, the red cliff would brighten and call attention to its outstanding beauty. It would be one of the few times that Ben could remember watching the blazing cliff without his beloved Eileen at his side.

Trudy watched her father from the kitchen window. He was still a handsome man at age fifty-five, and displayed noticeable reminders of his past military background: a chin-up, chest-out, shoulders-back sort of man. His six-foot muscular frame showed only a slight bulge at his mid-section. She used to tell her friends that her Pop looked like Spencer Tracy with raven-black hair. Trudy was proud that she had inherited those large, bright amber, long-lashed eyes, but without their fighter pilot crow-feet wrinkles etched above his cheeks. It was a happy face, usually, but not now.

Their conversation during lunch was uncomfortable for both of them. Each wanted to talk of the obviously missing person, but neither wanted to rekindle the smoldering grief of the other. It was a natural feeling, although perhaps not a healthy one; a feeling that only time would ease.

After lunch, Ben sat at the kitchen table watching his daughter clean up the dishes. Her movements and looks reminded him of Eileen. Trudy was an inch or so taller, about five feet nine. Her shining brown hair was darker and longer than Eileen's pale blonde hair, falling to shoulder-length in loose curls. She had his amber eyes and high cheeks, but her strong, rounded jaw and chin were definitely Eileen's. Her most attractive facial feature was also Eileen's: beautiful, even, white teeth, and soft, puffy, red lips. Her well proportioned figure looked a bit more athletic than Eileen's, probably because Trudy exercised regularly. *These modern girls are going to change the world*, he thought, *but that's what people had said about modern women of the 20's too.*

Trudy wanted to ease the tension between them. "Pop, I've been thinking about you staying in this big house all alone after I leave. Why don't you take some time off, and go to D.C. with me?"

"Thanks, honey, but you and Kitty don't have room for me in your apartment, and I don't want to stay alone in some hotel. Besides, I'll be okay. I've been wanting to start my home-built airplane project. I already have the plans and materials, except for the engine. That'll keep me busy while I'm home."

"Wonderful! You've been talking about that for years. So you're finally going to do it, huh? Tell me about it."

Ben explained that the aircraft was supplied in a kit, and that it needed only to be assembled.

"Oh, I can hardly wait! Let me help you! I'm going to stay another week, so we can start right away. Please, Pop, we have to keep our minds busy on something, or we'll go crazy. I don't want to talk about Mom's murder now, and I don't want to think about it—its too soon. Let's go look...." She was interrupted by the door bell.

"I'll get it," Ben said.

A young man wearing a yellow blazer, and holding a microphone, stood close to the door. "Sir, are you Ben Two Bears?" He held the microphone out for Ben's answer.

Ben noticed a yellow van parked in his driveway, displaying "Channel Six News" on the side. A television cameraman stood nearby, directing his camera at the reporter, and then at Ben.

"Yes, I am. What can I do for you?"

"My name is Randy Sinclair, Channel Six News. I'd like to ask you some questions, sir. Is your daughter also here? I'd like to interview her, too, if you don't mind."

"What do you want to question me about, Mr. Sinclair?"

"It's about your deceased wife, Mr. Two Bears. We just found out from the coroner's report that Eileen Two Bears did not die of a heart attack, as we were led to believe. Sir, was Mrs. Two Bears' murder connected in any way to the women's liberation movement?"

Ben stepped back to close the door as another van turned into his driveway. "Young man, you're trespassing on my private property. Get away from here, and tell those other people to leave, too."

The reporter was persistent. "May I talk to your daughter, sir. We have an obligation to. . . ."

Ben closed and locked the door, and walked back to the kitchen. Trudy stood beside the table, angry and taut. Her small hands were clinched into tight little fists.

"Oh, that makes me so mad!" she said. "Now I know why the news media infuriated Mom so much!" Trudy looked out the window, then turned to Ben. "What do they intend to do, blockade the house?"

The vans had parked on both sides of the driveway, and they noticed that another was parking across the street.

"Not if I can help it!" Ben picked up the telephone receiver, and keyed the sheriff's number from memory. The anger in his voice had calmed somewhat by the time Sheriff Sam Lang reached the phone. Sheriff Lang expressed his sympathy, and assured Ben that a deputy would be sent out to disperse the newsmen. "Thanks Sam, we appreciate anything you can do." He hung up the receiver, and turned to Trudy, who had that look as if she knew that her Pop could do anything.

Ben owned fifteen long, fenced acres on the crest of an upsweeping ridge. A national forest bordered his property on the west, so his was the last private land at the end of the upward winding road. Within the hour a deputy arrived, and moved the newsmen away, but a few of the most persistent ones claimed their right to wait beyond Ben's eastern property line. A lone news helicopter hovered nearby for a while, noisily annoying, but it, too, soon left. There was no place that even a helicopter could land because of the towering pine trees.

"Pop, you're a wonder. I don't know how I'm

going to get along without you next week. Now, let's go have a look at your aircraft plans."

They walked into the shop where Ben had containers stacked almost to the ceiling. "Well, this is it," he said. "I've already taken care of the inventory, so all we have to do now is follow instructions."

"Gee, I had no idea there'd be this many parts. Where are we going to work, Pop? We can't build it in here; there isn't enough room."

"You figured that out all by yourself, did you?"

Trudy looked at him from the corner of her eyes, and he was smiling. It was good to see his sense of humor returning. It would take some time, but he was going to be all right. She smiled, and turned to face him. "Okay, my smart-aleck Pop, where do we work?"

"Remember the old rock barn up by the ledge?"

She recalled the old barn, only a short distance away, but hidden from the house by a dense grove of young pine trees. Beyond the barn was an outcropping of sandstone that she had once used as a shelter from the rain. "Sure, I remember, but the roof is all collapsed."

"Not any more. I had it all fixed up: new roof, new floor, electricity, telephone, running water, and even a toilet. How about that?"

"Well, I should've known! I suppose you even made a new door, big enough to bring out a new airplane. Never mind, I know you did."

When they had spread out the drawings and instruction manuals on the kitchen table, Ben turned serious for a moment. "Honey, I need to talk to you about something. Your Aunt Esther thought I needed some help with the house—you know how she is—so she hired a housekeeper for me. Is that all right with you?"

"Of course, Pop. Gee, I'm so thankful for Aunt Esther. That takes a big load off my mind. When does the new housekeeper start to work?"

"Maybe tomorrow, I think. I was afraid you might resent another woman coming in here so soon. I did, at first, but I don't know what else to do."

"Not at all. I like the idea very much. Now, explain these plans to me."

Leona, the new housekeeper, arrived by taxi early on the following morning. Trudy greeted her, and helped bring in her things.

"My goodness," Trudy said. "Did you come all the way up here in a taxi? Don't you have a car?"

Leona laughed loudly, for no particular reason that Trudy could see, and said, "Why would I need a car? I never go anywhere."

She spoke with a heavy cockney dialect, which told Trudy that Leona must be from the East End of London, possibly a recent immigrant. Furthermore, they were to learn that Leona laughed at almost everything, seeming to be constantly happy. She was very short, about five feet two; solidly plump; a small, round face with bright green eyes; small mouth and small teeth; and she wore her bright red hair in a tight bun at the back of her head. She was about fifty-five years old, twice widowed, and childless; apparently content to spend the rest of her life as a servant.

When introduced to Ben, Leona said, "Now, you mustn't worry, Mr. Two Bears, I shall take good care of your house!" Then she turned to Trudy. "You're so pretty, Miss Trudy, but you need to eat more. I shall take care of you. I'm a good cook!" She flashed a warm smile, and Trudy liked her immediately.

They finished moving the aircraft parts by ten o'clock, then stopped for a coffee break. "Gosh, it feels good to work," Trudy said. She set her cup on a work bench, and picked up the instruction manual. "Okay, here we go. Step number one." She read the instruction aloud, then repeated it after the parts were selected. The first sub-assembly, a very simple one, was finished after a few minutes, and she stepped back to examine their work. "See, this is a piece of cake. Nothing to it. We'll have this airplane flying by nightfall!"

By five o'clock, they agreed to quit for the day. Trudy again stepped back to examine their work.

"Gee, Pop, you'll never finish this thing! All that work, and it hasn't even begun to look like an airplane."

Time passed quickly, and the day arrived when Trudy had to return to Washington.

"I'm not ready to go back, Pop, but I must. You're doing just great—better than I expected—but now I'm afraid of what's ahead for me. Darrin hasn't called me for the last three days. I had to call him last night to ask if he wanted to meet me at the airport. Frankly, I'm beginning to wonder about that guy. It really hurt my feelings when he didn't come with me to Mom's funeral. He could've gotten away for at least one day if he'd wanted to. Do you know what I mean, Pop? Am I being too selfish?"

"I'd rather not criticize Darrin, honey, but I don't think you're being too selfish. Try not to worry about it, because I'm sure that everything will work out right."

"Oh, I guess so. But you're right. It won't help to worry about it. Let me say good-bye to Leona, and then we'll go to the airport. Will that bother you—the airport?"

He held his daughter in a close hug, and kissed her forehead. "Well, I suppose it will, but we can't bury our heads in the sand, can we? Don't worry about me, but I want you to promise that you'll call me if you run into any problems, or if you need my help."

Her smile was everything that he could ask for. "Okay, Pop, I promise."

As they left the mountain, Trudy's mind saw the image of a tall man in the distance. She was very relaxed; her head was resting against the back support; her eyes were closed. But he was there, suspended in black space before her; yet, too far away to distinguish features. He was not moving; just standing with his hands on his hips. His hair was pure white. Then he was gone. She knew that the same vision had previously appeared to her, but she could not understand why it seemed to be significant.

CHAPTER 3

Fortunately, there were no reporters to bother them at the Springwater airport. Trudy said a reluctant good-bye to her father, knowing that he would wait until her plane was out of sight before returning home.

She always had the same thought while boarding a commercial aircraft: *where are all these people going?*

After stowing her small tote bag under the middle seat in front of her, Trudy leaned back to relax. An extremely overweight young woman wearing skin-tight, cut-off denim shorts, struggled into the aisle seat on her left. Then, shortly afterward, a red-faced, gray headed man excused himself, and asked if he might be allowed to pass over to the window seat. Both women had to get up and step into the aisle while he made his way to the seat. *If the airlines were smart*, she thought, *they'd find a way to seat people in a more efficient manner.* Then she laughed at herself, realizing that Darrin would have been thinking the exact same thing, and would have probably gotten angry about it. Was she becoming as cynical as her fiance? The woman on her left draped her huge arms on both armrests.

The man on her right leaned close. "Hey, wanna' hear a cute little joke?"

"No, thank you. I just want to rest."

"Okay, honey, su'cher self. Just thought'cha might wanna' be friendly." His foul breath was almost more than Trudy could bear.

Once airborne, she adjusted the backrest as comfortably as possible, and tried to relax. Could this be the very same airplane in which her mother had died? Trudy's imagination pictured her mother in the last moments of life, and tears blurred her vision. Why would anyone want to kill her lovely mother, who would never even think of harming another person?

Trudy tried to force her mind to think logically. Agent Drake had given a small bit of information; surely the F.B.I. must know a great deal more. Why hadn't she thought to ask how they knew so quickly that her mother had been murdered? A small adhesive patch on her forearm would not seem to be much of a clue; lots of people use those things. And what about the sleep-inducing drug? Someone had given her a drug before she arrived at the airport. Who had she seen, and how did she get to the airport? A taxi? Or did someone else take her?

Also, she had told Pop on the phone that she had taken a trip to India. No, that's wrong. She had only said that India had been giving her trouble. A women's lib movement in India? Or a rival organization, opposed to women's lib? Or maybe the Indian government?

"Excuse me, honey. Would you tell that little girl ta' bring me a beer?" The red-faced man had broken her thoughts.

"Sir, I can't get out, either. If you can wait, she'll be back here in a moment, and you can ask her yourself."

"Okay, okay, sorry ta' trouble you."

It's impossible to concentrate on an airplane, Trudy thought. *Besides, the more I think about it, the more confused I get.*

But it also seemed impossible *not* to think about it. She decided to make an appointment with Marcella, the woman who was going to take over some of her mother's responsibility. Maybe Marcella would have some answers.

Congressman Darrin Snell was never late for anything. He arrived at the airport a few minutes early, allowing time for parking, and the long walk through the concourse to the gate where he would meet Trudy. Nothing about him was haphazard or unplanned, a characteristic that had caused problems with Trudy on several occasions. He recognized that he was a perfectionist; yet, he felt that it was a good trait for someone in his profession. He was, in fact, the ideal person for politics: tall, good-looking, intelligent, well-mannered, and a good talker.

He loved Trudy, but he often wondered if she was suited for a life of politics. Not that she wasn't a good hostess, or a good conversationalist—in those attributes she excelled. But she seemed to be too stubborn, even hardheaded at times—definitely not like his first wife, who had died in an automobile accident during his first term in Congress. Deborah had been too flexible, never having a solid opinion about anything.

Trudy's airplane was to be fifteen minutes late in arriving. That was always a great exasperation to Darrin. Why couldn't those people run an airline on schedule?

When Trudy walked into the concourse, she saw Darrin talking and laughing with a group of reporters. She waved, and he came to her immediately, took her hand luggage, and kissed her on the cheek.

"Well, that was a nice brotherly kiss," she said. "You act as if I have a big sore on my lip. What's wrong, Darrin?"

"I'm sorry. Please don't be so crude, Trudy. There are some reporters here who want to interview you."

She had been trying to shield her eyes from the camera flashes.

"Yes, that's quite obvious. Please get rid of them for me, Darrin."

"But why? They only want. . . ." He was

interrupted by one of the reporters.

"Miss Two Bears, please give us some statements about your mother's death. Who do you...."

"No! I will *not* give you any statements! Leave me alone!" She walked away, leaving Darrin standing with an incredulous look on his face.

He caught up with her, and took her arm. "Trudy, I can't believe this." He tried to smile as he hissed the words between his teeth. "These people are important to me." She kept walking. "Don't do this to me, Trudy. Don't you hear me?"

"Of course I hear you, Darrin. Tell them to leave me alone."

A television cameraman ran ahead, then turned around to record the scene as he walked backwards.

"Miss Two Bears, is there any truth to the rumor that there was a lot of jealousy within the leadership of your mother's organization?"

Trudy began to run, and the reporters hesitated. Darrin was visibly shaken, but stopped to make a statement. "Hey, listen, I'm sorry. Miss Two Bears is very upset about her mother's murder. This isn't like her. I'm sure she'll be glad to talk to you later, okay? Thanks for your cooperation."

He caught up with her in the baggage area.

"Trudy...."

"Don't wait for me, Darrin. I'll take a taxi."

"I *will* wait, and I'll take you to your apartment." He took a deep breath to calm his anger, realizing that the situation now called for intelligent strategy. "Trudy, be reasonable. They're not going to bother you any more now. Let's calm down and not make a scene. I'll bring the car around and load your baggage. Okay?"

She looked down to the floor, seeming to be in deep thought. Finally, with a much resigned voice, she replied, "All right, Darrin."

They spoke very little in the car as Darrin made his way through the heavy traffic. She watched his face, and knew that he was still angry because of the way his jaw muscles tightened. No matter, she was mad at him, too.

It was not their first argument. She remembered the time, at an important dinner party, when she had embarrassed him by arguing against his support of a military budget reduction.

"If you can't support me, then please don't argue against my views in public. It just doesn't look right for the future wife of a congressman to oppose his views." He had been upset with her for several days. Actually, her political opinions were conservative in some respects, and liberal in others.

"Darrin, do you think we should break our engagement?"

"Please, Trudy, let's not discuss that now. We're both angry, and this isn't a good time to talk about it."

They remained quiet until they entered Trudy's apartment. Kitty met them, and gave Trudy a great, long hug. She had attended Eileen's funeral, but had to return to Washington immediately afterward. "I've missed you so much, Trudy. Are you doing okay?"

"I'm doing fine, Kitty, and I've missed you, too. What's been going on?"

They sat and talked, Darrin acting as though he and Trudy had never had an argument.

"Trudy, the telephone has been ringing constantly—mostly reporters, wanting to know your father's unlisted phone number. Of course I didn't tell them. I hope they haven't been pestering you."

"Let's not talk about reporters now. That's a bad subject at the moment." She looked at Darrin, who quickly looked down at his hands.

"Oh, something else," Kitty said. "Senator Mary

Armstrong's secretary called yesterday. Senator Armstrong wants you to have lunch with her soon. She asked that you call her for an appointment. You never told me that you knew Senator Mary—that's what everyone calls her."

"I don't. All I know about her is that she is a very active leader in the women's lib movement. Mom spoke of her many times. Do you know her, Darrin?" Trudy tried to make her question sound friendly.

"Oh, sure. I'll introduce you to her if you like. She's a very headstrong lady. You two should get-along well together." He winced, and gritted his teeth after his remark.

Trudy could not help laughing. "All right, Darrin, I know how hardheaded I am, and I'm sorry that I embarrassed you, but you tried to sacrifice me to those hungry reporters. I'll forgive you, if you'll take Kitty and me to dinner."

He slapped his hands together. "It's a deal. You girls go put on your faces while I call for a reservation."

Two days later, at noon on Tuesday, Darrin ushered Trudy into Senator Mary Armstrong's offices. They were greeted by a tall, beautiful black woman, the most strikingly beautiful woman that Trudy had ever seen. She was dressed in a well-coordinated white jacket, navy silk bow blouse, a slim front-pleated white skirt, gold chain belt, and a two-strand necklace of freshwater pearls. Her beauty was accentuated by an unforced, pleasant smile.

"Well, it's nice to see you again, Congressman Snell." She offered her hand to Darrin, then to Trudy. "I'm Icy Brooks, Senator Armstrong's secretary. You must be Miss Two Bears. I'm pleased to meet you. Senator Armstrong asked me to show you in immediately."

She led the way as Trudy whispered, "Oh, Darrin, isn't she stunning? I could hardly take my eyes off her."

The senator was standing beside her desk reading a

letter as the door opened. She looked over her half-glasses, then smiled.

"Darrin, I'm so glad to see you."

"It's always a pleasure to see you, Senator Mary. May I present my fiance, Miss Trudy Two Bears."

"I'm most delighted to meet you, Trudy. And you look so much like your mother. My dear, I was terribly saddened when I heard of your mother's death. It was just dreadful. May I ask, are you recovering all right?"

"Yes, I'm doing fine, thank you. And I'm pleased to meet you too, Senator Armstrong. My mother spoke highly of you."

"Please, just call me Mary, or Senator Mary if you prefer. Sometimes I find it hard to accept the puffed-up formality in this city. Well, my dear, do you mind eating in our dining room, or would you prefer someplace else?"

"Please, let's eat in the Senate dining room. I've never been there before."

"Of course. They do tend to pamper us a great deal. You'll find the food to be excellent. Darrin, please join us, won't you?"

"No thanks, Senator Mary. I have an appointment for a late lunch. You two have a nice visit. I'll see you later, Trudy." He kissed her on the cheek, then left.

Trudy marveled at the material luxury of the senate office building. *So that's how they spend our money*, she thought. It was one of the many things that had exasperated her mother: how our government officials continually promised an austere federal budget, but insisted on luxuries for themselves.

Mary Armstrong had been a winning politician for the past thirty-five years. Mary's husband had been their state senator for a number of years before his death. Mary had then been appointed to fill the position for the remainder of his term. Upon the insistence of the party, she ran for the post at the next election, and won handily. She had been winning ever since, and had spent the last twenty-five years in Washington. She was growing old in public service. She had quit trying, many years ago, to impress people with her physical appearance. Now, at age sixty-five, Mary looked like a little gray-headed lady running the feed store back home. She held a position of tremendous power in Washington.

"My dear, I wanted to talk privately with you because I want you to know, as well as I know, that our women's liberation organization had absolutely nothing to do with your mother's unfortunate death." She looked thoughtful while spreading a generous amount of butter on her bread.

"I'm well aware of the malicious rumors going around, and it is very important to me that you do not believe such drivel. I have promised absolute cooperation with the F.B.I.. My dear, I want the person responsible for this vile crime to be punished as much as you do."

"Thank you so much for saying that," Trudy replied. She wiped her eyes to clear away sudden tears. "Oh, I'm so confused. I have confidence in the federal investigators, but I can't seem to think of anything else. I want to know who, and why?"

"Of course you do. Trudy, I must tell you something before you hear it from someone else. Your mother arranged a meeting before she left Washington. The meeting was held here, in my office. There were four women at the meeting, including your mother and another leader from her organization. The F.B.I. has been informed of every detail. I cannot believe that anyone at that meeting could be responsible for your mother's death."

"But I was under the impression that the F.B.I. didn't know who my mother was with. Would you please tell me their names?"

"Of course, but I would advise against your

contacting any of them, dear. You should not get involved. Please let the investigators handle it."

"I know that your advice is well intended, Senator Mary, and I believe you're sincere, but no one seems to understand how impossible it is for me to remain uninvolved. I haven't heard from the F.B.I. since our interview; I don't know who to call, and for all I know, my mother's murderer may never be caught. Please, if you don't mind, may I ask you some questions?"

"Well, if you must, of course. My dear, you must believe that I want to be your friend, and that I want to help you in any way that I can. But first, let me caution you: if you persist in this search, you will learn some awful things about politics, and about the unpleasant, often ugly, manner of some of the people we deal with. There are things happening underground in this issue of women's rights that even I don't understand. You may discover something about your mother that you will regret, although I would find that difficult to believe. Eileen always conducted herself in a respectable manner. What I'm trying to say, dear, is this: if you insist on pursuing your own investigation, please be cautious, and expect to be disappointed. I must say, also, that I think I do understand your need to know. I would probably feel the same as you do, under the same circumstances. But, for your sake, I urge you to be patient. You must not do anything that might interfere with proper investigation."

"But I won't. All I want is information."

Senator Mary was thoughtful for a moment, then smiled at Trudy. "My dear, you're so much like your mother. How may I help you?"

"Senator Mary, my father and I were told that my mother had ingested a sleep-inducing drug, probably before arriving at the airport. Of course, she might have taken the drug herself, but that doesn't seem logical. Do you know anything about who she was with, or what she did just before arriving at the airport?"

"Yes, I do know." Senator Mary noticed that Trudy seemed to relax, as if a weight had been removed from her. "Our meeting required more time than your mother had prepared for, so she had to rush to the airport immediately after leaving. She was accompanied by her associate, Mrs. Marcella Silman, who was also at the meeting. My chauffeur drove them to the airport in order to save time. To the best of my knowledge, they did not stop anywhere on the way, and Mrs. Silman was still in the car when your mother got out at the airport.

"The F.B.I. agents also informed me about the drug. This is difficult to explain, my dear, and I have given it much thought. You must be thinking that your mother might have been given the drug while in my office. In truth, it does seem logical; however, I cannot see how. Eileen never left her chair during the meeting, and she was very alert. We all had coffee about fifteen minutes before the meeting ended." Trudy appeared to become tense. "My dear, I poured and served the coffee, myself. It isn't possible that the coffee was drugged.

"You and I have known each other for only a few minutes, Trudy, but I sense that you believe I'm telling you the truth. Your mother and I had very strong arguments, but I always respected her, and I would never have wished her any harm."

Trudy looked down for a moment, then back to Senator Mary's eyes. "Yes, I do believe you, Senator Mary. Now, if I may have the name of the other woman at the meeting, I promise not to bother you with more questions on this subject."

Senator Mary's eyes twinkled. "I do believe you have a bit of politician in you, dear. The other woman was my secretary, whom I know very well, and whom I trust completely. Now, if I may change the subject, you're a very charming young lady, and I would like to know more about you."

They finished lunch with more pleasant conversation, each impressed with the other's acumen. Finally, Trudy asked to be excused, saying that she had to get back to work.

"My dear, it's been so refreshing to visit with a genuinely nice person for a change. I shall insist that Darrin bring you to my home for dinner, very soon."

CHAPTER 4

The rest of Trudy's afternoon was almost unproductive. Her work had always been interesting, even enjoyable, but now it was difficult to concentrate on her project.

For the past three years, she had been Dr. Mel Bonner's assistant; a coveted position, as viewed by her co-workers. Dr. Bonner became famous early in his career for his contributions to physical research, especially his experiments dealing with Einstein's theories. Now, at age seventy-six, his body was failing, but his mind was still clear and sharp. He had a marvelous sense of humor, and a remarkable attitude of life. Everyone loved him. He had never married, nor even hinted of a secret romance, stating that there had never been time in his life for a family.

Dr. Bonner was lured to Ball Labs ten years previously with a promise that he could choose his own research projects, virtually unrestricted by management. The research manager, Dr. Owen Smith, later had second thoughts about that decision, however, when Dr. Bonner had selected Trudy as his assistant for a new project. Dr. Smith had already promised the job to another female physicist, but was forced to back down by Dr. Bonner's insistence. Trudy was embarrassed when she later heard of the incident, but Dr. Bonner had only smiled and said, "All of those people were also well qualified, but I chose you because I like you." The matter was closed.

Dr. Bonner's early association with Albert Einstein had profoundly affected his thinking; especially Einstein's search for a *unified field theory*, which supposedly linked electromagnetism and gravitation in a single mathematical equation. But Einstein's theory was wrong, in Dr. Bonner's opinion; yet, it was only after his friend's death that Dr. Bonner was able to deduce a logical solution to the problem.

The problem, in his opinion, began when scientists first experimented with the curious results of attractive and repulsive static electric charges—even as far back as Thales of Greece, in the sixth century B.C.. Experimental work on static electric charges was made popular by Benjamin Franklin, who first assigned positive and negative electric polarity to the different charges in the 1740's. However, the first scientific documentation of the law of force between such charges is attributed to the eighteenth-century French physicist, Charles Coulomb, who supposedly proved that unlike charges (positive and negative) are attracted to each other, while like charges (positive and positive, or negative and negative) are repelled by each other. Coulomb's 'proof' was based on his observation that a hard rubber rod stroked with fur left an excess of negative charges on the rubber rod, which repelled other negatively charged objects, and attracted positively charged objects. The fur was proven to have a positive charge after stroking the rubber rod. Why, then, would the different materials exchange charges, if opposite kinds of charges are strongly attracted to each other? It was concluded that rubber has an *affinity* of some kind for negative charges, and fur an *affinity* for positive charges, so that, when rubbed together, each tends to pick up a different kind of charge.

A more logical reason, as concluded by Dr. Bonner, is that positive and negative forces are actually a result of *two opposite kinds of energy*. Attraction, which only occurs between *like* positive electric charges (the opposite of

Coulomb's observation), is a result of positive energy, while repulsion, which only occurs between like negative electric charges, is a result of negative energy. He defined positive energy as a behavior of *matter*, and negative energy as a behavior of *anti-matter*. His obvious conclusion was that anti-matter would also be *anti-gravitational* because of the repellent force.

Trudy was fascinated by Dr. Bonner's theory, and had worked very hard to help him support the theory with experimental research. It had taken three years to design, fabricate, and assemble the equipment that was needed. The actual experiment was scheduled to begin in about six months.

Her mother's death had been a tragic shock to Trudy. She knew that it had also affected her work and the project. When she had spoken to Dr. Bonner about it, his response had been sympathetic and reassuring.

"Your emotions were quite predictable, Trudy, and very normal. You and I have worked closely together for a long time; so you see, I know you quite well. I would not expect you to react otherwise, and neither should you. You must not think that your personal tragedy will upset the project. We have planned well, and kept very detailed records. So, you see, our project will continue, even without you or me."

It was almost five o'clock, and Trudy was writing notes in her journal when Dr. Owen Smith, the research manager, entered the room. Dr. Bonner had already gone.

"How's it going, Trudy?"

"Oh, hi, Dr. Smith. Everything is fine. I'm just about finished for the day."

Dr. Smith was silent for a moment as Trudy continued writing. He was an average looking man: about five feet ten, middle aged, wavy black hair, very light-complexioned; in most respects, good-looking. But Trudy did not like him. In fact, most of his subordinates did not like him. He had been employed by Ball Labs since its beginning, almost twenty years previously. His superiors knew of his unpopularity, but kept him in his position because he 'ran a tight ship'. He was also a 'womanizer', something that his superiors did not know, or chose to ignore, but the female employees knew very well.

"Hey, are you still going out with Congressman Snell?"

Trudy looked up with a frown. "Dr. Smith, why did you ask that question?"

"No reason, just conversation. The latest rumor is that you two aren't getting along very well. Is that true?"

Trudy did not answer, but continued her frowning look.

"Well," he continued, "I came in here to ask if you'd go out with me tonight—maybe dinner, but you don't seem to. . . ."

Try as she might, Trudy could no longer hold her anger, and Owen Smith, who just happened to be in the wrong place at the wrong time, became the recipient of her repressed emotions.

"Don't say any more, Dr. Smith. Since you came in here to ask a personal question, I'll give you a personal answer. My answer is the same as the last time, and the time before that, but this time I want it clearly understood: I won't go out with you tonight, or any other night. My personal life is none of your business. I've tried to maintain a polite professional relationship with you, but you've refused to let it remain that way. Now, I'm going to record this conversation in my journal. Is there anything else that I should add?"

His white face quickly changed to red, but he said no more. Then he turned, and walked from the room.

Trudy sat for a few minutes, thinking. Her work

would be much more pleasant if she never had to see that man. But maybe she had been too impatient. Maybe he was only trying to be a friend. She had actually been very rude to him, so she decided not to note the incident. After slamming her journal closed, it occurred to her that she suddenly felt much better. With a suppressed giggle, she thought, *a lot better than poor Dr. Smith, I'll bet.*

CHAPTER 5

It was Saturday afternoon in mid-August, three months after her mother's death. Trudy was thinking of her father while shopping through the mall. She had called him at least once every week, and he had called her more often. *Poor Pop*, she thought. *He's working himself sick, trying to keep his mind occupied. I wish I could be home with him, but I'm glad he has Leona to take care of the house. At least, I don't have to worry about him not eating good meals.* The thought of Leona made her smile. She was still thinking of Pop when someone called her name.

"Well, Miss Two Bears, is this your 'chores' day, or do you just enjoy bumping around in the crowd?" It was Icy Brooks, looking even more beautiful than the last time that Trudy had seen her.

"Oh, hi, Icy! Please call me Trudy. To be honest, I just love to shop. Do you come here often?"

"Only when I have to. I hate crowds. Frankly, I saw you from the next level up, and I've been trying to catch-up with you. Buy you a drink?"

"Thanks, but I don't drink alcohol. I'm a nut for coffee though, if you'd like a drink."

"That's okay . . . what I'd really like is a private talk with you. Do you have time for a chat?"

"Oooh, sounds mysterious. Sure, I have time."

"I was thinking of the little park outside. Maybe we could commandeer a secluded bench. Do you mind?"

Trudy laughed. "Goodness! Now you've aroused my curiosity. Let's go."

They found a bench in the shade of a large tree. A group of children were romping noisily, but far enough away not to be disturbing.

Trudy smiled as they sat down. "Why do I have the feeling that you're about to drop a bomb on me?"

Icy laughed, "Oh, it's nothing quite so drastic!" Her smile completely swept away any doubt of friendliness. "To put your mind at ease, I'll get right to the point, Trudy. I already know that you're in favor of equality for women. Have you ever heard of the women's organization called W.E.B. (Women Escape Bondage)?" Icy was 'fishing'. She knew that Trudy was not an active member of any women's lib group, but she wanted to determine the depth of Trudy's interest.

Trudy looked surprised, then she laughed. "Bondage? Sounds a bit melodramatic." Then her smile faded. "I'm sorry. You're serious about this, aren't you?"

Icy held her smile. "I suppose it does sound corny, but . . . yes, I'm quite serious. Shall I continue?"

"By all means! You've certainly captured my interest. Is this something you're involved in?"

Icy was now committed; she had to continue. "Yes. It's a very secret women's society."

"But now it's no longer a secret, to me, is it? Somehow I have the feeling that this meeting was planned. Want to explain?"

Icy laughed. "You're very perceptive, Trudy, and absolutely correct. But I didn't really lie to you. I saw you in the mall, by chance, then made a quick decision that now was a good time to approach you. I do my research very thoroughly, and I know you quite well—much better than you realize. So, I'm convinced that you would be a great asset to our society; hence, the reason I accosted you. I wanted to invite you to join our organization."

"Well, now you'll have to tell me about it. Obviously, the secret part is working. But why secret? And what's it all about—your doctrine?"

"Okay, let's start with what it's all about. We believe that women all over the world are suppressed, simply because the old traditions cast them as the weaker sex. Our objective is to change that condition. We believe that women are not only equal to men, but superior. As to secrecy, our society is secret, simply because it *must* be. Otherwise, it would be destroyed, even before it's organized."

"Destroyed by whom?"

"By the enemy, of course—men."

"Oh, Icy! I couldn't view men as my enemy. How could the human species continue without our relationship with men?"

"We aren't talking about the same thing, Trudy. Certainly we must coexist with men. We aren't against romance, love, and personal relationships—that's entirely another subject. I'm talking about the repression of women. Just hear me out, and then think about it. Okay?"

"Okay, I'm sorry. But while we're on the subject of secrecy, aren't you afraid that someone within the society might defect and tell all? That would seem to be a distinct possibility if your organization is very large."

"A very astute observation. This is the hardest part to explain. Our membership is organized in tiers of rank, like a pyramid. New members enter at the basic level, or the learning tier. Each new member is assigned to a host member, who's always a member of the second tier. That host may be responsible for as many as three basics, but the basics are usually unknown to each other. A host of the third tier may be responsible for three members of the second tier, and so-on, up to the top. In most cases, no member is acquainted with any other member, except her host. I'm an exception because it's my duty to recruit and test new members."

"But how do you communicate information? Don't you have meetings?"

"There are never any meetings. All information is communicated orally, either upward or downward, by a host." [Here, she lied. Her explanation to Trudy applied to members in the third tier and below. Members above the third tier held regular meetings, and were well known to each other. Trudy had no need to know that yet, so Icy felt that her lie was justified.] "So, you see, even if a host defects, she can only name five other members, including her own host and me. The organization cannot fail. We do have a weakness in the structure, however, but it isn't a serious one. It's possible that a potential recruit may be an informant—that's *my* problem. But, as I said, I do my research very thoroughly before I expose the society."

"How do you know that I won't expose you?"

"Oh, I don't know. But you have no reason to expose us, do you? And besides, what information could you expose—the idea that we want to help women?"

Trudy laughed. "I see what you mean. Well, you've certainly aroused my interest. How do you plan to bring about this great change to uplift women?"

"Ah! Now you've asked a forbidden question. I can't tell you the answer at this time. That must come later as part of your learning experience."

"Okay, but I still have other questions. How big is your society; I mean, how extensive?"

"Well, I couldn't tell you that yet, even if I knew. But I can tell you that we're international, even though we've been organized for only a few years."

"All right, now the big question: Why do you need me? How would I be an asset?"

"Frankly, I can't think of a reason why you *wouldn't* be an asset. But first, let me tell you that a great number of our members are professional business women. Many of them are scientists, like yourself. I think you'd be surprised to learn who some of them are. But we're especially interested in you because you're a physicist. Beyond that, I can say no more at this time. We intend to be well-diversified."

"Uh-oh, now you've hit a sensitive area. Since you seem to know me so well, then you must know that my work is highly classified. I'd never, in any way, jeopardize the security of our country."

"Oh, come on, Trudy!" Icy was still smiling. "We're *all* patriotic women! We wouldn't want you if you felt differently."

Trudy looked down, feeling a bit intimidated.

Icy immediately saw that Trudy was very sensitive about loyalty. *Excellent*, she thought, and then said, "Maybe that was a bit too strong, Trudy. Of course we'd never expect you to compromise your loyalty."

Trudy was thinking of her next question, expecting that it would not be answered. She studied Icy's expression. "Icy, is Senator Mary a member of your society? Does she know that you're a member?"

Icy's expression indicated no surprise at the question. Her self-control was extraordinary. She smiled. "I really should refuse to answer that question, but I won't because I sense that my answer might determine whether or not you decide to join us. Actually, I doubt that Senator Armstrong is a member because she's so involved in the women's lib movement. I also strongly doubt that she knows of my involvement. However, my answer to both questions could be wrong if she is a member in a tier above me. I really have no way of knowing, but if she *is* a member, then we're very fortunate."

"Thank you. Now, if you don't mind, I'd like to change the subject for a moment." She waited for Icy's nod, then continued. "You were in the meeting with my mother and Senator Mary on the day that my mother was murdered.

Mrs. Silman was also present. Is there anything that you can tell me that might help to ease my mind about it? I know that she was drugged sometime that evening."

Icy appeared to relax. "Well, I'm glad you brought up the subject, Trudy. I didn't know if I should speak of it. First, I want to say how sorry I am . . . about your mother's death. I've wished many times that I'd spoken to her about the W.E.B. society. I'm sure she would have approved. Her objection to the women's lib movement was directed at their nitpicking politics, not women's rights. And I agreed with her—those women are just wasting their time by quibbling. Our W.E.B organization intends to *do* something for women! I'm sorry, Trudy. I tend to get a little upset about that subject. About your mother, I'm afraid that I can't offer you anything but speculation, and that isn't what you want."

"Oh, but it is! So far, I've gotten nothing but a few isolated facts, and they've led to nowhere! I'd like very much to hear your opinion."

Icy was apprehensive. "Really, Trudy, I. . . . Very well, have you spoken to Marcella Silman?"

"No. I've written to her, trying to set-up an appointment, but she hasn't responded. Why?"

"I'll probably regret saying this, Trudy, but maybe you shouldn't try to see her." Icy seemed to be fighting with her conscience. "Everyone knows that Marcella was jealous of your mother—they fought continuously. Didn't you know that?"

Trudy's eyes grew larger. "No, I had no idea. Mom never talked to me about it. But surely the F.B.I. must know. . . ."

"I'm sure they do. Listen, Trudy, this is no good. It's only speculation on my part, and it serves no purpose, other than to upset you. I'd rather not say any more." She looked at her watch. "Darn! I'm supposed to meet someone. Please excuse me, Trudy. Is there anything else you'd like to know about the W.E.B. society?"

Trudy was obviously disappointed, and faltered in her next sentence. "Oh . . . no, I guess not. I'm impressed, Icy. But you'll have to allow me a lot of time to think about it. I'm very careful in making decisions of this kind. Thank you for considering me."

"It's been my pleasure, Trudy. Believe me, I'm impressed with you, too. Don't hurry your decision. This is much too important to rush into. In the meantime, if you have more questions, please feel free to give me a call, and I'll meet you again. But don't mention names. We never discuss the society over the telephone. Well, thanks for your time. I'll keep in touch." Icy left, feeling satisfied, and in control of the situation. She had planted the seed, now it must have time to grow.

Trudy lay awake for several hours that night, thinking about Icy and the secret W.E.B. society. Icy's statement about the suppression of women was true; she had experienced it in her own life, both personally and professionally. Even Darrin was suppressive. How many times had he left in a sullen or angry mood, simply because she had refused to be dominated?

Ball Labs was the only place she had worked professionally, but she had often seen first-hand evidence of female suppression there. Owen Smith was a prime example: it was almost an every day joking matter that some female employee had felt the pressure of his influence. *If I've seen it in my own life, as a small example*, she thought, *just imagine how widespread it is across the whole country—the whole world, in fact*. But was it really that bad, or did it appear to be so, only because of the attention given to it by the news media, talk shows, and the recent flood of books on the subject? And, if female mistreatment was as bad as the publicity indicated, did it justify the extreme solution suggested by Icy Brooks?

Another thought suddenly entered Trudy's mind. Icy's W.E.B. society was deliberately kept secret. Agent Drake had spoken of a group of not-so-well-meaning fanatics that used the women's lib movement as a shield. Also, Senator Mary had mentioned that there were things happening underground in the issue of women's rights that even she did not understand. Could Icy's secret society be that mysterious organization: the one responsible for her mother's death? There was no logical reason to support such thoughts, and Icy seemed like a very nice person. It just didn't make sense.

Then Trudy suddenly sat up in bed, pressing her palms to her forehead. *Trudy, you fool. Wake up! You're not a child. Things aren't the way you'd like them to be. This is the real world — the world exactly as it's shown on the television news; greed, selfishness, pain, hunger, disease, narcotics, and crime.* The realization of her predicament caused a cold sweat to ooze from her skin. Agent Drake and Senator Mary were right. They had tried to warn her. What else could they do, lead her around by the hand?

What do I do now?, she asked herself. Obviously, she would have to be very cautious. If her suspicions of Icy Brooks were correct, then she must stall the decision to join the secret society for as long as possible; yet, she must hide her nervousness, and appear to be interested, but undecided. If the secret society was vicious enough to condone murder (evidently, several murders, as implied by Agent Drake), then her own life might very possibly be in danger.

She tried to relax; to forget her problems. She'd never get to sleep with those kinds of ideas in mind. Another thought crept in: *What am I going to do about Darrin? Do I really love that jerk?* She laughed at herself. *Well, he really is a jerk.* But Darrin was just another problem, so she forced him out of her mind.

She slowly relaxed, and closed her eyes. Presently,

the tall man of her previous visions again appeared before her. This time he was much closer, but she still could not distinguish his features. His hair was pure white, and she could see the shine of a gold band around his head. A name actually popped into her mind for an instant, then it was gone, and she could not remember. He just stood there with his hands on his hips, but his presence seemed to allow her to relax even more. Then, as quickly as he appeared, he was gone. It was very strange; yet, not at all distressing. Somehow, the thought of him was very soothing to her mind. *A space ship? Goodness! How did that thought enter my mind? What does all this mean? Why these recurring visions, and why the same figure every time?* Trudy's mind finally relaxed completely, and she drifted off into a deep, restful sleep.

CHAPTER 6

Trudy still could not get Marcella Silman out of her thoughts, and in a telephone conversation with another of Eileen's former associates, she learned that Marcella had given up her position, and was no longer active in the movement. She had virtually secluded herself to the confines of her home. The latest rumor was that Marcella had suffered a nervous breakdown, and had refused to see or talk with anyone.

A month later, Trudy made a hasty decision, and drove to Richmond where Marcella lived. Maybe it was a foolish thought, but Trudy reasoned that, if her mother and Mrs. Silman had, indeed, fought over the leadership of their movement, then Mrs. Silman would not have given up the opportunity to take charge after Eileen's death.

It was just after noon when she finally located Marcella's home, and parked in the driveway. All was quiet. The drapes were drawn, and the lawn had been badly neglected. She noticed, by chance, after slamming her car door closed, that one of the window drapes moved slightly aside, then quickly closed again.

Trudy pressed the doorbell button, heard the muffled chimes inside, and waited. She pressed the button again, but still no answer.

"Mrs. Silman, if you can hear me, I'm Trudy Two Bears. I know you're home. Please let me talk with you."

She knocked on the door, and heard a faint sob from the other side. "I mean you no harm, Mrs. Silman. I only want to talk."

She waited for several minutes, knocking and ringing the doorbell, then dejectedly gave up and walked back to her car.

Oh, Eileen, please don't leave — I'm so afraid! Trudy was shocked; there had been no sound of a voice — only a distressed message in her mind. She hurried back to the door.

"Mrs. Silman, I heard you. Please don't be afraid of me, I want to help you."

A moment passed, then she heard the door lock click, and the door opened. She quickly stepped inside as the door closed behind her. The room was dark. Marcella stepped away, keeping her eyes on Trudy.

What a pitiful sight! Marcella had obviously not bathed for several days, at least. Her eyes were baggy and bloodshot, her teeth and fingers were stained from smoking too much, and the house reeked of stale cigarette smoke. Her gray hair hung greasily, and her dressing gown was filthy from having been worn for many days.

"Oh, Mrs. Silman, you look . . . [Trudy almost used the word 'terrible', then caught herself] so frightened. Is there anything I can do for you? I'd like to help."

"No. What do you want?" Then, with a sudden change of attitude, she motioned for Trudy to follow her. "I'll make us some coffee, Eileen."

Trudy followed her to the kitchen, which was much better lighted, but cluttered and dirty. Marcella turned, smiling. "I've missed you so much. . . ." She recoiled in fright. "You're not Eileen! Who are you?"

"Mrs. Silman, I'm Trudy — Eileen's daughter. Please don't be afraid."

"Trudy?" Marcella's mind fought for control, then she approached, and touched Trudy's face. "You look like

Eileen. You're Eileen's daughter?"

"Yes, and I'm your friend." She stroked Marcella's arm, then led her to a chair at the kitchen table. "Why don't you sit down, and let me make the coffee. Okay?" Marcella smiled, and sat down to light another cigarette.

Trudy opened a door that led outside to an open porch. "I'm just going to let-in some fresh air." She smiled. "Have you had lunch? May I fix you something to eat? You look starved."

Marcella's eyes followed Trudy's every move, but she said nothing. Trudy searched until she found some canned vegetable soup and crackers, then went about fixing it for lunch. When it was ready, she placed the small meal before Marcella, and brought a cup of coffee for each of them.

Marcella ate the soup and crackers hungrily, then sat back to smoke, and watch Trudy. "I miss your mother very much, Trudy." As if there was no more to say about it, she changed the subject. "I'm sorry, but you can't stay long—I'm very ill. How may I help you?"

Trudy was caught off-guard by Marcella's sudden composure. "Oh, I . . . I only came to ask a few questions." She hesitated for a moment, while trying to think. "Do you remember what happened to my mother?"

"Of course. She was murdered." Marcella was evidently lucid, at least for the present time.

"Mrs. Silman, before my mother boarded the airplane that night, she spoke with my father on the telephone. She talked very strangely. Do you know that she'd been drugged?"

Marcella raised one eyebrow, and puckered her lips. "I see. Trudy, had I known that you were going to pursue an investigation, I would have refused to let you in. You tricked me!"

"No, I thought it would be okay. You seemed to be feeling better. Mrs. Silman, I don't want to cause you any problems, but—please, you were my mother's friend. Can't you understand how I feel?"

Marcella sat quietly for several seconds. She rested her elbow on the table, and bowed her head to touch her brow. "Yes, I suppose I can understand that." She sighed deeply, then paused before saying more. "I'm sorry, Trudy. You can see the filthy mess I'm in. Please accept my apology. To be honest with you, I was afraid I was going crazy, but I'm okay now. Seeing you has been a strain on my nerves. I actually thought that you were Eileen. I do miss your mother. She never seemed to let things bother her." Another deep sigh. "I learned from the F.B.I. investigators that Eileen had been drugged. They questioned me for quite a long time. The reporters. . . . Well, I'm sure you know about them. I'm so sorry, Trudy. You must be hurting terribly."

Trudy reached across the table to take Marcella's hand. "It's all right, Mrs. Silman, I'm fine. But I'm honestly worried about you. Is there anything I can do? May I take you to see a doctor?"

"No, I'm okay now. I think it's helping me to talk." She frowned at the cigarette in her fingers. "These darned cigarettes are killing me!" She coughed while mashing it out in the ash tray. "Trudy, are you rushed for time?"

"No, I'm in no hurry. May I do something for you?"

"No, there's nothing you can do, but I can't stand this embarrassing filth any longer. Do you mind if I clean myself up? Then we can talk."

Trudy smiled. "Okay, then I'll clean up the kitchen while I'm waiting."

Marcella appeared to be feeling better as she left the room.

The change was amazing. Marcella smiled when she reentered the kitchen. She had bathed, put on a nice dress, made up her face, and fixed her hair into a neat pageboy style. "The kitchen looks as good as I feel. Thank you, Trudy. Now I'll have another cup of that coffee, and we can talk."

After they settled back at the table, Marcella continued. "Let me start by telling you of the meeting. Do you know of the meeting in Senator Armstrong's office?"

Trudy nodded. "I only know that a meeting was held, and the names of the women present."

"Well, it began badly and ended badly. Everyone seemed to be in a sour mood. Your mother called for the meeting in order to prevent a lot of trouble because of that latest outbreak of abortion clinic bombings. Your mother and Senator Armstrong tried to remain calm, but I'm afraid I.... Well, it was that heartless, smiling *India* who made me furious. That woman...."

"Wait! What did you say? India?" Trudy was obviously alarmed by the word.

Marcella was puzzled. "Why, yes. India Brooks. India is...."

Trudy gently bumped her head on the table. "Awww, geee. Of course! 'Icy' is only a nickname, isn't it?"

"Trudy, what on earth is wrong?"

"I don't know, Mrs. Silman. Mom told my Pop that 'India' had been giving her trouble. We assumed that she was talking about the country."

"Ha! The country of India would be hard pressed to match anyone as vile as India Brooks. The nickname—very appropriate, indeed—came from her initials: I. C. Brooks."

Trudy brought her hand to her forehead. "I must be terribly confused, Mrs. Silman. You *are* speaking of Senator Mary's secretary, aren't you?"

"Yes, I certainly am. Listen, Trudy, I don't know if you're associated with India Brooks, but if you are, then I must advise you to choose your friends more carefully."

Marcella had abandoned her guard.

"I've only seen her twice, but she seemed to be such a nice person."

"Then I'm glad to have the opportunity to enlighten you. Your mother was beginning to collect a nice fat file on that 'nice' person. For beginners, India Brooks owns a very exclusive, very illegal gambling casino only a few miles from Washington. It doesn't require much imagination to think of the influence that she must have with some of Washington's elite."

Trudy was dumbfounded. "I believe I've been quite naive, Mrs. Silman. It isn't a very flattering feeling. Please go on."

Marcella fought hard to regain her composure. "I was going to tell you about the meeting, wasn't I? Your mother and I were terribly upset about those despicable abortion clinic bombings. No right-thinking person would attempt to solve the problem with such violence; yet, our organization was being blamed.

"But to begin: we were shocked when we entered Senator Armstrong's reception office. India Brooks received us. Of course, she was all smiles, and she said, 'Oh, *really*, ladies—*bombs?*' Then she laughed, and motioned for us to follow her into Senator Armstrong's office. Trudy, I was furious! India walked to Senator Armstrong's side, and turned toward us with nothing but calm innocence on her face. And there stood Eileen and I, looking as if we wanted to fight the Senator. Well, we were speechless!"

Trudy could not believe her ears. It seemed impossible that they could be speaking of the same woman. She felt that her entire experience and association with people had taught her nothing; that she could never again trust her judgments of character.

Marcella lowered her head, and covered her face with her hands for a long while. Then she looked up and continued. Her voice was weak, and she spoke with difficulty. "Oh, India is very smart—I won't deny that. She certainly made us look foolish, which, I'm sure was her intention. But we were able, somehow, to get on with our meeting. Then Eileen brought up the subject of an underground group of women, whom she thought were the true villains. I particularly watched India's expression, but there was no indication of surprise; nor was Senator Armstrong surprised. The Senator said she'd heard of the group, but that she knew of no proof that such an organization existed.

"That's when I made a terrible mistake. I said, 'Oh, we have the proof, all right', *and I patted Eileen's briefcase!* Oh Trudy, I can't ask you to forgive me because I can't forgive myself. Your mother's murder was my fault! That's why I couldn't go to her funeral. That's why I couldn't call you or your father." Tears streamed down her cheeks.

"Oh, no, Mrs. Silman!" Trudy reached for Marcella's hands. "No. You can't blame yourself. How could you have known? No wonder you've been so depressed!"

She allowed Marcella time to recover. "Mrs. Silman, it took a great deal of courage for you to tell me that, and I thank you with all my heart. Look, let's go for a walk. You need to get this out of your system, and I need some answers. Okay?"

They left the house, and walked down the street to a small park. The sky was overcast, threatening rain. A light wind scattered scraps of paper over the lawn. They walked slowly, Trudy holding Marcella's arm.

"Mrs. Silman, did you tell the F.B.I. investigators everything that you've just told me?"

"No, Trudy, and I'm so ashamed. But I just couldn't tell them what I knew of the W.E.B.." She explained her knowledge of the W.E.B. society to Trudy.

"Could you tell me—were the investigators Agents Drake and Miller?"

"Yes, they told me that they'd talked to you and your father."

"I don't understand. Mrs. Silman, please, I don't want to alarm you, but if the W.E.B. organization was so desperate to murder my mother—because of what she might know—then, why have they left *you* alone? They surely knew that you would be questioned by the F.B.I.."

"Why, indeed? Don't think I haven't been worried about it. That's why I didn't tell the investigators. Trudy, don't you see? Agent Miller is a woman. What if she's a W.E.B. member? Maybe the only reason I'm alive today is because I've kept my mouth shut." She stopped walking, and squeezed Trudy's arm. "But I'm talking to you, aren't I? Oh, Trudy, please tell me that I can trust you."

Trudy hugged her new friend, and patted her gently on the back. "Of course you can trust me." She looked up when she felt a drop of rain, and suggested that they return to Marcella's home.

When they were back in the kitchen, Trudy continued with her questions. "You said that the meeting ended badly. What happened?"

"Why, your mother all but accused India Brooks of being a member of that underground group."

"Was that before, or after Senator Mary served the coffee?"

"It was before. India remained cool, naturally, but the Senator almost lost her temper, and demanded that Eileen should produce proof if she intended to accuse anyone. Eileen said that she wasn't yet ready to produce proof; that she was reluctant to disclose her source of information. Then she smoothed everything over, and we were able to have coffee without fighting. Your mother was like that; she was very tactful and diplomatic."

"Tell me more about the coffee. Who made it?"

"I suppose India brewed it. She left the meeting and brought it in, but the Senator poured and served it. Oh, I've thought about it over and over, Trudy. I'm sure I've missed nothing. Eileen *must* have been drugged by the coffee. But, if so, why weren't the rest of us affected? I didn't feel anything, and I know that India and Senator Armstrong were not affected, either. The Senator's chauffeur drove us to the airport, and Eileen's flight was almost ready, so she had no time to even get a drink. It *must* have been the coffee! Why haven't they been arrested?"

"Well, I assume it's because they don't have enough proof. Why would Senator Mary be so protective of her secretary? I should think she'd want to know the truth."

"Why, Trudy, didn't your mother tell you? Senator Armstrong was India Brooks' benefactress since childhood. She raised the girl as a foster child, then paid for her support and education through college."

"No, I didn't know. But why? How did you know that?"

"You'd be surprised at how many people step forward to offer information to us, especially if they sympathize with our movement. In a way, I feel sorry for India Brooks—certainly as a child. Her mother and stepfather abused her horribly and frequently, until she was taken away from them at the age of eight. Maybe that's reason enough for her present behavior." Marcella took a deep breath, and expelled it slowly. "So, Senator Armstrong heard of the child's misfortune, and took her into her own home. The child's destiny was completely reversed: from rags to riches, you might say."

"Yes, I see what you mean," Trudy responded. "It's an incredible story. I find myself hating her at one moment, and loving her the next. What a terrible tragedy!"

Both women thought quietly to themselves for a

while, then Trudy asked, "Mrs. Silman, who was my mother's informant?"

"I have no idea, Trudy. Eileen never told me. But you can be sure that, whomever it was, that person's life is very much in danger."

CHAPTER 7

The days had passed too slowly for Ben, and the nights had seemed to last forever, but the grief was finally bearable. He was able to sleep through the night; to awake the next morning without remembering the horribly swollen face and body of his dead wife. *Why have I remembered the ugliness?* he thought. *Why can't I only remember her beauty?* He was thankful that he had insisted that her dead body not be displayed; that he had not allowed Trudy to see her mother's corpse.

It was near the end of September, a Friday that Ben would never forget. That day he had forced a change in his life that he was determined not to regret. He marveled that his decision to retire was so uncomplicated; that he had simply called a meeting of the board, and announced his decision. They had given him a grand farewell luncheon, as had always been customary when someone retired, and it was over.

Now it was simple, for he had only one plan for his future: to see that Eileen's death was avenged. The law had been too slow, and his patience had a limit. He had analyzed his thoughts very carefully. Was he being fanatically vindictive? Was he driven by bitterness and hate? Could he be happy or content again when Eileen's murder was solved? Should he confide his mission to Trudy? Would Trudy approve? Such were his thoughts as he parked his car in the garage, and entered his home.

Ben had not spoken to Leona of his retirement, but now he felt like talking, and Leona had been a great help to him. He thought it strange that she had not greeted him as usual when he entered the house, but then it occurred to him that it was only two o'clock in the afternoon. She would not expect him to be home so soon.

For some reason, he felt nervous and apprehensive. Was he already thinking that his retirement was a mistake? He made a cup of instant coffee, and sat down at the table. The coffee was not what he really wanted, so he shoved it aside. His airplane project—it was almost finished, but he had neglected it, lately. Not today. He was not in the right mood for it. Maybe this would be a good time to examine the files in his office. Eileen had occasionally used his office; maybe she had left him a clue, or at least a note.

As he climbed the stairs, he heard a slight noise from one of the upstairs rooms. *So Leona is in the house after all*, he thought. *Probably cleaning.* The noise sounded again. It came from his office. There was a click, then the sound of a file drawer sliding open.

Ben was totally unprepared for what he saw as he entered the office. He stopped suddenly, raised his arm and pointed, but could not speak. Before him, standing beside the file cabinet with her back turned slightly toward him, was a woman he did not recognize. His first thought was that the woman was a man. She was almost six feet tall; had rather short, straight, blonde hair; she was dressed in a loose-fitting olive sweat shirt, khaki hiking shorts, olive socks rolled down above high-topped hiking boots, and she carried a beige colored knapsack strapped to her back.

Ben finally spoke: "What . . . who're you? What's going on here?"

She turned her head quickly toward him, then calmly replaced the folder that she had been examining, and turned her body to face him.

"Mr. Two Bears, how unfortunate. You're off-schedule today." She appeared to be very calm, and spoke as if she were addressing an old friend. Her voice was deep, for a woman.

Ben noticed her appearance more closely. She had plain facial features, certainly not unpleasant, and she wore no make-up. Her bare legs were stout, but very muscular, and her arms and upper body seemed very muscular, too, even beneath the loose-fitting sweat shirt. *This is the woman who killed my Eileen!*

Suddenly, he leaped at her. He was crazed with fury. He wanted to throw her to the floor, and smash her face and body. All his frustrations, up to that moment, came rushing from his lungs in a horrible, growling scream. Both of his arms stretched for her. His fingers spread and curved, as if they were claws. But he missed. The woman was not there.

Ben had reacted wildly, and without thinking, but the woman responded quickly and surely, with practiced skill. Her movements were all in one motion as Ben lunged. She took a step forward to meet him, then sidestepped to his left, turned her body, and slammed the edge of her stiffened right hand into his throat with a quick chopping action. As Ben bent forward and grabbed his throat, she continued the turn of her body, and brought her left elbow down hard to the back of his neck. Her motions were like a ballerina, dancing to long-rehearsed steps.

Ben fell heavily to the floor. The woman straddled his body. Leaning over, she carefully turned him onto his back. He was not dead, as she knew he would not be, but his eyes glared, and his mouth tried to snarl the obvious hatred on his face. Try as he might, Ben could not move his arms or his legs. He was paralyzed from the neck down.

It had all happened so quickly. Ben's mind was still in a rage, but he could see, and he slowly became conscious of what was happening. His eyes focused on the woman as he watched her step away from him to remove her knapsack. He could hear her as she spoke.

"You were very foolish, Mr. Two Bears. I didn't wish to harm you, but now, you see, I have no choice. Your wife was very beautiful. I think that I could have loved her."

Ben watched her as she knelt on one knee beside him, and stretched out his left arm. He tried to scream at her, but his voice was gone. He tried to make a fist, to flex his arm, to kick, but he could not move. He knew most certainly that she was going to kill him, and he knew exactly how she would do it. How many times had his mind imagined the way this woman had murdered his Eileen?

He watched her hands as the woman unzipped the flap of her knapsack; as she removed a small metal box that she placed on the floor beside her. Then, of all things unexpected, he watched her as she knelt on both knees, clasped her hands together before her breasts, closed her eyes, and prayed.

"Oh, Lord, this man has done me no harm. Receive him, not as my enemy, but as a lost friend. Amen."

She reached again into the knapsack, removed a pair of plastic gloves, and put them on her hands. Then, as if performing some sacred ritual, she opened the box, and removed a small plastic packet.

Ben's eyes suddenly shifted toward the doorway to see Leona standing there. She was wearing dirty, white coveralls, and her hands and face were covered with sweat and dust, but Ben saw her as a guardian angel at that moment.

The woman beside him looked around as Leona thrust out her arms, seeming to shove the woman away from him. Leona was at least ten feet away, but the woman beside Ben tumbled across the floor, and hit hard against the metal filing cabinet.

Leona did not look at the woman again, but she spoke over her shoulder to someone else as she rushed to Ben's side.

"Tie that woman up very carefully, then please call for an ambulance and Sheriff Lang." Then, to Ben, she said, "I'm sorry, Mr. Two Bears, I came as soon as I heard your distress call. Don't worry, we'll get you to the hospital. You'll be okay." She placed her hand gently on his forehead.

Ben's fear and rage suddenly vanished. He watched her through tear-blurred eyes, and knew that Leona was telling him the truth. *Is that really Leona?* he thought. *She sure doesn't talk like Leona.*

The first thing that Ben saw when he awoke the next day was Trudy. She was standing at the foot of his bed watching some goings-on near his head that he could not see. Her eyes were red and puffy from crying, but she was a lovely sight to him. He tried to ask her what was wrong, then remembered that he could not speak. Obviously, he was in a hospital. *How long have I been here? Am I dying?* Then, the horror returned, and he recalled the woman in his office.

"Oh, Pop! Doctor, he's awake!" Trudy could see the terror in his eyes, and it alarmed her. "Pop, you're okay!"

The doctor's face moved into Ben's view. A hand touched his forehead. "Easy there, Mr. Two Bears. Try to relax." It was the doctor's voice. "I'm Doctor Vance. We'll take care of you. Just try to relax."

Ben looked again at Trudy. Her mouth was open; her hands pressed tightly against her cheeks. Then she brightened and smiled, and clasped her hands together beneath her chin. Her smile told him everything. He was okay. His breathing slowly returned to normal as he watched the doctor's stethoscope being moved around on his chest. But there was no feeling. He could not feel the doctor's touch. A nurse scurried back and forth within his field of vision. The doctor spoke something softly to Trudy, and she walked around the bed to Ben's side, staying within his view. She took his hand, and stroked it gently, but there was no feeling. The reassurance came from her smile.

"Pop, the doctor wants me to step outside for a minute. Don't worry, you're going to get well. I'll be back with you in a moment."

Trudy stayed by his bedside for the next four days. He slept most of the time, but she was there when he awoke. On the fourth day, he felt a tingly, burning sensation that started in his arms, then slowly moved through his body to his legs and feet. On that day he was moved from the intensive care unit to a private room.

"Pop, I have to go back to Washington tonight. Don't worry about anything. Doctor Vance says your feeling will return in a few days, but don't try to talk yet. I'll be back as soon as I can, and while I'm gone Leona will stay with you. Pop, there's so much I want to talk with you about. Can you believe Leona? She's just not the same person anymore. But I love her dearly, even though she won't tell me about everything that happened. She says I must wait until you can talk about it." She smiled, and said, "Gee, Pop, you look terrible! You should see yourself with this contraption trying to pull you apart."

Ben smiled for the first time since his mishap, and formed silent words with his mouth.

Trudy beamed, "I know you do, Pop, and I love you too."

CHAPTER 8

Ben remained in traction while the cervical vertebrae in his neck healed. Fortunately, there had been no permanent damage to his spinal cord, and glorious feeling gradually returned to his body. The damaged larynx and vocal cords also healed slowly. His biggest problem was frustration. Ben thought that he could endure the long wait for bone and tissue to heal, but he wanted desperately to be able to talk; to ask questions; to yell at Leona because she would not voluntarily tell him everything that he wanted to know.

The process of rehabilitation would take time, possibly months. First, they began with physical therapy as soon as possible. Finally, Ben was allowed to try his voice in speaking. He called Trudy to tell her the good news himself, but his voice was weak, and he could not talk long. Then, after a rest, he asked to speak with Leona, alone.

"Leona . . . God knows, I can't thank you enough . . . for saving my life, but . . . I don't understand." His voice was hoarse, and barely above a whisper. "Who are you? How'd you do that?"

Leona took his hand and patted it, then released it, and walked to the foot of his bed where he could see her easily. She spoke in a quiet voice to prevent anyone outside the room from hearing.

"Mr. Two Bears, I'm still Leona—that's my real name—and I'm still your housekeeper. Now wait, I know that isn't what you meant." She paused longer than he felt it necessary, so he looked exasperated and started to speak. She held up her hand to quiet him.

"Very well. You're a most impatient man." She wagged her finger at him. "If I don't explain, you'll yell at me and damage your voice. If I do explain, you'll still yell because you won't believe me."

"Try me," he interrupted.

"Your sister recommended me to you because of my past work references. I must tell you now that my references were not exactly honest. My former employers, whom your sister called, did not actually employ me; they were a part of a plan to get me into your home."

Ben raised his eyebrows, and opened his mouth, but Leona wagged her finger again. "Shhh, have I not been a good housekeeper?"

He only glared at her, and motioned for her to continue.

"I came to you at a very trying time in your life. You needed my help, but it was also a convenient time for us—please be patient, Mr. Two Bears—because we needed time to search the mountainside above your home. You see, some of us; that is, a few unique Earth people, were selected to be specially educated and trained to perform certain assignments on our own planet."

Ben could hold back no longer. "Great Scott, Leona! Do you expect me to believe what I'm hearing?"

Leona again wagged her finger at him. "You see, I told you so! All right, Mr. Two Bears, then don't believe me. I'll think up another story to tell you."

Ben moaned. "Leona, don't call me 'Mr. Two Bears' any more. Call me Ben." He moaned again. "How the heck can I pay you to be my housekeeper again, after this?"

"Don't worry about it, Ben. I intend to remain your housekeeper until you're completely recovered. Then. . . .

Well, we'll cross that bridge when we come to it. But now you must rest. You may think about what I've told you, but please don't speak of it to anyone, not even to Trudy. You'll be asked to describe how the woman in your office was captured. I'm sorry, sir, but you must lie. You must say that you don't remember. Please be patient, Ben. All of your questions will be answered."

"But I have a hundred, a thousand questions to ask. How...." A knock sounded on the door.

Leona wagged her finger again, then walked to the door, and opened it. A nurse entered, and spoke to Ben.

"Mr. Two Bears, you *must* rest now. Sheriff Lang insists on talking with you, but that will have to wait until tomorrow. I think you may have already overexerted yourself."

Sheriff Sam Lang was at least sixty, but still a man's man. He stood six-four in walking-heeled boots, and was somewhat overweight, especially around the middle; yet, he carried his big frame with ease. He was a stereotypical western sheriff, originally from the big-ranch country of northern Texas.

He entered Ben's hospital room with his large western hat in his hand. "Ben, I shore am glad ta' see ye! How ye feelin', 'ol hoss?" His wide smile was honestly sincere.

Ben weakly shook the sheriff's hand, and returned the smile. "Doing better, Sam. Thanks for the help. Do you still have that amazon in the hoosegow?"

Sam's laugh sounded like a series of wheezes, and his large belly shook up and down. "Well, she wuz there when I left, but I wouldn't swear that she's still there now." He looked down, and his face turned serious. "Ben, that's one heck of a woman. Like I said, I'm shore glad ta' see ye. Yer mighty lucky ta' be alive. If ye don't mind talkin' about it, I'd like ta' know jist what-all happened."

Ben cleared his throat. "I wish I could help you, Sam. Fact is, I can't seem to remember much. I got home from work early—I retired that day, you know—and caught her going through my files. I didn't know who she was, at first, but then it came to me, and I knew that she was the woman who killed Eileen."

"What happened then? Did she jump ye right off?"

"No, she didn't. It's funny, Sam, but now that I think about it, she acted almost friendly. She wasn't surprised, and she wasn't afraid, but I just went crazy, and rushed her. Sam, I tried to kill her, but it back-fired, and she almost killed me, instead."

"Well, I don't blame ye. What happened then?"

"Sorry, Sam. The next thing I remember was seeing Leona, just before you got there."

"Okay, Ben. That woman we got in the brig won't tell us anythin'. All she says is that Leona is a witch—that's all. Know anythin' about that?"

"I wouldn't know about that. Leona has been an excellent housekeeper for me, and she saved my life. That's all I know. Have you talked to her?"

"Yeah, I talked to her. Ye say she saved yer' life? How's that?"

Ben suddenly felt trapped. What had he said? "Well, I guess she did, didn't she? She hasn't told me about it yet, but I didn't see anyone else around. What did she tell you?"

The sheriff grinned. "Wonder ta' me that ye saw anythin' a'tall. Naw, Leona said that big tow-headed feller done it—knocked that woman fer a spin inta' tha' file cabinet. I rekin' that's how it was. Leona wouldn't stand a chance aginst that big woman."

"Sam, what the heck are you talking about? What big tow-headed fellow?"

Sam looked questionably at Ben. "Well, I figgered ye knew 'im. Leona said he was her nephew. Last name's

O'Brien. Ye mean ye ain't talked ta' Leona about all this?"

"Nope. I haven't had a chance to talk to her. They hardly let me open my mouth, but I'm sure going to start asking some questions."

"Well, I'm much obliged ta' ye, Ben. That sassy nurse told me not ta' stay long." He turned around to leave the room, then stopped at the door to look back. "Take care o' ye'self, Ben. An' say 'hidy' ta' Trudy fer me." He waved his hat as he left.

Ben did not have an opportunity to speak privately with Leona again for several days. Dr. Vance, the nurses, the therapists, or someone else was always in the room. He did not ask to speak with her privately, fearing that, to do so, would attract suspicion. Also, it seemed that Leona avoided opportune times to be alone with him. She no longer sat with him overnight, since his condition was not critical.

Drat that woman, he thought. *I'm going to fire her as soon as I get out of this hospital!* But he could not stay angry at her. She was constantly cheerful, and she always brought him his mail, opened it for him, and even read it to him if he was tired. Most of his mail was 'get-well' cards and letters, and his room was too cluttered with flowers and potted plants. She took some of them home for him every day when she left.

Leona was especially cheerful one morning when she entered Ben's room with a stack of mail. He was no longer in traction, but his neck and upper body were confined in a cast. He was sitting up in bed, breathing hard after a tiring session of physical therapy. A nurse was taking his blood pressure.

"Good morning, Ben. Guess what I've brought you."

He knew. "Good morning, Leona. You'd better have a letter from Trudy. If not, you'd better turn around, and go back home."

She felt like teasing him, but he seemed to be in a sour mood, so she opened the letter from Trudy, and handed it to him.

> Dear Pop,
>
> I was so thrilled when you called. Oh, I knew you were going to get well, but hearing your voice was like a blessing from heaven. Now, you be careful, and don't overdo it. Besides, I've already instructed Leona to make sure that you behave yourself. I know you very well, you see, and I don't trust you for a minute.
>
> Everything is okay here. Well, maybe not everything. Darrin and I finally broke up for good. I can't say that I'm really sorry about it, or that I was surprised. Actually, I'm surprised that our relationship lasted as long as it did. But you knew it all along, didn't you—that it wouldn't last? You were just too kind to say so. Mom told me one time that Darrin and I were wrong for each other. We had a big fuss about it. Now I see that she (God bless her) was right. Maybe wisdom really does come with age.
>
> It's so funny, the way it happened—not so funny, either. Darrin was supposed to meet me at the airport when I returned from visiting with you in the hospital, but he didn't show up. Then he called me right after I got home, and explained that he'd intentionally not met me because he knew that there would be a lot of reporters around; that he knew I'd embarrass him. And he was the one who decided that we shouldn't see each other any more. Since next year is an election year, he felt that I was a source of too much negative publicity for him. Pop, he actually

said that! Believe me, if it weren't for you and Dr. Bonner, and maybe a few more, I could very easily turn into a man-hater. Well, enough of Congressman Darrin Snell. I'm putting him out of my mind.

Pop, I'm taking a chance in writing this letter—actually, two chances. The first is that I'm afraid that what I'm going to tell you will upset you. I love you too much to let my problems cause you to worry. The second is that I'm afraid that this letter might fall into the wrong hands. But I have to let you know what I've learned since Mom's death. I can't talk about it on the telephone because I think our phones may be 'bugged'.

When I learned that you were almost killed by that dreadful woman who murdered Mom, I nearly fell apart. Sheriff Lang was the one who called me. Bless his heart, he was so kind and thoughtful. I was worried to death about you, and when he told me that the woman had been captured and put in jail, I felt relieved and a little relaxed, but Pop, we *can't* relax. That woman is only a small part of a very big problem.

You and I didn't know it, but Mom was gathering information to expose an underground women's organization known as the W.E.B. society (Women Escape Bondage). They call themselves 'Women of the Web', and they actually have a small red hourglass tattooed on their bellies. Do you understand the symbolism? Their objective is to subjugate the world's male population. Please don't take this lightly, Pop. I know it sounds ridiculous, but you must believe me.

I've decided to try to contact Agent Drake,

and tell him what I've learned, but somehow, I have a feeling that the F.B.I. already knows of all this.

Pop, I know that you'll be distressed as you read this, but please don't do anything foolish. I've told you this, only because you must be on guard for yourself. I'm okay, really. You know that I've done some stupid things during my life, but I've suddenly grown up, and I'm now using my head.

I have much more to tell you, but the rest will have to wait. It's now six a.m. here, and I must get this letter in the mail. I don't dare leave it lying around. Please have Leona destroy it as soon as possible. I trust her completely.

All my love,

Trudy

Ben had begun shaking half-way through the letter; now he was turning purple. He looked around the room, and saw that he and Leona were alone. "Leona, I've got to get out of this place. I've got to help my girl!"

Leona rushed to his side, and took his hands in hers. "Ben, you must calm down."

"But Trudy's in trouble! She needs me. Here, read this!" He shoved the letter at her.

"I don't need to read it; you've already told me what the letter said. Yes, there are times when I can read your thoughts—anyone's thoughts—especially when the mind is in a state of anxiety. There isn't enough time to explain now. You'll be allowed to go home soon. Then—I promise you—I'll answer all of your questions. But, for now, please trust me."

She glanced at the door to make sure that no one

could hear. "You must also trust Trudy. You don't know, and she doesn't yet know it, but your Trudy is gifted with an unusual extrasensory mind. The unfortunate recent events in your lives have been very stressful to both of you. In your case, it's been depressing, but, for Trudy, it's begun an awakening of her subconscious mind."

Ben did not know what to say. He was tired, worried about Trudy, and utterly confused, but this woman had a remarkably soothing influence on his mind.

CHAPTER 9

Georgette did not waste time. Her capture had simply been a hindrance to her mission, and her confinement in jail provided time for meditation. She had not been careless, nor had she made a mistake. Ben Two Bears' untimely entrance could not have been foreseen; therefore, there had been no error on her part.

It was not a matter of pride that she withheld information from her captors; it was a matter of superiority. Interrogation was her expertise, and she despised the incompetence of her present captors. She knew the usefulness of torture and mind-altering drugs, and she knew how to condition her own mind to resist even those methods. In Vietnam and Laos she had known the best, and she had been one of the best, herself.

Georgette had grown up in the jungles of southeast Asia, where both of her parents had been American missionaries. Her parents were both killed when she was twelve years old, and she had been tortured and taken prisoner by the Vietcong. She survived, and grew strong to earn the respect of her captors, who taught her to fight and survive, or escape and evade. She became a Vietcong guerrilla fighter.

Later, when her guerrilla band was captured by American troops, she used her Caucasian appearance and American citizenship as an advantage; claiming that she was a prisoner of the Vietcong, and requested to be sent to her

American relatives in Panama. She became a mercenary, fighting in various Central American uprisings; finally in Nicaragua, where she joined the Sandinistas.

A short time later, someone within the Sandinistas leadership 'discovered' Georgette, and saw her real value to their revolution. Her superior talents had been wasted as a jungle fighter: here was an American woman whose loyalty had been purchased; whose real worth had been hidden among the expendable soldiers. Her true value to the revolution was the publicity that she would receive as a political defector, and there was no better exposure than as a hero of the revolution.

She spent months in special training to become a helicopter pilot because she preferred the action above the talking. Then, more time was required in grooming her for public exposure. As a final step in her preparation, they 'planted' her in various heroic situations, always making sure that the news media stood nearby.

Georgette soon became bored with the assignment. She felt no need to nourish her ego, and she hated the publicity; therefore, the timing could not have been better when Icy Brooks entered the scene. Icy was there, at the time, with Senator Mary Armstrong, who was on a fact-finding mission.

After a short discussion between the two, Icy invited Georgette to Washington for a clandestine meeting; all expenses paid by the W.E.B. society. It turned out beneficially to both: Georgette got the job of her dreams, and the W.E.B. society got it's most proficient assassin. She advanced rapidly up the tiers of rank to become Icy's most trusted lieutenant.

Georgette seldom thought of her past life. She remembered her parents, but there was no remembrance of mourning over their death. She remembered that her father had taught her to pray for the soul when someone died. She saw no sin in killing, although she did not particularly enjoy killing. The thrill was in the planning and stalking, and evading capture after the kill.

She thought of Ben Two Bears. Her only regret was that her mission had failed. Then she thought of the witch, the woman who had caused her to fail. What had happened? What strange power did the witch possess? Could she, herself, obtain such power?

Now she must plan her escape. When the time was right, Icy would come to her rescue. She must then learn the secret of the witch's power.

CHAPTER 10

Icy Brooks was not worried. Her enterprise, superbly planned and organized, could not fail. So what? If one member of her organization failed, the rest would be strengthened by the failure. True, Georgette had been a great asset to the society. Her strength and ice-cold temerity had served many times to eliminate opposition. Should she attempt a rescue? Not a good idea. Federal agents were now in charge. A rescue attempt at this time would be too risky. Besides, Georgette was a professional; she could take care of herself, and she would not expose the society. On the other hand, Georgette could not be easily replaced. Others could be sacrificed without a great loss, but Icy's plans relied heavily on Georgette's skills. Perhaps it would be wise to reconsider.

Icy reviewed events: Eileen Two Bears had been getting too close. As a diversion, the W.E.B. society had accomplished a second series of abortion clinic bombings in order to place Eileen's organization in an unpopular situation. It had worked, but by sheer accident, and the simple stupidity of Marcella Silman, Icy learned that Eileen had obtained information that would expose the society's identity, including Icy's own involvement. Such information would have been extremely injurious to the society at that time. Eventually, their presence would be announced, but by the society itself, and at an opportune time decided by the society.

Icy had been pressured to act quickly; to remove Eileen and the briefcase before the information could be disclosed. When Icy left the meeting to get coffee, she had quickly telephoned Georgette. She instructed Georgette, using a previously devised code, to eliminate Eileen. Then she put a tasteless form of sleeping drug into the coffee *cream*, knowing that Eileen was the only woman present who used cream with her coffee. All evidence had been easily removed after the meeting.

Marcella Silman would not be a problem. Eileen's organization would deteriorate with Marcella at its head. Also, Icy's information sources had assured her that Marcella could prove nothing; that her extreme fear was actually an asset to the W.E.B. society at that time.

Unfortunately, Eileen's daughter, Trudy, was much needed by the society, and Icy had been maneuvering to enlist Trudy for some time. Trudy's recruitment had been made more difficult by Eileen's unavoidable murder. It became a delicate situation, but one that Icy could handle with expert diplomacy and more time.

Trudy was a physicist, and the W.E.B. society needed a physicist with her unique qualifications. She sympathized with the plight of women; yet, more importantly, she specialized in the theory of anti-matter. Icy smiled at the thought. Trudy would indeed be surprised if she knew how much Icy knew about her.

Icy realized that the opportunity of recruiting Trudy would be lost if she ever learned the truth about her mother's death. But Trudy was a scientist, and her mind would not accept mere suspicion as fact.

Icy knew, however, that information leaks would occur, and that a final countdown of time had already begun. For that reason, Georgette's untimely arrest might turn out to be more of a problem than originally thought. Georgette would not talk—Icy was sure of that—but the tattoo. . . . Icy felt a sudden tinge of doubt regarding the symbolic hourglass tattoo. She had once thought of the idea as a stroke of genius; it served as a bond, like the mixing of blood, to unite the members of the society. It also served as a brand. Once branded, a member would be reluctant to desert the society, knowing that she could always be identified as once a member. In this case, however, if Trudy learned of the tattoo, it would be a certain indication that her mother's murderer was a member of the society.

Now there was no doubt. Trudy must be recruited as soon as possible, so that her brain could be picked for the benefit of the society. The wheels had already been set in motion. Trudy's recent break-up with Darrin Snell had been no accident; it had been deliberately planned by Icy. Icy collected her I.O.U.'s when necessary, and Darrin had been blackmailed. Trudy would be coerced to join if she could be convinced that men were reprehensible; however, her will and her spirit must be broken. She must be forced to welcome Icy as her savior.

Now it was time to apply more pressure. Icy must use her ace-in-the-hole.

CHAPTER 11

It was again Saturday, a day that Trudy usually set aside for shopping, or for running errands that she did not have time for on work days. The Washington area weather had turned unusually cold for early December, and there was a threat of snow in the low clouds. She drove into a service garage as instructed by Agent Drake.

"Change the oil and filter, please. I'll wait." She gave her name to the service manager, who acknowledged his recognition of the name with a nod, then led her to an office, and opened the door.

Agent Drake, obviously having just arrived also, was removing his topcoat and gloves.

"Good morning, ma'am." Then, to the service manager, "Thanks, Harry. How old is the coffee?"

"Just made it. Help yourself." The service manager closed the door behind him as he left.

Trudy removed her own coat while Drake poured the coffee into foam cups. He smiled as he handed her one of the cups.

"Don't be deceived by the china. This is a classy joint."

She returned the smile as he continued. "I'm glad you called, ma'am, but I'm curious as to why you wanted me to be alone."

"I'm not sure I can give you a good reason for that, Mr. Drake. I called you from work yesterday because I think my home phone may be 'bugged'. Is that the proper term?" Drake smiled his answer. "As for asking you to come alone—call it intuition if you want—but I've had a *lot* of strange 'intuition' lately." She seemed to be nervous.

"What's wrong, Miss Two Bears? Are you in trouble?"

"Yes, I believe so, but first—and I never thought I'd say this—I don't know who to trust anymore. Especially women. Even my own room-mate . . . and I've always trusted Kitty. Oh, I have absolutely no reason to suspect her, but I just don't know. Anyway, that's why I asked you to come alone."

"I think I understand. This intuition of yours—does it have anything to do with Agent Miller?"

Trudy nodded. "You feel it too, don't you?"

He did not answer the question. "What can you tell me, Miss Two Bears?"

She took a deep breath. "Mr. Drake, my mind is going faster than I can keep up with it, and I can't seem to let go of this investigation. Everyone has advised me not to get involved, but no one seems to understand." She shook her head, then changed the subject.

"Senator Armstrong invited me to lunch soon after I came back from my mother's funeral. We briefly discussed events leading to the murder. She told me that a meeting was held, and the names of the women present, but not much else.

"Later, I ran into Icy—India Brooks—at the mall. She asked me to join a secret organization called the W.E.B. society. Do you know about that?"

"About the W.E.B. society? Yes, I know a little. Please go on."

"I was very impressed with Icy, and her secret society made sense, to a point. Then I had a long visit with Marcella Silman in her home. Oh, that poor woman. I felt so sorry for her.

"Mr. Drake, my mother was murdered because she knew certain information about the W.E.B. society, but Marcella Silman also knew the same information; yet, she still lives."

Drake interrupted. "I think you may have been misinformed about that. Mrs. Silman's knowledge of the W.E.B. society is extremely vague. Evidently, your mother didn't share that information with her."

"Mrs. Silman lied to you, Mr. Drake, in order to protect her own life. She believes that she's alive today, only because the W.E.B. society knows that she refused to disclose her information. If she's correct, then, how did the W.E.B. society know that, unless they knew exactly what Mrs. Silman told you?"

Agent Drake looked away, and nibbled at his lower lip. He suddenly looked very tired. "Miss Two Bears, we can't just *assume* that the W.E.B. society knew that Mrs. Silman lied to us. We need real evidence."

"They *did* know, because Icy Brooks knew it. Icy knew it because she was in the meeting when it was discussed. Mrs. Silman plainly implied in the meeting that my mother's evidence of the society's existence, and Icy's involvement, was in my mother's briefcase. And why did that awful woman break into by father's home? What was she searching for?"

Trudy did not wait for Drake's response. "I'll tell you why: it was because the information they wanted was *not* in my mother's briefcase. They murdered her for *nothing!* All they want now is the name of my mother's informant, and they still don't know. Now they *can't* kill Mrs. Silman because they have to assume that she *does* know who the informant is, but won't talk." Trudy knew that she was on the verge of shouting, so she abruptly stopped talking.

Drake frowned. "I see. It seems I'm a little short on all the facts. Thank you, ma'am." He waited a moment, thinking about how much he should say before speaking again.

"We've had suspicions of India Brooks for some time, but she's clever. There is simply no proof. The woman seems to read our minds."

"Don't say that. I've had some weird feelings lately, about mind reading. Mr. Drake, does that woman—the one who almost killed my father last month—does she have a red hourglass tattoo on her abdomen?"

"Her name is Georgette Adams, and yes, she does. That ties her in with this W.E.B. organization, but that's no help to us yet. We can't just go around inspecting women's bellies, so where does that leave us?"

"Well, wouldn't you like to know if Icy Brooks has a red hourglass tattoo? If I could find that out for you, could you arrest her?"

"No, ma'am, we still. . . ."

"Oh, for heaven's sake, stop calling me 'ma'am'!"

"Yes, ma'am." He winced, then shrugged his shoulders. "Sorry, just a habit. Of course it would be useful information, but knowing it wouldn't be of any help at this time. The arrest of Georgette Adams was a lucky break; yet, frankly, we know little more now than we did before her arrest. What we need is the name of your mother's informant. You can guess our chances of getting that. You see, the case of your mother's murder, and probably others, will apparently be closed with the conviction of Georgette Adams, but we know that it's much more complicated than that. I shouldn't say this: our system of justice does not favor law enforcement at this time. This W.E.B. organization isn't legally guilty of any crime—only one of its alleged members. Do you understand?"

"Oh, sure! I understand, all right!" Trudy was visibly exasperated. "But it sure as heck isn't right!" She jumped up from her chair to leave, but Drake also stood, and touched her arm.

"Miss Two Bears, please wait," he spoke gently.

She stopped, but turned away from him. He waited for her to calm down, then both took their seats again.

"I'm sorry, Mr. Drake." She took a tissue from her purse, and dabbed tears from her eyes. "I'm scared—for my Pop, and for myself—and there isn't anyone who can help us."

"Yes there is, ma'am." He rolled his eyes up at his mistake in calling her "ma'am" again. "You didn't know it, but you've had F.B.I. protection for some time—at a distance, of course. If you'd like, I can assign an agent to be directly with you."

"Oh, that's ridiculous! That would only draw attention to me, and I certainly don't need more attention." She thought for a moment. "Look, that Georgette woman is in jail now, and that's a big relief. The one I'm really worried about is Icy Brooks. I'll simply have to take control of myself, and start using my head. She wants me to join her darn spider web, so—okay, I join—that would take the heat off. Right? And I might get some real evidence for you."

"Miss Two Bears, you aren't thinking. Have you thought about *why* she wants you to join?"

Trudy's expression turned blank. "Of course I have. She needs all the help she can get to pull-off this ridiculous plan to enslave. . . . Wait! Are you suggesting that. . . . How stupid of me. She needs my knowledge! Of. . . ." It suddenly dawned on her that Icy must know of her top-secret project at the lab. *But how?* she thought. *Who would divulge such information?*

She seemed to be looking through Agent Drake, then her attention returned to him. "Mr. Drake, I have to go home and think. Is there anything else?"

"Only this: whatever you do, be very careful. We'll be with you, but we can't keep you in sight at all times. Think before you act, and scream as loud as you can if you need help quickly."

They were chilling words, but she shook his extended hand, and smiled.

That night, when she lay in bed with her eyes closed, he appeared again: that mysterious white-haired man with no distinguishing features. But she felt a warming, and a calming sensation emanating from him. Again, he just stood there with his hands on his hips. There seemed to be a message coming from him, but she could not consciously make out what it was. Then he was gone. Trudy felt more relaxed than she had in a long time, and drifted, as she had before, into a deep and restful sleep.

CHAPTER 12

By Monday morning, the whirling sensation in Trudy's brain had ceased. She entered the lab with a clear mind, and a smile for Dr. Bonner. He had been reading Trudy's journal, but looked up as she approached. His expression was grave.

"Good morning, Dr. Bonner. How're you this. . . ." She sensed that something was wrong. "My goodness, are you okay? What's wrong?"

He replaced the journal on her desk. "I'm afraid we have a large problem, Trudy. Yes, yes . . . a problem. This is very distressing to me. It seems that you've been fired."

She looked at the journal on her desk, then back at his face. It felt as though she could not breathe. Her voice came out as a whisper. "Oooh, no. This can't happen. It's too much."

Dr. Bonner's shoulders sagged. "I'm very sorry, Trudy." He held up his hand, and beckoned to someone behind her.

Trudy looked over her shoulder. It was Carl, the security guard she joked with every day. She turned, and waved him away. "Wait, Carl! Dr. Bonner, you have to talk to me. You have to explain."

It was a tense moment for all of them, then Dr. Bonner nodded, and Carl retreated to the outer door of the entrance.

Trudy walked to Dr. Bonner, grasped both of his

arms, and looked into his eyes. "Please, what have I done wrong?" Her voice was pleading.

He led her to a work table where they both sat down. "My dear young friend, you have done absolutely nothing wrong." She started to speak, but he signaled her to wait. "You must understand that, in our business, we must keep a low profile. Trudy, you are a victim of circumstances. You had no control of your destiny."

It all came back to her: her mother's murder, her father's near-murder, her estrangement with Darrin, the reporters—always the reporters. Her life had been opened up for public inspection.

She nodded, started to cry silently, and kept nodding. "Yes, it couldn't be helped." When her crying stopped, she stood, and looked around the lab. Everything in the room had felt her touch. The project would go on without her. When she looked back at Dr. Bonner, she could see tears in his eyes. *Dear old man*, she thought, *you couldn't have done this.*

"Dr. Bonner, this isn't your doing. Who's responsible for firing me?"

He looked down, and shook his head. "It can't be stopped now, Trudy. I could do nothing to help you."

"I know, but listen to me—look at me, please. Dr. Bonner, someone in this building has talked outside. I can't tell you any more than that, but I think our project has been disclosed. You must be very careful."

"But. . . ."

"No, I can't say any more because I have no proof." She walked to him, and offered her hand. "You're a brilliant man, Dr. Bonner, and I've enjoyed working with you. Well, where am I supposed to go now?"

He stood, and opened his arms for her. "Carl will take you to Dr. Smith. Please take your journal to him." He watched as she walked to her desk to pick up the journal. She took one last look around, then followed Carl out of the room.

The short meeting with Dr. Smith was anticlimactic. She handed her journal to him, and stood quietly as he talked. He stressed the importance of secrecy, warning her of the consequences should she disclose any information regarding the project. He gave her a box containing all of her personal effects, and handed her a final pay check, which he said was very generous. Then he offered his hand, saying, "No hard feelings, Trudy?" She ignored his extended hand, and left the office without having said a single word. Carl, who waited outside the door, escorted her from the building, and spoke an embarrassed farewell before returning to his routine rounds of inspection. They had not even allowed her to say good-bye to her friends.

Dr. Smith waited fifteen minutes, then unbuttoned his shirt, and shoved Trudy's journal inside his trousers behind the belt. After rebuttoning his shirt, he put his jacket on, and examined himself in a mirror. It would be necessary to suck in his stomach in order to look natural. He keyed Dr. Bonner's number on the telephone.

"Dr. Bonner, I must remind you again—please send Trudy's journal to my office." After a short wait, "What? She did *not* bring it to me!" Another longer wait, then, "Are you sure? Okay, don't get excited, I'll take care of it."

He touched the disconnect button, then keyed security. "This is Dr. Smith. Send someone over to Dr. Bonner's lab to search for Miss Two Bears' journal. Do it quickly, and call me back—this is important."

Five minutes later, he heard the chief security officer's voice calling out orders to the area guard as he hurried along the hallway. Owen met the officer at his door.

"It's gone, Dr. Smith. We'll have to. . . ."

Owen swore, and slapped the top of his desk. "All right, I know where she lives. Come on, we can't waste any time!"

They ran through the security check-points together, out of the building, to the guard house at the parking lot. The guard had the gate open, waiting for them.

"Follow behind me, and use your siren!" Owen ran to his car, and almost laughed aloud as he unbuttoned his shirt, and squealed tires while leaving the parking area.

"Stupid idiots!" In the excitement and confusion, he could have stolen a whole safe full of secret journals.

CHAPTER 13

Trudy decided not to go back to her apartment; instead, she felt an unexplainable need to get out of the city. She was dressed comfortably enough in a light-blue jump suit, her usual work-day attire, and she had an insulated ski jacket for warmth.
A freeway sign ahead indicated the exit for Annapolis and Chesapeake Bay. She decided quickly. The Bay was one of her favorite places.

The events of the past six months had seemed to extract the gaiety from Trudy's personality. She had grown up as one of the few people on earth who experienced life as uncomplicated and worry-free. Her's had been an existence of love, laughter, and the joyous benefits of good parentage. She had not felt especially protected, or insulated from major problems; it was more akin to good fortune. As she saw it now, all of her previous life had been the life of another person. What had happened? When had the change begun? Why?
She felt no need to go back over the same questions that had plagued the past weekend. The 'why me?' question led to no answer, and she refused to dwell on it, but there were other questions that did have answers. Those tragic events had not been a matter of fate or destiny; they had been planned and executed by people, for a purpose.
Her mother's needless murder had only been a

means of keeping her from disclosing information. The brutal assault on her father, with the intent to murder, had only happened because of accidental discovery, but, even then, it could have been avoided. Trudy could not comprehend, under any circumstance, a justification for such violent behavior.

Why, then, did Icy Brooks' W.E.B. society resort to such violence in order to achieve its goal to enslave men? The goal, itself, seemed ludicrous and impossible. Yet, was it really impossible? Did the goal seem ludicrous merely because it concerned women? There were many famous women in history. Some of them were women of great power. Helen of Troy was a woman; so was Cleopatra of Egypt, Queen Isabella of Spain, and Catherine of Russia. More modern women included Golda Meir, and Margaret Thatcher, and many other outstanding people. The list could go on and on. Icy wanted power; more power than she could ever get in conventional politics, and she would stop at nothing in order to get it.

Women outnumber men in population, they control the wealth, they live longer than men, and they have begun to compete seriously with men in athletic skills and feats of strength. Women are shouting their discontent at discrimination. There is the well known saying that 'Hell hath no fury like a women scorned.'. As for violence, it is also well known that terrorism has always been an effective method of achieving political power.

Icy Brooks is extremely intelligent, possibly a genius; therefore, her ability and determination to succeed must not be underestimated. The W.E.B. society has been growing for several years, and is well organized, but could it be seriously considered as a major threat? How about the great conquerors: Genghis Khan, Napoleon Bonaparte, Adolf Hitler? Why not a woman?

Should women's rights end only with equality? Women have been suppressed during the entire history of mankind. Was it not their turn to have the pendulum swing to their side? Trudy was amazed by her thoughts. Had she, herself, been treated fairly by men?

These thoughts so dominated her mind that she almost missed the exit to her favorite beach. *Goodness! What have I been doing? I probably ran a dozen red lights without realizing it.*

The weather was changing fast, and getting worse. Light, powdery snow occasionally stuck and melted on the windshield. *Trudy, this is crazy. You promised Pop that you wouldn't do anything foolish, so why are you doing this?*

Then, a most remarkable thought came to her. *Leona. Here I am, Leona!* It was such an unexpected thought that she suddenly became very alert. She looked far ahead down the highway, then in the rear view mirror. No other car was in sight. Strangely, her F.B.I. protectors entered her mind. She had left work so unexpectedly that she had lost them. Was she in danger?

Chesapeake Bay was all around her as she parked the car on a small peninsula. She sat still for a while, thinking how the melancholic scene so well matched her mood. She wanted to walk, so she picked up her jacket, and stepped outside to put it on. Not a single, living creature could be seen anywhere. The low clouds overhead looked dark and threatening.

She zipped up her jacket, and turned, head down, to protect her face from the cold wind, and almost bumped into another car parked behind her own. It was *not* a car! The surprise was so sudden that she screamed, and staggered backward. She looked again. The first thought that struck her brain was *flying saucer!* And if she could trust her eyes, she saw a glassy-dark bubble-canopy snap open to reveal a white-haired, smiling, human-type young man. He agilely leaped out to the ground, and straightened up to a full six and a half feet of height.

She screamed her anger at him. "Cotton O'Brien, are you crazy? You almost scared me to death!"

Then she realized what she had just said. *Trudy, you're the one who's crazy! You never saw this man before in your life, and you just called him by name.* But she then realized that she did know him. *He's the man who's been appearing in your visions!*

He again smiled broadly, revealing even, white teeth, and an arrogant self-esteem. Then she noticed that he was wearing the thin gold band around his head that she had seen in her visions.

"Girl, you've been awful hard to find. You ought to show a little more appreciation for all my trouble."

Not only could she not believe her eyes, she also could not believe her ears. This big abomination had just addressed her as if she were his little lost sister, and he was now walking toward her.

"Stay away from me, you. . . . I didn't ask you to find me. Why were you looking for me, anyway?"

He stopped walking, and lifted his hands to his hips, just as in her vision, but he was still smiling. "Leona sent me. Do you have any more clothes, or anything to take with you? I came to take you home."

It was such a matter-of-fact statement that it left her searching for a reply. "No way, big boy! I'm not *about* to get in that thing with you! And if you really know Leona, you can. . . ."

Cotton wheeled around as they heard a distant fast-moving car scattering gravel around a turn in the road.

He ran for Trudy, grabbed her up in his arms, and raced back to his 'flying saucer'. "I don't have time to argue about it now, Trudy." He literally pitched her into the passenger seat, and hopped in beside her. The overhead canopy snapped closed.

Trudy had landed awkwardly in the seat, and had

bounced and fallen with her head and arms forward into the foot-well, with her lower body and legs in the seat. She tried to right herself, while yelling at Cotton, but was unable to move because she felt suddenly pressed hard-downward against the floor. It lasted for a few seconds only, and she was finally able to turn her head to look up at Cotton sitting in the other seat.

"Trudy, get up off the floor. You don't look lady-like, all sprawled out like that." He was shaking with laughter.

"I hate you, Cotton O'Brien! And I didn't even get to see what was happening." Then she started to laugh, too, and was amazed to discover that she felt no fear or anxiety. "Well, you don't look so good from down here, either."

She finally righted herself, and looked around at her little prison. It now appeared to be much roomier than at first, and very comfortable. Her seat was separated from Cotton's by a console that extended forward into a brightly displayed instrument panel. Behind their seats, at a level with the tops of their backrests, was a deck. The whole craft was circular in shape, much like a discus. Overhead was a dome-like canopy, extremely transparent now, but she had seen it as glassy-dark from the outside. She looked outside. All around them was blue sky, and she could see the tops of smooth, bright clouds below them.

"Oh, it's breath-taking. We're traveling so fast!"

"Yep. Nice, ain't it" Look ahead."

She had turned around, her knees in the seat, to look behind them. Now she turned back, and sat again in the seat. Ahead, still far away, appeared the top of a large, snow-capped mountain.

"Looks like you. Where'd you get that white hair? Did someone scare you?"

"Nope, I was born with red hair, but when I was a little kid, I was locked in the cellar for a month. After a while, with no sunlight, my hair got moldy. It just stayed that way."

Trudy could not decide if she should laugh, or not. His face was dead-pan at that moment. She giggled, then broke out in laughter. He winked at her. "I'm not laughing at you, I'm laughing at myself. I almost believed you."

He pointed ahead. Trudy looked, and fell back in her seat, startled. The great mountain loomed before them. They seemed to be racing head-on to certain disaster. The craft quickly slowed, and stopped only a few feet from the rocky surface, then hovered there. Its rate of deceleration had almost forced Trudy from her seat. She expelled her breath, and looked at Cotton, who sat there doing nothing. There was no control stick in his hand, no throttle, no pedals, levers, or knobs—nothing visible by which he controlled the little craft.

"Cotton, that wasn't funny."

He had done a very foolish thing, and she saw the regret in his face. "I'm sorry, Trudy. Showing-off, I guess. Maybe I just wanted to impress you."

"I *am* impressed. I'm extremely impressed with this ... whatever it is, but not with you. Please take me home."

"Sorry again. I can't take you home, yet. We'll have to wait for awhile."

Trudy jerked around in her seat, and clinched her fists. "I knew it! You never did intend to take me home, did you?" She was yelling at him. "So, now what? Do you take me to your cave?"

Cotton smiled. "Girl, you sure have a short fuse. Maybe you don't know it, but you're in big trouble. You're a fugitive now."

"Fugitive? You're using the wrong word, moldy head! *Captive* is what you should have said. And I know I'm in big trouble. What chance do I have against a big bully like you?"

"Trudy, it isn't me you have to worry about, it's the law. They think you stole your lab journal."

Her expression showed disbelief. "But I *didn't!* I gave it to Dr. Smith! How'd *you* know about that?"

"I know a lot of things—mostly because Leona tells me. Now, just hold it, will you?" She had jumped to her knees in the seat, and looked as if she were going to yell at him again. "Wait a minute, Trudy. I'm going to park this baby."

He looked outside at the mountain, as if searching for just the right spot. The craft moved upward, then stopped again near the peak of the mountain at a flat, snow-covered ledge. It moved forward, hovered above the ledge, rotated around, then settled down, and backed gently into the snow bank. Their view was spectacular. Trudy seemed to forget her anger, and marveled at the scene below them. They were far above the tree line, but she could see a few gnarled, wind-shaped survivors scattered here and there, thousands of feet below. Great wisps of snow were being blown from the mountain by wind, and clouds were building up from the lower elevations. A blizzard was working its way toward them.

Cotton removed his gold headband, held it in his right hand, then leaned back, draped his right arm over the back-rest, and brought his right leg upward to place his boot on the seat. He gestured with his left hand. "Now, this isn't so bad, is it? If you'd just relax, you might find it enjoyable."

His smiling, handsome face, almost rugged because of its angular features, was not unpleasant to look at, but Trudy could think only of his arrogance. She knew, however, that her feelings were shifting back and forth, and were not reliable at the moment. She changed the subject.

"How do you control this thing?"

He chuckled at her description of his most prized possession. "She reads my mind, and does what I tell her to do."

Trudy interrupted before he could continue. "Does it

have anything to do with that gold band?"

"You got it, first try. Without this gold band we'd be 'dead in the water', but it wouldn't work for just anybody. This little band tells her that it's me who's giving the orders. Here, try it. Tell her to do something."

Trudy took the band, turned it around in her hands, and examined it. Obviously, it was not gold; it was much too light. It was about the width of her little finger, and very thin, but she could see inconspicuous, small lumps at various places on the inside surface. She placed it on her head, but had to hold it in place because it was made to fit Cotton's larger head. Presently, she handed it back to him.

"Well?" he asked.

Trudy giggled. "I told it to eject you."

"And *how* did you tell her?"

"I just thought, 'eject Cotton through the canopy'."

He slapped his knee. "Naw! That ain't the way you do it. You have to think an *image* of me shooting up through the canopy. Not words."

She giggled again, and put her hands over her mouth. "I am."

He smiled, then winked at her. "Anyway, she couldn't do it. She doesn't have ejection seats."

Trudy was silent for a moment as her mood changed. "Cotton, if they think I stole my journal, then I can't go home. They'll be looking everywhere for me. Kitty will be worried about me, and so will Pop."

"No they won't. Your father knows all about this—from Leona—and you can call your friend when you get home."

"You do know everything, don't you? Do you know what I'm thinking about at this very minute? Never mind, I'm confused and babbling. I'm scared, I'm miserable, I don't know what's happening, and I feel like I ought to be freezing to death, but I'm not. Why not? Here we are, half-buried in a snow bank on top of a mountain in the middle of winter, in a. . . . What do you call this funny looking thing, anyway? And why aren't we freezing?"

"Call her anything you want to. Sometimes I call her 'sweetheart', or 'baby', or 'darling'. You may not think she's beautiful, but it's like the old farmer said of his wife: 'She may not be so good to look at, but she's a sure-fire bargain for stout.'."

He laughed at his little analogy, but Trudy glared at him. After a moment, she replied, "You think that's so darn funny, don't you? I don't think it's funny at all. You're just like all men: you make jokes about women as if they were property! Go jump in the lake, Mr. Tow-Head O'Brien!" She folded her arms, pouted her lips, and turned away from him.

Cotton chuckled lightly, then changed his tone of voice. "So that's the way it is, is it? You've been burned pretty badly by men, have you? Well, don't be so sensitive, little lady. We aren't all rotten."

Trudy's mood changed again. She leaned forward, rested her elbows on her knees, and covered her face with her hands. "My father is the only good man I know, and I'm worried about him."

"Your father's okay—I mean, *really* okay. He's the toughest man I've ever met. Too bad you aren't more like him. Where's your spunk, girl? You couldn't be in a more safe place than you're in now. I'll take you to your father as soon as the time is right."

Trudy bounced back. "Spunk?" She was shouting again, and to make matters worse, Cotton smiled as if he liked it. "What do you know about spunk? It's another one of those words that men use to describe women and children!"

He held up his open hands. "Okay, okay. I suppose you're right. Settle down, will you? Maybe you're tougher than I thought. Look, let's change the subject. Ask me some questions about my amazing little baby space ship."

Again, Trudy changed moods as if on command. Cotton was delighted by her supple personality.

"All right, why aren't we freezing, and why does the air smell so fresh? Why do you call it 'her', as if it had female gender?"

He had expected a physicist to ask about the energy source, but her questions were typically female. He almost laughed. "I refer to her as 'her' because I'm in love with her. You wouldn't expect me to call it 'him' in that case, would you?"

Trudy closed her eyes, and slowly shook her head. She had no doubts regarding his masculinity.

Cotton continued, "This little tub had a thousand times more engineering put into it than the battleship Missouri. Her energy source has more energy in 'stand-by' than the Three Mile Island nuclear power plant has at full-heat." He watched her eyes open as if she were suddenly awakened. "There! I thought that might get your attention."

"'Don't misunderstand me, Mr. O'Brien. I've been thinking about your little tub's energy source ever since you forced me into it, and maybe I'm just jealous because someone else was far ahead of me. The only reasonable explanation is anti-gravity levitation. Your little darling is powered by anti-matter."

Her sarcastic reply took the wind out of his sails, and she could see it in his eyes. She almost wished that she could retract her statement, and rephrase it in a more friendly manner. But who was this man? Something within her mind told her that he was her friend—even her champion. Without knowing why, she had known from her first sight of him that he could be trusted. Why, then, was she rejecting him?

He had actually kidnapped her, but did she not need his help? Yes, she wanted to trust him, she needed him, and she definitely wanted to know more about his baby space ship. As these thoughts raced through her mind, she saw the disappointment fade from his expression, to be replaced by a smile. This man was different. She had to let him know that her own self-control was equal to his.

"Okay, Mr. Cotton O'Brien, you did get my attention, and I apologize for my caustic reply. You didn't deserve that. If you'll kindly continue, I'm dying to know all about her."

"Her, who?" He smiled easily. "Frankly, I was about to offer you my other cheek, but you surprised me. Thank you, Miss Two Bears. I'm most happy to continue. Do you really want to know why we're not freezing?"

It was Trudy's turn to smile. "Not really. I assume that, with so much energy available, it's a small matter to tap-off a little bit for air conditioning." She frowned, and shook her head. "No, it can't be that conventional. I want to know all the details about everything, but first, I want to know about the energy source. May I see it, and ask you to explain it?"

"I'd be happy to show you, but this little darling is pretty compact, as you can see, and I can't easily show it to you from the cockpit. Trudy, there's much more involved here than I can explain right now. There are beings, known to us as *Ezekiens*, that are responsible for this ship, and a lot more. They have a large colony ship out in space—don't look so startled—I know it's difficult for you to believe.

"But it's all true, and everything will be fully explained to you at another time. When you do understand and believe, if you don't mind, I'd like to show you around their colony in space, and explain it to you then; providing that Leona approves, of course."

It suddenly hit Trudy, and the enormity of her present experience caused her to tremble. She gasped, covered her mouth with her hands, and looked in horror at the man beside her.

"What? What did you say? Who are you? Are you some kind of outer-space alien? 'Colony in space'? Who *is*

Leona?"

Cotton was astounded by Trudy's sudden fright, and became concerned that her present condition might lead to shock. He had overestimated her strength, and underestimated all that she had recently endured.

"Take it easy, girl." He reached out to touch her arm, but she recoiled, and moved away from him. "Trudy, I'm sorry. I should have known you were taking this too well. Look, I'm not very good at this, but they've taught me a little."

He quickly put the gold band over his head, again reached out, and despite her withdrawing, gently placed his hand on her forehead. Her eyes rolled up, then slowly closed. Her trembling stopped, and she relaxed. When he released his hand, she opened her eyes, and spoke.

"Your hand felt so soothing. What did you do?"

"I don't know, Trudy. Honestly, I don't. It must be a form of hypnosis. I just *willed* you to relax. Do you feel okay now?"

She nodded. "I'm fine now, but I'm very, very confused. All that's happened lately. You, with the white hair—I've seen you before, you know. Visions. This space thingamajig. Colony in space. Leona. Cotton, I've got a whole lot of questions, but I'm not sure that I can handle the answers."

"Do you still want to know about the energy source?"

"No. I mean, sure I do, but I don't think I'm ready for that yet. I need other answers, first. Cotton, who are you? And who is Leona? I love her for what she's done for my father, but I don't know anything about her."

Cotton took a long moment before answering her questions, but Trudy was now relaxed and patient. He leaned back, and put his booted foot on the blank instrument panel before them. Outside, the leeward sides of a few jagged rocks appeared starkly black in contrast to the pure white blowing snow. Their view down the mountainside was no longer visible because of the blizzard. The overhead dome of the little space ship was so perfectly transparent that Trudy felt almost unprotected from the weather outside. It seemed that she needed only to reach out her arm to feel the cold wind and snow; yet, she was absolutely comfortable.

"Trudy, I can answer your questions now. Leona agrees, and goodness knows, you've earned the right to ask."

"Are you telling me that you've just communicated with Leona?"

"Well, yes and no. It's more accurate that Leona communicated with me. As much as I've tried, I've never been able to do that."

"But just a few moments ago you did. You got inside my brain and calmed me down."

"No. Sorry to disappoint you, but I only made it possible for you to read *my* mind, and even that came from Leona, not me."

"Well, crud! Now I *am* disappointed! So, what's so special about *you?*"

Cotton almost fell out of his seat with laughter. This girl had a sense of humor to match his own.

Trudy continued. "Hey, wait. You just said that I read *your* mind! Did Leona do that? Can she *control* my mind?"

"No, girl. Leona can do almost anything. She's a real V.I.P., but she can't control minds. Not even the Ezekiens can do that. Leona says that you have the gift. You can read minds, but you don't know it, yet."

Trudy's jaw fell open like a trap door. "Whoa, cotton-top. Back-up. Just one bullet at a time, please. *Who* are the *Ezekiens?*"

"Trudy. . . ." He sat up, and slapped his hand to his forehead. "Girl, this could take hours."

She smiled, hunched-up her shoulders, and spread

her open hands. "Well, you asked for it."

He returned the smile. "So I did. How 'bout I just tell you my own story, and let Leona explain the rest. Okay?"

She nodded her agreement, and he began.

"Okay, first things first. A minute ago, you asked what was so special about me." Again, he chuckled at the thought as he shook his head. "Well, since I have to explain it to you, I might as well tell you the truth before someone else denies it: I'm the best darned fighter pilot in this whole universe! That, I am! The only trouble with that is, there isn't anyone for me to fight with, so I'm stuck as a handyman and errand-boy for Leona. Don't worry, she only hears what she wants to."

Trudy smiled, and snuggled-up to her knees.

"My real name is Casey O'Brien. I was the oldest of six kids growing up in the hills of Tennessee. Mama died when I was ten. Papa blamed it on the baby, but he took it out on me. I was pretty badly abused, especially when he was drunk, and that was most of the time. The county sheriff finally took away the rest of the kids, but left me there, for some reason. I was so badly treated that I used to climb on top of the barn at night, and pray for a flying saucer to come down and pick me up. That was when I was twelve—hey, that was twenty years ago. Anyway, believe it or not, one night it really happened."

Cotton was fascinated by the expressions of Trudy's face. Her mouth, her eyes, her eyebrows signaled every feeling within her. The blizzard outside roared around them, but there was no sound inside, other than Cotton's voice.

"I wanted to get away from that place so badly that I could die. Well, when that bright, blue light shined down on me, I nearly did die—from fright! The next thing I knew, I was falling *up*, and into that flying saucer. It was big! Much bigger than our barn, and inside was as bright as daylight. I was breathing hard, and my heart was pounding, but I couldn't close my eyes." Trudy's eyes were wide-open. "As soon as I was inside, the door closed beneath my feet, and the light released me. The first person I saw was Johnny, a young man in his late teens at that time."

Trudy's eyes got even bigger. "Johnny?"

"Yep, Johnny J. Jones. Ugliest human I ever saw—ugly as home-made soap—but he's a fine person, and one of my best friends now."

"Did he speak to you?"

"Yep."

"Well? What did he say?"

"He said, 'Hi, kid, how you doin'?' Johnny's a real, live, cut-up."

"Cotton! Be serious. I'm trying to believe you."

"I *am* serious. Well, I was really scared, but Johnny calmed me down, just like I did with you, and he put a gold band on my head. Then, the Ezekien walked in. He was a little shorter than I was, and I wasn't very big at that time. They took me into a small room—a laboratory-looking room—and I climbed onto a table...."

Trudy raised her head. "Oh, Cotton, stop! If they hurt you, I don't want you to tell me about it. Tell me about the Ezekien. What did he look like?"

"Okay, do you know what a pod of okra looks like?"

"Sure do."

"Then, you know what his skin, or the outside of his body, looked like; except, maybe not such a bright green. More brownish-green, and maybe more ridges running lengthwise along his limbs."

"Did he have arms and legs, like ours?"

"For Pete's sake, Trudy! Let me finish!"

She smiled, and rested her chin back on her knees.

"They have arms and legs, but not like ours: much longer, in comparison to their short bodies. Their body structure is *exoskeleton*. That means that their body is supported from the outside—by the cover. They have no bones."

"Cotton, I know what 'exoskeleton' means."

He had actually forgotten, for the moment, that Trudy was an adult. She had seemed, for the moment only, to be a child; a beautiful, delightful, child. Perhaps it was her facial expressions. He had embarrassed himself.

"I beg your pardon. Of course you do." He looked outside, but could see nothing, only grayness. *Maybe I wanted her to be a child*, he thought. *Maybe I, myself, would like to be a child again. When compared to the Ezekiens, we are children; at least, intellectually. Never in my life have I felt more like a child, than this day.*

"Hey, you big snow-top, don't leave me hanging. Are you talking with Leona, or just daydreaming? Next time you do that, *I'm* going to read your mind."

"I wouldn't be surprised." She saw a momentary wistful look in his eyes, then it was gone.

"What about eyes, ears, mouth, fingers?"

The feeling retreated, but, for the rest of his life, it would never leave him. He tried to fake exasperation.

"Trudy, if you keep interrupting, I'll never get through. Besides, you'll find out for yourself." He looked at the panel clock. "Now, where was I?"

"They look like okra." She giggled, then assumed her former knee-hugging position.

Cotton put his foot back on the instrument panel, and again removed the gold band. "That's enough about how they look. As I said, you'll see for yourself."

Trudy stuck out her lower lip, and frowned, but said nothing.

"What I want you to realize is that they're not to be feared. Their only mission is to help *us* to make Earth a better place to live. Back to my story: As soon as I stood before the Ezekien, I lost all of my fear. I know it wasn't mind-control. It was more like I helped you a few minutes ago, except that he never touched me. He just *told* me that I had nothing to fear."

Trudy's hand shot up, as a signal that she wanted to ask a question.

He laughed again. "I know. You want to ask how he spoke, and did he speak English." Her hand came down. "Well, he didn't speak to me in words. He didn't actually speak, at all. I just knew what he wanted me to know. You see, we speak to each other with words, and we usually think with words, but we could communicate with each other much better if we could speak with images, and that's what the Ezekiens do. No language is involved, and speech isn't necessary. They *telecommunicate*. Do you understand?"

She responded by rolling her eyes upward.

"For Pete's sake, Trudy, I know you're smart! I just keep forgetting. Now, wait a minute! What you just did is a perfect example that I never thought of before. I knew immediately what you meant when you rolled those beautiful eyes. See how smart I am?"

His reference to her beautiful eyes came back like a punch in the chest. *Cotton, old boy, you'd better get away from here before it's too late. Those eyes are going to haunt you*, he thought. He looked at the clock again.

"We'd better go, Trudy. You want to go home, don't you?"

She looked hurt. "No, Cotton . . . I mean, yes. I want to go home more than anything, but you haven't finished with your story. We're okay, aren't we? I mean, we're not going to freeze to death, and we're safe here. You won't have to jump-start this thing, will you?"

His laugh was joyous. "Trudy. . . ." He wanted to grab her, but never in his life had he felt more restrained by such a good feeling. *Be cool, Cotton, this girl is different*.

"All right, girl, anything you say. Just tell me when you're ready to go."

He stretched his body, then leaned back in his seat, and put both feet on the instrument panel.

"They strapped me onto that table, but it wasn't to keep me from fighting; it was to keep me from floating off. We were already up in free-space, you see. They didn't hurt me at all, and I learned later that they always examine everyone before they're allowed to enter the Colony. Also, that's when I was neutralized."

Trudy's expression indicated that she wanted more information about 'neutralized'.

"Okay, the reason. . . ."

"Wait! Cotton, I can't just sit here and say nothing. It's impossible. I think I understand: you had to be *atomically neutralized* before you could enter an anti-matter condition. Is that correct?"

"Absolutely correct. Girl, I might as well throw in the towel. You're way ahead of me."

Trudy beamed her pleasure. Then her expression changed to a look of puzzlement. "But, if that's true, then I must be neutralized now. Don't patronize me, Cotton. Was I wrong when I guessed that this little space ship is powered by anti-matter?"

"Nope. You were right-on, but this little fighter—and that's what we should call her—is pushed by a *propulsive-type* power source. Only her thrust-rods are converted to anti-matter for propulsion. But the structure is now matter, the same as this mountain that we're dug into. When we return to the Colony, this whole fighter, including us, will have to be neutralized. Got it?"

"Got it! Then, the colony ship has a different type of anti-matter energy source. What's the difference?"

"The colony ship was designed only for interspace travel. Its energy source makes the entire ship either attractive or repulsive: matter, or gravity, being attractive; anti-matter, or anti-gravity, being repulsive."

Trudy became very excited. "Oh, I knew it! Dr.

Bonner is right." She clapped her hands over her mouth, but the excitement shone from her eyes.

Cotton could not help laughing. "Either energy source serves its purpose well. The colony ship repels and attracts its way very efficiently from one star system to another, but it isn't easily maneuverable. This little fighter, on the other hand, can tie knots in the sky." He held up his hand, and formed a circle with his thumb and forefinger. Trudy returned the 'okay' signal.

"I keep drifting off the subject. Now, try to save up your questions for a while, girl." Trudy snaked her tongue out at him as he continued. "Every day was school day. Back home, I hated school because I didn't go very often. I was always behind the other kids, and they made fun of me, but the Colony was different. I couldn't get enough. I was hungry for knowledge. Nobody made fun of my ignorance, and I was treated like a prince. Sure, it took me a while to get used to things. Zero-gravity was a problem, at first, but they made me exercise every day to keep myself physically strong. Now, that's something the Ezekiens don't do. They're physically weak because they've lived their whole lives at zero-gee, maybe for thousands of generations. Their food isn't very good either, so they brought in special Earth food for us. I always pig-out on beef steaks when I come back to Earth.

"My education was different from yours. You've noticed that my language skills and my manners are perfect. Well, that's because Leona taught me.

"I had other human teachers too, in the basic education classes, but the Ezekiens, mostly, polished me up, and taught me everything else.

"The Ezekiens don't look funny to me, anymore. They're like my own folks. I feel at home when I go back to the Colony. Well, look what they've done for me! You don't realize yet how special I am, but I feel like the most singled-out, special person on this earth."

Trudy broke-out in laughter. "Now I see it! Your white head is bigger than you are."

Cotton laughed with her. "Well, I'm just teasing you a little bit, but there's some truth to that statement, too.

"They taught me mathematics, physics, biology, geology, medicine, and how to do my own laundry. Then, after I grew up, they taught me all the skills of warfare, even though they're the most peaceful folks in the universe.

"I had human playmates, too. In my age group, fourteen of us grew up together—all races, and different ethnic backgrounds. I even had a childhood sweetheart, but you wouldn't be interested in that." Trudy wrinkled up her nose.

"Leona spends most of her time here on Earth, but she used to bring me down here with her a lot, so I wouldn't forget human ways. I wasn't the only one, though. Leona brought all of us down here at one time or another. She was more of a mother to me than my real mother. I also have an Ezekien mother, whom I love almost as much as Leona."

Trudy had tears in her eyes. He wanted to cup her face in his hands. *Stay cool, Cotton. This girl breaks too easily, and she's already been hurt more than she deserves.*

He spoke softly. "Are you ready to go home?"

She straightened up, stretched, shook herself, and looked around. As before, she was fascinated by the protective dome overhead. Inside was brightly lit, but she could not see the source of the light. Outside was now dark, with a heavy overcast sky; yet, she could see no glare or reflections from the surface of the canopy.

When she looked back at him, her smile was almost sad. "I'm trying not to remember anything before the last few hours. Thank you, Cotton, for helping me forget." Then she forced her expression to brighten. "Okay, best darned fighter pilot in the universe, take me home."

Cotton smiled and winked. "Got your seat belt fastened?" He straightened up, fastened his own safety harness, placed the gold band snugly on his head, and faced the instrument panel. Suddenly, the whole panel lit up with a display of colored lights. There were bars, dots, and odd symbols everywhere, and right in the middle of the panel appeared a life-sized, full-color, three-dimensional image of Trudy's smiling face. Then the image changed, and showed her tongue snake-out as she had done before.

"Look!" Trudy screamed her delight, and pointed at the image. She was as happy as if she had just received a wonderful birthday present.

The image faded away, and was replaced by a terrestrial display of the surrounding area, also in three-dimensional, full color.

"Oh, how did you do that?" She was radiant with delight.

"Simple. It was just a recorded visual display of my mind's image at that time, and it was my way of thanking you for being good company."

He took one more look at her radiant face. "Ready?"

She nodded.

There was no jerking, or bumping, or weird noises of any kind. Trudy felt only a moderate, momentary heaviness in the seat before she looked outside. A carbon-black sky full of brilliant, glittering stars surrounded them. Far below, she could see the dimly-lit tops of the clouds they had just left, and many miles ahead, where the clouds broke up, were the lights of some large city.

CHAPTER 14

Icy was smug in the appraisal of her plan. She had used Dr. Owen Smith, another I.O.U. collection, for the final degradation of Trudy's resistance. It would now be only a matter of time until Trudy submitted. But, to strengthen her assurance, Icy now called upon the help of Kitty Yamada. Also, Kitty's loyalty to the W.E.B. society had been brought up for question. There still remained the mystery of who had supplied information to Eileen Two Bears.

Kitty had no idea of what to expect. She had only been told to wait in room fourteen of the Starlight Motel, where a man would deliver a package to her at about midnight. She was then to stay there until Icy arrived later.

It was 11:30 when Kitty entered the room. There was one double bed, a dressing table and mirror, two armchairs, and a television set, but no man. She sat on the edge of the bed, thought about turning on the TV, then decided not to do so. It was times like this, especially during idle moments, that Kitty thought of her parents, both of whom were lost at sea during a sailing accident while she was in her first year of college. Since that time, Trudy and her parents had informally 'adopted' her as a member of their own family.

Meeting an unknown man was no problem to Kitty because she had no fear of physical attack. She was an only child, so her father had taught her, beginning at a very young age, the traditional martial skills of the Japanese samurai.

Kitty was still unaware that Trudy had been fired that day. She worked full time as a chemist during the day, and instructed the martial arts every Monday night at a public gym, so she had not been home since early morning.

Owen Smith was nervous; in fact, he was trembling. *How was I supposed to know I'd be blackmailed*, he thought. *When this is over, I'll have to kill that woman.*

It had been a terrible day for Owen. First, he had been forced into firing Trudy, which he had not wanted to do, because he still had hopes that she would change her mind about him. Then, to top it off, Icy had made him steal Trudy's journal. Stealing the secrets did not bother him so much, but falling into a blackmail trap was another thing. He thought of himself as being much smarter than that.

Owen knocked on the door, and was let in by Kitty. He was surprised, expecting to meet Icy.

"Uh . . . I was expecting to see someone else. Am I in the wrong room, sweetheart?"

"Whom were you expecting, sir?"

"Icy."

"Icy will be here later." Kitty stepped back, allowing Owen to enter and close the door behind him. "I believe you were supposed to deliver some papers to me. May I have them, please?"

Owen shook his head. "No way, baby. This is a business deal. I trade only with Icy."

He looked her over. "So, Icy sent you over to keep me company until she gets here, right?"

"No, sir. I was only instructed to receive your papers. You may leave after you've given them to me."

"Oh, I *may*, may I? He placed his briefcase on the dresser, and reached for her, but Kitty stepped back. "Don't be shy, baby, I like oriental beauties."

He reached again. Kitty deftly grabbed his hand, gave it a twist, and bent his wrist almost to the breaking-point. Owen cried out as she forced him to his knees.

At that moment, Icy opened the door, and stepped into the room. "Oh, how nice. I see you two have introduced yourselves." She removed her coat and gloves.

Owen was in great pain. "Tell her to let me go!"

Icy nodded. Kitty released his hand, then took a long step backward, away from him.

Owen got back to his feet while rubbing his hurting wrist. He sneered at Kitty, then glared at Icy. "What's going on here? Your little slant-eyed courier almost broke my wrist!"

Icy gave him her sweetest smile. "Nothing's going on, Owen. You simply forgot your manners, as usual. Shame on you." Her smile faded as she looked at his briefcase. "Do you have Trudy's journal?"

He grabbed the briefcase, and jerked it to his body. Kitty tensed, then looked at Icy. She started to speak, but Icy interrupted.

"Oh, you didn't know, did you, hon? Allow me to introduce your little room-mate's boss, Dr. Owen Smith."

"Trudy?" Kitty was obviously confused. "What do you know of Trudy? She has nothing to do with you."

"Oh, but she does! Trudy...."

"Hold it!" Owen interrupted. "I don't know what this is all about, and I don't care. We made a deal. You get the journal, and I get the videos. No more blackmail!"

Icy was smiling again. "Down, boy. Owen, you're really not very bright, are you? I get the journal, sure, but I'll keep the videos for a while longer, thank you. Now, let's have the journal."

Owen looked at her with contempt, then nervously unsnapped the lid of the case. He reached inside, and drew out a handgun, pointing it at Icy. It was a .22 caliber revolver equipped with a silencer. Kitty reacted quickly and instinctively, with a kick to his sore wrist. The gun flew out of his hand, bounced from the ceiling, and fell on the bed. Icy snatched it up, and pointed it at Owen.

"Exactly as I expected. Now, the journal, please."

Owen dropped the case, and Trudy's journal slid out onto the floor. Icy fired the gun, point-blank. Owen fell backward, hit the wall, and slid to the floor.

Kitty covered her face, then slowly withdrew her hands as she looked at Icy. "That wasn't necessary. You didn't have to kill him. You murdered him!"

Icy swung the gun around, pointing it at Kitty. "Take it easy. . . ." Kitty crouched. "Don't do it, hon! You and I are going to talk. You sit in that chair, and I'll take the bed." Neither of them said anything as they warily took their places.

Kitty was the first to speak. "What were you going to say about Trudy?"

Icy raised her chin. "You don't know your roomie as well as you thought, do you?"

"Oh, yes, I know her very well."

"But you didn't know that she intends to join our W.E.B. society, did you?"

Kitty lost her composure. "You lie! Trudy would *never* join your rotten web!"

"Ahhh . . . rotten? So, now we know, don't we? *You're* the informer. *You* were the one who supplied information to Eileen Two Bears!"

Icy stood up, and aimed the gun. Kitty lunged from the chair as the gun fired, then fell heavily to the floor, blood streaming from the side and back of her head.

"Too bad, honey. You were good, and I really needed you, but I need Trudy more." Icy was still as calm as when she first entered the room. She wiped her fingerprints from the gun, then firmly placed it in Kitty's limp hand before dropping it aside. *The head shot was lucky. Looks like a suicide.*

She put on her coat and gloves, picked up Trudy's journal, glanced at the room, and looked carefully around outside before leaving.

An hour later, Kitty stirred, then struggled to her hands and knees. She was a bloody mess, and her head felt like an explosion. "Trudy. Oh, Trudy, you've got to hear me." She fell back to the floor, but struggled up again, crawled to the door, and opened it. *I have to warn Trudy.* Then, she fell outside, and lay still.

It was another half-hour before Kitty awoke again, in the trauma center of the hospital. She was aware of people working hurriedly around her.

"I saw a case like this once before," she heard someone say. "Happens more often than you'd think. The bullet enters, travels around between the skin and skull, then comes out half-way around the head. This is one tough little lady."

Icy heard the news on her car radio while driving to work. Kitty was alive! Not only alive, but conscious and aware, and she was now telling everything to the police. *Impossible!* Icy thought. *How could it be? I saw where the bullet entered, and where it came out. Well, this changes everything!* Icy was not one who dwelled on disappointment; her mind was totally positive. If a plan failed, she always had alternatives. She changed lanes, and took an exit to return home. *No, I can't go back home. It may be a trap. So, it has to be The Tunnel.*

'The Tunnel' was headquarters for the W.E.B. organization. It was an old, abandoned, underground arsenal in western Virginia, used by the army during World War II. She had purchased the property through a second party, and named it 'The Tunnel' because it had two entrances, one on each side of a mountain ridge. It had originally been a natural cavern.

Icy worked her way through heavy traffic to a society-owned warehouse. There, she gave hurried orders to another society member, then changed to a different car, and drove safely from the city. It never occurred to Icy that she had been lucky not to have been stopped by the police. Luck was never a factor. She had simply taken advantage of the early morning heavy traffic, and used good judgment.

So, now the lid was off. It was almost a relief to Icy. Now she could push the buttons, and initiate her well-prepared plans to control the world. Women would, at last, assume their proper roll as masters, not mistresses, of men.

Her plan to enlist Trudy must now be abandoned, but it had been a risky plan from the beginning. Trudy would have learned, sooner or later, that the W.E.B. society had been responsible for her mother's death. Icy felt a tinge of regret. *Too bad. I really needed her. So now I'll have to rely on Nadezhda.* But there would be problems: Nadezhda was a Russian physicist, who was also searching for the anti-matter solution. She would have to be smuggled out of Russia, and brought to the United States; that was difficult enough. Then, there was the language difference, which would require interpreters. There were other problems, none of which were too great, provided there was enough time.

On the other hand, there were the advantages of importing Nadezhda. She was already a 'woman of the web', and she was ready for a promotion to the fifth tier. The Tunnel's lab was equipped and waiting, for it was Nadezhda's brain and remote instructions that had allowed work to begin on *the bomb*. So far, the theory had not worked. There was an error somewhere in the atomic conversion module. Icy had been counting on Trudy's knowledge to correct the error, but Trudy was now out of the plan. However, Icy did have Trudy's lab journal, which might provide Nadezhda with enough information to solve the problem.

It was now early December. Icy had almost two months left to make the bomb work. It might just be enough time; if not, she would have to wait another year.

CHAPTER 15

Trudy's reunion with her father was both happy and sad. Happy, because Ben's health was almost back to normal. He seemed to be himself again, now that his daughter was home; yet, it was also a sad time for both of them because they were not yet accustomed to reuniting without Eileen's presence.

Trudy was glad that Leona had not yet appeared. She wanted to visit alone with her father for a while, but also, she did not know how to greet Leona. Finally, she knew that she had to ask.

"Pop, what do you know about Leona?"

"Well, I'll tell you something, honey; she isn't the same Leona you knew before. It's taken me a long time to get used to the change. I liked the way she used to laugh all the time, you know, but she doesn't do that anymore. I kinda' miss it."

"Maybe it's because of what happened to you."

"Maybe. Has Cotton told you anything about her?"

"Pop, I don't know *anything!* Cotton talked as if she were some kind of superwoman, but he wouldn't tell me about her."

"Well, she is a super woman, I guess. She sure saved my life, and I still don't understand it all."

"How did she save you?"

"Honey, Leona didn't even lay a hand on that woman, but she threw her across the room, and knocked her out. I saw it happen. Another thing, she can read my mind. Now, if *that* wouldn't keep a man off balance, I don't know what would!"

Trudy giggled. "Well, you'd better get used to it because I'm starting to read minds, too." Then her expression turned solemn. "I didn't tell you this before, but I knew that you were hurt before Sheriff Lang called me. Your distress alerted me, and I thought I saw it as it happened, but I wasn't sure until now." She gripped his hand. "Pop, this is scary stuff."

They both turned, as Leona knocked and entered the room. There was a marked change in her appearance since Trudy had last seen her. She seemed taller, somehow. Her red hair was now neatly styled, and her face, very plain before, was now almost pretty. She even walked differently.

"Ben, am I interrupting?"

Trudy stood. "Leona, is that you?"

Leona's smile was spontaneous and delightful. "Yes, it's me."

"Oh, I don't know whether to curtsy, or fall to my knees." Then she laughed. "But I'm so glad to see you."

Leona laughed also, the way she used to, and held out her arms as she approached Trudy.

Trudy almost wept as they embraced. She stepped back to look at both of them. "Leona, Pop, you have to tell me everything. Cotton explained. . . ." She looked around the room. "Where *is* that tow-head?"

Leona's smile was all-knowing. "He wouldn't stay, Trudy. I think he wants to be alone for a while, but he'll be back."

Trudy looked puzzled for a moment as they took seats. "Leona, he said that you'd explain everything. Please tell me who you really are."

Leona looked at Ben.

"Go ahead, Leona. I'd like to hear it again, myself."

"Very well. My real name is Leona Braun, as you know. Braun was my late husband's name." She smiled. "My latest late husband. But I was born Leona Graham. I'm an emissary of the Ezekien Colony, and my mission is to help save our planet from ourselves."

"But you aren't an Ezekien?"

Leona smiled, and shook her head. "No, dear. My parents were Irish, but I was reared in London; that is, until I was nine years old, when I was rescued by the Ezekiens."

"Goodness, I was worried! Cotton's description made the Ezekiens sound *ugly*." She put her hand over her mouth. "I'm sorry, Leona. I hope that wasn't offensive."

Leona laughed. "Not at all. The Ezekiens wouldn't be offended. I'm sure they must think we're ugly, by comparison. But, really, I don't notice their difference any more. They're my family."

"That's exactly what Cotton said. I think I'm beginning to like them. Would you mind telling me about your life with them? You were only a child when they adopted you, but. . . ." She clapped her mouth again. "Excuse me. Cotton got annoyed at me because I asked so many questions."

Ben laughed, and slapped his leg. "Here it comes, Leona. She won't quit until she knows everything."

Trudy wrinkled her nose at her father. "Pop, you're not being nice."

Leona smiled. She would not be concerned any more about Ben and his daughter. They only needed to be together again. She continued.

"As I was saying, I was only nine when they rescued me." She told how she became orphaned, and about the horrifying London Blitz. "We were all unfortunate children, in one way or another, when we were rescued. They sometimes take adults, but rarely; children are pliable, more easily educated, but mostly because the Ezekiens just have a kind feeling for children. They truly want to help us."

Ben interrupted. "Where'd they come from, Leona, and how long have they been here?" Trudy shook her finger at him.

"They're from a star system nearer to the center of our galaxy. Their planet, Ezekia, was probably a billion years older than Earth. It was destroyed more than a million years ago when their sun exploded." She smiled at Trudy. "You want to know, since they have no language, how they came to be called *Ezekiens*." Trudy nodded.

"They were given the name by another human, many years ago. It had something to do with a description from the book of Ezekiel in our Judeo-Christian Scriptures. One of the books that we had for study was the Christian Bible, along with other religious books. The Ezekiens attempted to make sure that our education was well-rounded, and even encouraged those coming back to Earth to engage in the religions of their choice. I don't remember all of the passages from Ezekiel, but I have one that's been my favorite. Would you like to hear it?"

Ben and Trudy both nodded. Leona was quiet for a moment, getting her thoughts together, then she began to recite:

"This is taken from the 36th chapter, verses 24-26, of the Book of Ezekiel:

> 'For I will take you from among the heathen, and gather you out of all countries, and will bring you into your own land. Then will I sprinkle clean water upon you, for ye shall be clean: from all your filthiness, and from all your idols, will I cleanse you. A new heart also will I give you, and a new spirit will I put within you: and I will take away the stony heart out of your flesh, and I will give you an heart of flesh.' (KJV)

This, I think, tells pretty much of what the Ezekiens are

trying to accomplish. They don't think of themselves as our Saviors, but more as our rescuers.

"You'll find this difficult to appreciate or understand, but the Ezekiens have been observing our Earth longer than intelligent human life has existed. They can't live here, however, because our gravity is much too strong for them. Some of them can survive, now, for short durations only, then they must return to zero-gravity conditions."

"Then, that's why they must rely on us to help ourselves," Trudy said. "Leona, you must be terribly discouraged. Your mission must seem to be impossible. We're so stupid!"

Ben could not resist. "Speak for yourself, kid. *I'm* not stupid."

She giggled, and leaned over to kiss him heartily on the cheek. "You may insult me all you want to. I love you dearly."

Ben squeezed his daughter with a hug, then turned to question Leona. "I've been forgetting to ask you this: you told me that you'd been searching for something on the mountain. What're you looking for?"

"Cotton and I have been trying to locate a very ancient Ezekien exploration craft. Cotton's little fighter ship is equipped with a detector for locating its energy source, but the craft has been buried in the earth so long that the whole area around here indicates activity."

Trudy sat up, very interested. "How long?"

"Maybe a million years. At least before the *great flood.*"

"Oh, wow! Do you mean the Ezekiens are *that* far ahead of us? They've had anti-matter energy for that long?"

"Dear, the Ezekiens discovered anti-matter energy long before they were forced to abandon their planet. Otherwise, they couldn't have escaped."

Trudy blew out her breath, and fell back in her chair. "Leona, I can't ask any more questions. This is too much.

No! I want to know about mind-reading, and how you saved Pop."

"Telepathy is a gift, Trudy. We few humans who possess the gift cannot explain why we're different, only that we are. Most of us, at some time, have felt that we knew what someone else was thinking—like coincidental thought, which probably is a form of mind reading. Telepathy, however, means *communication* from one mind to another. I've known of my own ability as far back as I can remember. Others may possess the gift in latent form. I'm sure it must be quite startling to discover it suddenly."

"You mean, like me?"

"Yes, dear. How long have you known it?"

"I don't know—and I'm still not really convinced that I *have* experienced it. But I *must* have; otherwise, I wouldn't have known about Pop, or Cotton. Now, that's a strange one: I *knew* Cotton, but I never met him before this afternoon. He's a big, conceited bully, Leona. Why didn't you teach him some manners?" Trudy laughed with Ben and Leona.

"I'm sure you do have the gift, Trudy, and you mustn't be afraid of it. You should practice, and try to develop it."

"I'm not sure that I want to. I think I'd feel terrible if I intruded on someone's personal thoughts." She looked at her father. "Pop?"

Ben looked uneasy. He knew that Trudy was handing him an opportunity. "Well, Leona, I've been meaning to talk to you about that. It's been bothering me some that you could know all of my thoughts. Just doesn't seem right, you know?"

Leona's face appeared to drain. "Oh, Ben. Is *that* it? I knew something was wrong, but I didn't think I should ask. No, Ben, I wouldn't do that. I learned many years ago not to intrude on people's private thoughts. Please trust me."

He managed a grin. "All right, Leona, I will. Thanks for setting me straight."

Trudy was not satisfied. "But I need to know, Leona. If I use this gift, as you say, then I must know how to control it."

"There'll be times when you have no control, Trudy, as when your father was so distressed. A distress call may penetrate all other thoughts. At other times, you may have to concentrate extremely hard in order to get through. It can be very tiring, mentally." She smiled. "Don't worry, it isn't like tuning a radio.

"You're so innocent, Trudy—so undeserving of your troubles. You should be allowed to live an uncomplicated life, but life isn't that kind to us, is it? I almost wish that you didn't possess the gift. On the other hand, you have the character and strength that our world so desperately needs." Leona then waited for Trudy's response.

It took a moment to sink-in, then Trudy was overwhelmed. She pressed her hands to her chest, as if to say, *who, me?* "Oh, Leona! What're you saying? Are you asking me to participate in your impossible mission?" She looked at her father. "Pop? Did you hear what she said?"

Ben's expression also showed disbelief, but Leona did not wait for his response.

"Please, both of you. I can't ask you, Trudy. I can only present the idea, but please think about it, and discuss it with your father. Cotton and I must leave soon, to continue our work, but you must take all the time that you need, to decide."

The conversation ended. Trudy and Ben looked at each other. Leona asked to be excused, saying that she must not have a part in Trudy's decision. Ben and Trudy sat together silently for several minutes, until she finally spoke. "Pop, I'm exhausted, and I can't think now. Do you still have some of Mom's things? Cotton didn't even give me enough time to get my purse."

Trudy could not sleep. She tossed and turned, and punched her pillow in vain. She looked at the alarm clock beside her bed. *Only 10:30?* Then she remembered the difference in time zones. It was 12:30 a.m. in Washington, D.C.. Suddenly, she was startled to full awareness. *Kitty!* Something terrible was happening! Kitty was crawling on her hands and knees. She was hurting, and calling Trudy's name.

Trudy jumped out of bed, and put on her mother's robe as she ran through the hall to her father's bedroom. She pounded on the door, then opened it, and turned on the lights. Ben was already throwing off the bed covers.

"Pop! Something bad has happened to Kitty!" She turned, before Ben could respond, and ran back down the hall to the stairway. Leona was running up the stairs. "Leona, something terrible has happened to Kitty—my room-mate in D.C.. She's been shot in the head!"

Leona grabbed Trudy's hand. "You must be calm, Trudy. Here, let's sit down." Trudy began to relax as they sat on the stair steps. Ben stood before them.

"I'm okay now, thank you." She squeezed Leona's hand.

"Try to concentrate, Trudy. What's happening to your friend now?"

Trudy lowered her head, and touched her fingers to her brow. A moment passed. "Nothing. She's just lying there. Is she dead?"

Leona stroked Trudy's hand. "I don't know, dear. You must tell me."

"No, she isn't dead! Someone else is there now, to help."

CHAPTER 16

Ben stood at the kitchen window sipping his coffee, while watching the cliff turn red from the morning sun. The weathered cracks and crevices, still in dark shadows, formed changing patterns as the sun rose. Trudy and Leona sat at the table with their coffee.

"But I panicked, Leona. How could you possibly depend on someone who falls apart in a crisis? If you hadn't calmed me, like Cotton did, I would have blown up."

"I didn't calm you, Trudy. You did it yourself."

"I did?" She seemed to be amazed.

"You most certainly did. What happened during your fathers crisis? Did you fall apart then?"

"No, I suppose not, but I was worried to death. Anyway, I didn't know then what I know now. I thought, then, that my imagination was just running wild."

Trudy got up, and walked idly to her father. She put her arms around his waist, and leaned her head on his chest. "What do you think, Pop?"

"About what, honey?"

"About me joining Leona." She raised her head to look into his eyes. "You knew what I meant."

He kissed her forehead, and walked her back to the table where they both sat down. "It isn't my decision, Trudy."

He seldom used her name, and by that, she knew that he was being serious. "I know I'll worry about you—you're all I have left—but I have to remember back when I was your age. My parents couldn't have held me back with an anchor chain. This old world is a good place to live, honey. If the Ezekiens think it's worth saving, and if you want to try it, then I couldn't stand in your way. Is that what you've decided to do?"

Her answer was given as seriously as his statement. "Yes, Pop." She squeezed his hand. "I love you." Then she looked at Leona. "Okay, chief. Do you furnish uniforms? I don't even have a change of clothes."

Leona smiled, then looked at Ben. "Thank you, Ben. We'll take good care of her."

The telephone rang, and Ben picked up the receiver. "Hello. Yeah, Sam. How is she? Well, that's good news. Yeah, she's still here. Okay, Sam, see you later."

He hung up the receiver, and spoke to Trudy. "Kitty's doing just fine, honey. Sam said she's in the hospital with heavy police protection. He's coming right up."

Sheriff Lang arrived in less than thirty minutes. They spoke their greetings, then returned to the kitchen. Trudy poured the sheriff a big mug of coffee.

"Thanks, Trudy. Ye shore are lookin' good. Didn't sleep much last night, did ye?"

"No, it was a terrible night." She had great respect for the sheriff, but decided that it would be best not to tell him any more than necessary.

"Sheriff Lang, I can't easily describe how I knew. All I can tell you is that my mind went wild, and I *knew* that Kitty had been badly hurt. Is that okay?"

"You bet. I've heard 'o that happenin', but cain't say as I've ever known anybody before who could do it." He glanced at Leona, then back to Trudy. "Yer friend Kitty told the police a whoppin' big story. Seems there's a bunch 'o women goin' ta' take-over the world. They wouldn't ordinarily tell me all this, me bein' only a sheriff, but I've got a few friends here and there. Yer friend sez' a woman named India Brooks is head 'o those women. Sez' she's the one killed yer' boss."

Trudy gasped. "Killed my boss? You mean Dr. Bonner?"

"Nope. His name was Smith. Is that right?"

"Yes. Oh, my goodness! That's terrible!"

"She also said India Brooks was the one who had yer' secret journal. Smith stole it. Some kinda' blackmail scheme."

Trudy covered her face. "I can't believe all this is happening. Sheriff Lang, how was Kitty involved in that mess?"

"She said she was a member of India Brooks' organization. They call it 'the W.E.B. society'."

Trudy spoke aloud to herself while trying to collect her thoughts. "Oh, Kitty, why didn't you tell me?" She took a deep breath, then returned her attention to the sheriff. "What happens now? Do the authorities know that I'm here? Did you tell them?"

The sheriff grinned, and patted her hand. "Trudy, I wouldn't wear this badge if I couldn't use my own judgment. Nobody knows you're here, but we need ta' let 'em know that you're safe. Ye did disappear kinda' sudden-like, ye know. Those F.B.I. body guards 'o yours are fit ta' be tied. Do ye think ye still need 'em?"

"No, sir. I won't be going back, and I'm safe here."

"Fine. Ye ought ta' call yer friend, too. They said she kept askin' about ye. She must be purty worried, by now."

"Oh, I know! Will they let me speak to her on the phone?"

"Maybe. I'll see what I can do."

The sheriff placed the call, and Trudy spoke with Kitty for a few minutes. Tears filled her eyes as she hung-up the receiver. She turned to her father. "Bless her heart, she was worried about *me*."

Sheriff Lang stood, and picked up his hat. "Guess I'd better go and let 'em know that you're okay, Trudy." He hesitated a moment, then spoke again. "Ye shore do git-around in a hurry, Trudy. No record 'o ye comin' in by plane last night."

She looked embarrassed. "I have a friend with a private plane, Sheriff Lang." Then she smiled.

He returned the smile. "Shore. I never thought 'o that." He said goodbye to Leona and Trudy, and Ben walked with him to the door.

The morning paper printed only a short article about Kitty's incident on an inside page. The authorities were obviously skeptical about her story, and played down its importance. There was no mention of Icy Brooks' name. The television network news made no mention of it at all.

Trudy was furious. "Oh, how stupid can they be? Kitty's story should be big news! Leona, what can we do?"

"You mustn't let it excite you that way, Trudy. Do you think it would be better to announce a world-wide catastrophe?"

Trudy dropped her shoulders, and cocked her head. "Leona, you're so wise. Do you think I'll ever learn?"

Cotton returned the next morning, and entered the kitchen as Trudy was helping Leona clean up the breakfast dishes.

Trudy was in a teasing mood. "Well, well . . . the great white hunter returns. Where've *you* been?"

He stood with a smile on his face and his hands on his hips, as she so well remembered him.

"None of your business. Wanna' fight?"

She laughed, and shook her head. "Touche'. I deserved that. Want some breakfast?" She felt good.

"Got a steak?"

"Sure do. Want some eggs with it?"

"About half a dozen, scrambled."

He sat down at the table. Leona brought him a cup of coffee, kissed him on the forehead, and ruffled his white hair. Then she left the two young people alone, saying that she had to start house-cleaning. Ben was outside watching the sunrise.

They bantered teasing insults to each other, until he finished his breakfast. She took his dishes to the sink, and brought him another cup of coffee. Then she poured herself another cup, and sat down opposite him.

She could not keep from smiling. "Guess what."

"What?"

"I'm going to work for the Ezekiens."

His expression did not change. "Guess who's going to be your teacher."

"Oh, you big kill-joy! I thought you'd be surprised!" She tried to pout. "Who's going to be my teacher?"

"Who's the best darned fighter pilot in the universe?"

She was the surprised one. "You?"

"You got it. When do you want to start?"

"Start what? No, I mean, really. I don't know what I'm supposed to do."

"How 'bout a trip to the Colony. Want to start there?"

Trudy could not contain her excitement. "Yes! Oh, I've got to go tell Pop! When can we leave?"

"Depends on when you're ready."

She jumped up, and ran outside to her father. Cotton shook his head, and bumped his forehead on the table top.

Cotton, 'ol boy, that little talk you had with yourself didn't help at all. You're in love!

CHAPTER 17

They left the house before dawn the next morning. The moon had already set behind the mountain, and the glow from the city was not enough to light their way. Trudy could not see where to step.

"Cotton, why don't you use a flashlight?"

He whispered. "Don't want to. Somebody might be watching."

She felt blindly for his presence, then held onto his arm. It was the first time they had touched since Cotton had 'calmed' her by placing his hand on her forehead. He felt deeply stirred by the simple action of her touch.

When they got to the barn, Cotton opened the doors, and put the band on his head. The little fighter's canopy snapped open.

"I can't see," she whispered. "You'll have to help me, but don't you dare pitch me in, this time." She had to suppress her laugh.

Cotton felt his way around to the passenger side, placed his hands around her waist, and gently eased her onto the seat. The craft floated through the doorway, then stopped. She could hear him as he closed the barn doors. He hopped into his seat, and the canopy closed.

"You control it, even from the outside?"

"You don't have to whisper now, Trudy. As long as I'm wearing this band, she obeys me, no matter how far away."

The cockpit flooded with light, and the instrument panel displayed its odd symbols.

"Better fasten your harness this time." He fastened his, while Trudy watched, then she did the same.

"Ready?"

She smiled, and nodded. Cotton looked around, then upward. Trudy felt a gentle, but constant pressure in her seat as the little craft accelerated straight up for a while, then rolled over on its side, and smoothly changed to forward motion. She looked outside, and to her right. The city lights rapidly moved behind them, then disappeared from her sight as the full moon came into view ahead. Several minutes passed. She continued to feel pressured against her backrest, which told her that they were still accelerating. It was amazing. The acceleration steadily increased until Trudy finally complained.

"Cotton, I can't breathe."

Her statement alarmed him, and he reacted quickly. The acceleration decreased to a comfortable level again.

"I'm sorry, Trudy. I was concentrating on our position. Is this better?"

"Yes, thank you. This is magnificent! Look at that bright, bright moon! Oh, Cotton, I'll never, ever forget this."

She babbled, exclaimed her delight about different sights in the heavens, and asked many questions. Cotton patiently answered each of them. Her excitement wore down after an hour, and she became more serious about the new experience.

When their acceleration began to decrease, she said, "So, now we've reached escape velocity. Is that correct?"

Cotton's smile showed his continued amazement at her versatility. "You're pretty smart, for a girl." Then he quickly held up his hand and laughed, knowing that she was about to bite off his head.

"We don't have to worry about escape velocity in this little sweetheart. Fuel is no problem, so we could *creep* away from Earth's gravity if we wanted to. Hold onto your hat, Trudy. We're now flying away from Earth at a mere velocity of one hundred and eighteen thousand miles per hour."

Trudy whistled. "No. You're teasing me again."

"Okay, judge it by the size of the moon, and look at the Earth now."

The moon did appear much larger, and when she turned around to look at Earth, she could see it in full eclipse.

"All right, I believe you."

"We could go much faster, but we'll have to decelerate later on, and I don't want it to be too much for you."

Their acceleration stopped completely, and Trudy felt weightless for the first time. Cotton was fascinated by her gleeful, child-like reaction. A few minutes later, her expression changed, and she began to look puzzled.

"Uh-oh, I think we have a problem. This is awful, Cotton. I think I'm going to throw-up."

"Well, we sure can't let *that* happen." He removed a small vial from a compartment in the console, and handed it to her. "Here, take a sniff of this stuff."

She held it to her nose, and cautiously smelled it, then inhaled more deeply. After a second sniff, she held it out to look at it.

"Hey, boy, this stuff is amazing. I feel better already." He told her to keep the vial, and use it whenever it was needed.

She shook her head in wonderment. "If my mom could only see me now. If *I* could only see me now!" She was continually having to brush her hair aside in order to see. There was no gravity to hold it down. "Why didn't you tell me to cut my hair before we left?"

"You can have it done when we get to the Colony." He reached into another compartment of the console, and handed her a gold band, very similar to the one he wore. "Maybe this will help. Merry almost-Christmas. It's yours."

Trudy smiled broadly, and placed the band on her head. It fit perfectly. "Cotton, you're sweet. Thank you."

Girl, he thought, *I'm going to kiss you one of these days, and that'll be the end of Cotton O'Brien!* He continued to watch as she arranged her hair.

She leaned back to face forward again. Her eyes glanced at the instrument panel, then outside. A moment passed before her head jerked back to take a second look at the instruments. The mysterious symbols were no longer mysterious. She read their velocity, their distance from Earth, the cockpit temperature, the time, even their exact position in space. She took the band from her head, and looked at the instruments again. Mysterious symbols! She put the band back on, and the symbols again had meaning.

"Moldy head! How long have you had this?"

"I picked it up last night at the Colony. We'll have it coded just for you, later."

"But why? Do you mean I can *fly* this thing now?"

He laughed. "No way! Not yet, girl. It's only a translator, but you should wear it at all times while we're with the Ezekiens." After a short pause, he directed her attention to the count-down clock on the panel. "Deceleration is coming up in a few seconds. Watch the clock."

She counted to herself as the craft rolled around to face backward, then called-out the seconds. "Five . . . four . . . three . . . two . . . one . . . decelerate!" She felt the pressure at her back begin.

The navigation display fascinated Trudy, and she pointed.

"Are we the little blue ball?"

"Yep. You're doing great."

"And the red triangle?"

"That's the Colony's shuttle craft. The same one that picked me off the barn twenty years ago."

"That's where we're going now, huh?"

"Yep. And the white ring is the mother ship—the Colony."

"And here's the moon, and here's Earth, right? And the mother ship stays hidden from Earth behind the moon. Oh, I'm so impressed!"

"Me, too. You're beginning to make me feel like the student."

She giggled. "You don't mean that. Want me to be quiet?"

"Nope. I don't ever want you to be quiet."

Nevertheless, they both quit talking because the force of deceleration soon became uncomfortable. Trudy continued to read the instruments, and to observe their progress on the navigation display.

It was almost an hour later that she felt a change in motion that indicated a course correction to carry them behind the moon. Then the little fighter rotated around again to give them a view ahead. Trudy saw the moon as another dark world below them, and directly ahead was the shuttle. She felt a rush of excitement, realizing that its dark form could not have been easily seen, had it not been well lighted. Her imagination pictured it hovering silently above the barn where Cotton was drawn up, twenty years earlier.

As they drew nearer, its lighted silhouette gave it shape, and the appearance of a field athlete's discus. Cotton maneuvered the fighter toward a bright, open chamber at its center. Trudy had imagined that the little fighter would be taken completely inside the shuttle, but when they were only a few yards away, it became obvious that the outer opening of the circular chamber was recessed for a close fit of the outer rim of the little fighter.

When the fighter squeezed inside, and the docking was complete, Trudy felt as though she had been swallowed. Cotton's voice almost startled her.

"Like a 'plug in a jug', Trudy. This is an air-lock. We'll have to wait here a few seconds while it pressurizes."

After a short time, a door slid open above them, and a large, circular room appeared. Cotton cautioned her as the canopy snapped open, "Be careful, Trudy, and don't make any sudden moves. We're stationary above the moon's surface, so we feel its gravity, but it isn't much. If you don't mind, just follow me, and do as I do. Okay?"

"Okay, teacher. I'm with you."

Trudy noticed the low-gravity condition immediately as she crawled out of the cockpit. Cotton was already out, and around on her side to help. Then she watched as he pulled himself, hand-over-hand, up a ladder to the upper room. She followed his example, and easily climbed out of the chamber. Cotton helped her over the edge, and to her feet, but her attention was distracted by her first sight of *the Ezekien*.

He was not at all as she had expected. He stood upright on two legs, and he had a body with two arms, a neck, and a head, but that was as far as any human similarity could go. Everything about him was outstanding, but the eyes were his most striking feature. They were very large, in proportion to his human-sized head, and almost cat-like, with an upward slant. The pupils were large, and shiny black. The irises, also large, were rusty-brown. The top of his head was egg-shaped.

He had small, almost prominent cheeks; a small, pointed chin; and a large *smiling* mouth, with human-like soft lips. His teeth were not separate and individual, but upper and lower gleaming white solid bands. Trudy could see no ears behind the prominent eyes, nor did she see a nose.

His neck, rather long and stringy, disappeared into a

triangular, armor-like plate that covered his chest, shoulders, and back. The abdomen, narrow and bellows-shaped, extended down from beneath the breast-plate to blend with slightly wider hips.

Cotton's previous description of the arms and legs was more accurate. They were very thin, and jointed like insect limbs, appearing to be slightly longer than his body. There were three long, jointed fingers and a thumb on each of his hands *and* feet.

The sides of his thorax appeared to be soft leather bags that expanded and contracted for breathing. Many narrow, vertical slits in the bags opened and closed as he breathed.

His exoskeleton 'shell' appeared to be a hard, plastic-like material, waxy and shiny. Trudy thought of Cotton's description as a pod of okra, but her own description would be more as a mixture of okra, grasshopper, and human. He was definitely not ugly to look at.

Her appraisal of the Ezekien took only a moment, and in that short time she 'heard' his welcome greeting in her mind. Her attention shifted to a tall, slender man standing beside the Ezekien. His face was homely, but he held her look with soft, friendly eyes.

Cotton introduced them. "Friends, this great-looking young lady is Miss Trudy Two Bears, my humble student. Trudy, our Ezekien friend has been given the name Moses. We just call him 'Mo'. And the other handsome gentleman is Johnny J. Jones."

Johnny spoke his only word, 'ma'am', and both of them bowed deeply. Cotton also bowed, but Trudy was caught off-guard. She had not expected the salutation, and in her haste to follow Cotton's example, bent quickly at her waist, forgetting his warning not to make sudden movements in their low-gravity environment.

The reaction was unexpected: her feet left the deck,

and she actually turned a forward somersault, landing awkwardly on her bottom. She was extremely embarrassed, but her pride was hurt much worse than her posterior. She looked up at Cotton, who was laughing uproariously. He was also within reach, so she kicked. Cotton fell to the floor, and grabbed his left ankle, but he could not stop laughing.

Johnny rushed to Trudy, his homely face showing the seriousness of his concern for her. She looked at the Ezekien, wanting to apologize to him for the embarrassing incident, and he was *laughing!* There was no sound in his laughter, but his mirth was unmistakable.

Trudy finally got to her feet, clinging to Johnny's arm, when her memory of the ridiculous scene suddenly struck. She began to laugh also, and poor Johnny, the only one who now felt sorry for Trudy, was left wondering why it was so funny.

Trudy held her sides while laughing, and walked over to Cotton, who now had tears running down his cheeks. She touched his arm, then kneeled down to examine his ankle. Her laughter was soon controlled, and she was able to speak to him.

"Cotton, I'm so sorry. Do you think it could be broken?"

"It's okay, Trudy." He wiped his eyes with his fingers. "You'll have to do that again when we get to the Colony." Then his laughter started again.

Cotton's limp was exaggerated as they followed the Ezekien to the examination room. When she offered to help, he waved her off.

"Keep away, girl! You're dangerous."

She snaked her tongue out, then changed the subject, and whispered. "Cotton, he isn't ugly at all. I think he's beautiful. Can you imagine how evolution could produce a more appropriate being?"

Cotton smiled. "No need to whisper, Trudy. Mo knows what you're saying."

Trudy reclined on one table, with Cotton beside her on another. A glowing halo of red light projected down from an assortment of instruments above them, and quickly scanned her from toes to head. It moved back, and stopped for a short time above her right elbow, then moved over to scan Cotton, also hesitating above his left ankle.

"What's happening, Cotton?"

Before he could reply, Trudy received an answer from the Ezekien. She understood that her right elbow had suffered a mild abrasion from her fall, and that Cotton's ankle was slightly sprained.

The halo retracted, to be followed by a beam of yellow light that engulfed her right elbow for a moment, then repeated the same at Cotton's ankle.

After a few more similar examinations, a door opened, and the tables carried them into a small, lighted room. Trudy started to ask, then understood that they were being decontaminated. A moment later they were returned to the examination room, and Trudy was made aware that the examination was over.

She got off the table, and pulled up her sleeve to look at her right elbow. The abrasion was gone.

"Don't be surprised, Trudy. You'll find that we have quite a few benefits with this job. Want to meet the rest of the crew now?"

"Sure, but when do we get neutralized?"

"We *are* neutralized. It happened while we were in the air lock. I'm sorry, Trudy. This is so routine for me that I keep forgetting to tell you everything. I've never been a teacher before."

"*Humble* teacher, you mean." She could not let him forget his earlier introduction of her as his humble student.

She met two more Ezekiens and another human in the *mess*, or dining room. Again, everyone bowed, and

Trudy was very careful not to repeat her previous mistake.

She asked about the human-styled furniture in the mess room, and was made aware that the furniture was an accommodation for humans, but that it had been manufactured at the Colony. The mess room even contained human artistic work, usually creations by the human members of the crew, who were encouraged to pursue hobbies during their leisure time.

Then Trudy met her first female Ezekien. She did not realize it immediately, until Cotton announced the name, but she did realize that the Ezekien standing before her was different.

"Trudy, I'd like you to meet Helen." Again they bowed, but this time Trudy was compelled to bend down again, so that they were more near the same height. Helen placed her hands on Trudy's shoulders, and politely kissed her on the cheek. Trudy was delighted.

Helen was about four feet in height, which seemed to be about six inches shorter than the height of the three Ezekien males that Trudy had met. Each of them also had distinctive facial features and expressions, like humans, that gave them individuality, but there were also more obvious differences between Helen and the males. Helen's face *looked* feminine, and pretty, even by human standards.

Her soft lips were glistening and warm; her eyes were bright and beautifully rose-pink in color; and the bag-like covering of her sides was brightly colored, blending from pale-green at the back, to vivid turquoise at the front. Her body and limbs were more green than gray; whereas, the males were more gray. Mo's skin color was dark green, turning to brown.

Helen's message was pointedly candid: *You may feel me if you wish.*

Trudy blushed, and looked at Cotton.

"It's okay, Trudy. Don't be embarrassed. They

aren't shy, and touching the body has no sensual meaning to them."

Helen held out her hand for Trudy's inspection. Her three fingers and thumb seemed almost too long for the small hand, and surprisingly, they were not as hard as they looked. The palms and inner sides of the thumb and fingers were especially soft and warm. Her arms and legs did look very much like a pod of okra, with slightly raised ridges running lengthwise to insect-like joints. A firm skin covered the exoskeleton, and it felt slightly plastic and waxy. The entire body had a polished appearance. Helen turned around, obligingly, for Trudy's inspection, then again faced her.

"I almost envy you, Helen. How old are you?"

I'm almost five, in our years, but fifteen by your Earth years.

Trudy thought to herself for a moment, then *started* to ask how old Mo was.

Mo is eighty. Two hundred and forty of your years.

"My goodness!" Trudy looked at Cotton.

"I told you not to be surprised. Mo is old, but he still has a few years left."

Trudy looked back at Helen. "Then, you must be just. . . ."

Yes, I'm just a teenager. Her smile was pleasant. *With your permission, Trudy, I'd like very much to be your companion while you're with us. May I?*

"Oh, of course. I'm delighted to be with you." She looked at Cotton. "Do you mind?"

"Happy to have her along. Besides, it has already been planned that way, with your approval. Helen will be a good companion, and a good assistant, but it'll be mutual: you've been assigned to Helen as part of her education."

"Wonderful." Trudy then bent down and kissed Helen on the cheek. Helen smelled like roses.

CHAPTER 18

Trudy and Helen, strapped into seats before an observation port, held hands as the shuttle decelerated. Cotton had been given permission to pilot the craft for docking.

Helen was child-like and playful as they rotated around to allow forward view. She wanted to share in Trudy's excitement.

Close your eyes, Trudy. I want you to be surprised.

A minute passed as the excitement built up. Trudy tried to imagine how the colony ship must look.

All right, open your eyes now.

Trudy's mouth popped open, and she pressed her hands to her cheeks. "Oh!" She sensed a giggle of pleasure from Helen, but could not remove her eyes from the monstrous sight ahead. Her first close-up sight of the moon had not been overwhelming because she had expected it to be big, but her imagination had not prepared her for this.

The Colony ship was shaped exactly as she had guessed, a replica of the shuttle; yet, it appeared to be at least a mile in diameter. Its flat whiteness was dazzling in the bright sunlight; perhaps that made it appear larger, but the view of it almost filled their observation port, and it was still some distance away.

Large, darkened windows surrounded the periphery of the ship, some emitting bright, colored lights. Trudy was glad to see that their approach for docking was on the sunlit side, and that she would be able to watch it happen. Their full view of the massive ship soon outgrew the size of their observation port, and smaller details became more apparent. Its surface no longer looked smooth and flat, but wrinkled with annular corrugations. The answer came from Helen before Trudy had time to ask.

Their purpose is to increase the surface area. You'll learn more about that later.

"Heavens, Helen! I keep forgetting that you know what I'm thinking. You'll have to give me time to get used to this."

Of course. Your response time is very quick, for humans, I think. I'll try to help you improve your memory.

"Is it *that* bad? I thought my memory was pretty good."

All humans have very poor memory. It's because you haven't learned to employ your subconscious mind.

"Whoa, we'll have to get back to that one later." Trudy returned her interest to the docking. Her eyes picked out a large depression near the ship's periphery that appeared to be about the size and shape of the shuttle. "Is that where we're going to dock? I was expecting a big door to open, and we'd go inside, but it's like Cotton's fighter docked with the shuttle, isn't it?"

Yes. Air is very precious to our colony; this way, none is lost from a lock. The shuttle is taken inside only if external repairs are required.

The docking procedure was happening much too quickly for Trudy. She wanted more time to observe, and thought of asking Cotton to slow it down.

No, you mustn't, Trudy. Cotton should not be distracted at this time.

Trudy was only human. Her thought had been only an inclination; not something that she would have actually done, but Helen's logical reaction registered as a command in Trudy's mind, and she felt a tinge of resentment.

Helen bent forward in a bow. *Please forgive me, Trudy. I've offended you. I'll ask to be excused as soon as we go inside.*

Trudy was overtaken by instant regret, and the docking became unimportant. "Oh, Helen! I'm so sorry. I wasn't really offended. I want very much to be your friend, and I don't want anyone else to be my companion." She hesitated a moment. "Helen, I understand now what Cotton meant: that our education is mutual. Our human emotions may not be easily understood, and they're sometimes flighty. Maybe that's why we don't have, or shouldn't have, the ability to know what someone else is thinking. Some of our thoughts are very private, and not intended to be communicated. Please try to be patient. This telepathic stuff isn't going to be easy for me."

Helen raised her head to look into Trudy's eyes, then she smiled. *You're very correct. Thank you, Trudy. I again ask your forgiveness.*

"Nonsense!" Trudy laughed. "We're never going to get anywhere if we have to keep apologizing to each other."

The docking was complete, much to Trudy's surprise, before she realized it. Cotton floated before them, and stopped himself by grabbing a hand-railing.

"We're home, girls. What's going on?"

Trudy laughed at his weightless posture. "Nothing. Just girl-talk. Somebody tell me what to do."

"We'll help you until you get used to zero-gee, but Helen is the expert. Just follow her, and do as she does . . . if you can."

They unbuckled, and Trudy watched as Helen pushed forward to grab the hand-rail with her feet, and agilely walk along it. She then stopped, and turned around to watch Trudy.

Trudy laughed delightfully. "I couldn't do that, even without my shoes." She tried bravely to push herself to the railing, but sailed above it, instead. Cotton caught her, and brought her back for a hand-hold.

"Okay, just pull yourself along, and follow Helen. Remember, even a monkey has enough sense not to turn loose with both hands until he has a hand on another limb."

Helen led them through a maze of passageways, then upward, and into a small spherical room where others were waiting for them. Once inside, Trudy felt the room move; actually, it only rotated, then the single, circular hatch, through which they had entered, revolved into another round opening to disclose another passageway. They entered it, hand-over-hand along railings, as Cotton described events.

"We just went through a large ball valve, believe it or not, and we're now inside the colony ship.

Trudy was beginning to feel accustomed to her new mode of travel when they entered a long, open corridor. They were on a mezzanine, it seemed, overlooking the windows that she had seen while approaching the huge ship. Her view through the windows reminded her of the canopy above Cotton's little fighter; there seemed to be nothing between her and the space outside. Their mezzanine and the windows curved around and out of sight, like the horizon of an ocean.

They were not alone. Two Ezekiens stood nearby, whom she recognized as part of the shuttle's crew, and others, farther away, were either standing to watch the view, or skating along the rails. She leaned over the guard-rail to look below, and saw trains of tubular vehicles coming and going quietly in both directions.

Cotton and Helen watched her with big smiles on their faces. It was as if she were a child in a toy store, but Trudy did not care; she wanted to see everything.

She watched another train as it came over the horizon at her right. It lay on its side, traveling along the outside of the mezzanine guard-rail. This one was obviously a passenger vehicle. It stopped at another station farther up the line, allowing several passengers to depart, as others boarded.

Not knowing what to expect next, Trudy moved back to join Cotton and Helen. The train stopped at their station, and Helen again took the lead. She pushed forward, grabbed a hand-rail above a long, slotted opening, and pulled herself inside the transparent enclosure. Trudy followed the example, this time perfectly, and Cotton followed her.

"Good work, Trudy. Now hold onto the rail, and hook your toes under the floor-railing." There were no seats, but in zero-gee, they were not needed.

Cotton continued. "We're going to the human quarters now. It's been a long day for you, girl, and no one could've handled it any better than you did, but we need some rest. Are you hungry?"

"Starving. And I am pretty tired, but I'll be very surprised if I can sleep after *this* day."

Certainly there was no need for ceilings and floors, as such, in a weightless environment, but the human quarters were designed to make the guests feel at home. Trudy remembered, too, that most of the humans were only children when they first arrived, and the Ezekiens spared no effort to make the transition as comfortable as possible. Also, their objective had always been to return most of the humans to Earth, once they had been educated and trained for their mission; therefore, it was logical to provide them with a gravity environment.

Cotton explained as they traveled that the human facility was actually a very large centrifuge.

"Well, that makes a lot of sense, but I'm puzzled about something: If I'm going to live in a one-gee environment—for some time, it seems—then, how is Helen going to be my companion? You've already told me that the Ezekiens can't live in gravity conditions very long."

He smiled, and winked at Helen, who seemed to be eager.

Cotton, may I please explain? Trudy, I, and only a few others, are very special Ezekiens. We're the product of hundreds of years of Ezekien evolution. You see, we're the only ones who can sustain moderate amounts of gravitation for long periods of time. Our ancient ancestors, who lived on our home planet, were conditioned for very high gravity, but that was more than a million years ago, in your conception of time.

I'm the most fortunate, Trudy. I'm the only one of us who can live permanently at one gee. Perhaps, in another century or two, I, or my offspring, will be able to live on Earth.

Trudy could only shake her head. "That's incredible! But. . . ."

Oh, no. We have no intention of conquering your planet. If we should ever live on Earth, it must be as your guests. And we wouldn't want to live there as it is now.

Trudy wanted to continue their conversation, but they had arrived at their stop. As before, Helen led the way. They traveled along the rails of a corridor in a direction that led downward from their starting point at the mezzanine.

Funny, how I still want to think up-and-down, Trudy thought. *Where the heck is up and down, out here in space.*

Helen stopped at a large concourse where other corridors led off in different directions. In the center of the concourse was a round, rotating room with an open door. It did not appear to be rotating very fast, as Helen waited for the door to come back around, then pulled herself inside. Trudy and Cotton followed, and the door closed behind them. They each grasped a railing, and were gently pulled into rotation with the wall. Their sense of movement soon stopped, since there was no outside reference. Trudy felt a very slight force drawing her to the wall. She looked upward to see that they were inside a round tunnel, then at Cotton for an explanation.

"We're inside the hub of the centrifuge, Trudy. Keep following Helen, and I'll explain as we go."

They pulled along until they came to a square pit, about eight feet deep by six feet square, extending outward from the wall of the tunnel. Other similar pits could be seen farther down the tunnel. As they pulled inside, Cotton instructed Trudy to stand with her feet at the 'bottom' of the pit as Helen was then doing. She did as instructed, then noticed a closed door in one wall.

"If you haven't already guessed, this is an ordinary, human-type elevator, minus the ceiling. Hang onto your rail until you feel enough gravity to hold you down."

Then Trudy noticed the lighted push-buttons beside the door, and the overhead 'floor' numbers. "Why, it's just like home." After her recognition of such a familiar setting, her senses of up and down immediately returned.

The elevator began to move very slowly, but Trudy felt it necessary to push herself 'downward' in order to keep her feet on the floor. A few seconds later, she began to feel weight, and released the rail.

She thought of the elementary school experiment when she had first learned of centrifugal force; how she had spun around with a bucket of water at arms length, to discover that the water did not spill out. She imagined herself now, traveling down her arm toward the whirling bucket of water.

Five minutes, and ten floors later, Trudy felt the elevator stop. "This has to be the slowest elevator I've ever seen. Is it always this slow?"

Cotton answered as the door opened. "Only if we've been at low gravity for some time. How do you feel?"

"Heavy."

Helen caught Trudy's hand as they stepped out of the elevator.

Welcome to Little Earth, Trudy. Would you like to see our apartment before dinner?

"Thanks. Little Earth, huh?" They stopped while Trudy looked at a large painting on the wall in front of the elevator. "It's beautiful. Yes, please, I'd like to wash up, if you don't mind." She looked at Cotton.

"Sure. See you girls at the cafeteria in about twenty minutes."

Helen led to the left as Cotton went right. Trudy felt a strange sensation as she looked ahead. The floor and ceiling of the corridor curved upward, and out of sight. She looked behind them, noticing that Cotton also walked upward.

Helen giggled. *I was waiting for your reaction, Trudy. Remember, we're walking around the inside wall of a rotating cylinder. It's the only way that your conception of 'up' can always be over your head.*

"I know. It's what I expected, but it's the *sensation*. I feel as if we're walking up, but we're not. Helen, if this hallway goes all the way around, then I could be walking upside-down at the place opposite to where we are now. But it's wonderful. I'm so impressed that the Ezekiens would go to so much trouble for us."

Helen led into an intersecting corridor, and stopped at a door. The nameplate read, TRUDY TWO BEARS and HELEN. Helen stepped to the side. *Please, you go first.*

The apartment was small, but ample for two guests: a small drawing room, one bedroom with two single beds, a dressing room, and a bathroom. Trudy was pleased with the furnishings, and delighted when Helen pointed out a complete new wardrobe of clothing, and a varied assortment of cosmetic articles.

Cotton was waiting as they entered the cafeteria. It was a large, upward-curving room with a serving line and at least twenty tables arranged in rows along the axis of the centrifuge. It reminded Trudy of a typical school cafeteria on Earth: the smell of food, the rattle and clinking of dishes, and the talk and laughter of many children. Most of the rectangular tables seated five children, with an adult at each table—all human. Many of them shouted friendly greetings to Cotton and Helen, who waved back. Helen, especially, seemed to be very popular, and an accepted member of the group. She waved heartily when a teenaged group cheered her as they walked by.

Trudy directed her smile and question at Cotton. "Are they always this boisterous?"

"You mean, at dinner? Well, sure. This is the end of a hard, serious work day for them. It's a fun time."

Their selection of food was quite varied, although Trudy noticed that there was no meat. She watched as Helen helped herself to a small portion of steamed carrots and boiled potatoes. A teenaged boy brought her a special dish of food from the galley.

Would you like to try our Ezekien food, Trudy? Cotton calls it 'cactus doughnuts'—he doesn't like it—but, really, it's very nutritious.

"Sure, why not? 'When in Rome', you know." The boy brought Trudy a large smile with the dish. She also selected a plate of vegetables and fruit, then followed Helen to a table.

The 'cactus doughnut' did look like a flattened, greenish-yellow doughnut, and it smelled almost like bananas, but Trudy frowned when she tasted it.

"I'm sorry, Helen. Please don't be offended."

Helen laughed. *No problem. I don't like human food very much, either, but I eat some with every meal as part of my human conditioning. The only human foods that we positively can't eat are those containing animal fats. We're also very sensitive to petroleum products. They make us very ill. But you must consider our differences: humans are a product of animal evolution; whereas, we evolved from plants.*

Their conversation was cut short by a late-arriving

young couple, whom Cotton invited to join them. He introduced them, saying that they were newly wed, and soon to be transferred to Earth for their life's mission. They were very pleasant company, but almost overly persistent in questioning Trudy about her opinion of recent events on Earth. Obviously, the Colony was well informed of Earth's news.

After dinner, Cotton formally introduced Trudy to the group. The Ezekien custom of bowing was not taken into the human facility, as it was not a widespread custom of Earth. It soon became plain, however, that Trudy needed rest, and the gathering broke up after she was made welcome.

Cotton walked them to their apartment, and said good night to Helen, while holding Trudy back. Helen went inside.

"Just wanted to give you my personal welcome, Trudy." He bent down, and kissed her on the cheek. "I'll meet you for breakfast at seven. We'll have a full day tomorrow."

"Thank you, Cotton. Everyone is so nice, especially you." She put her hands on his shoulders, then reached up, and kissed him quickly and lightly on the lips. "Good night." She left him standing there as she closed the door behind her.

Cotton managed, somehow, to find his way back to his own apartment. *Adios, old scout. Might as well make a pot of coffee, 'cause you ain't gonna' sleep tonight!*

He felt happiness beyond bounds, yet devastation at the same time. How should he deal with his feelings? The Ezekiens had taught him how to cope with every imaginable situation, except for this one. He was hopelessly in love, and lost. But now what? Could he really be in love so quickly? Well, there was no doubt about that, but how did Trudy feel? Her innocent kiss must surely have been only an expression of simple gratitude. Or was it?

Whoa, boy! Get a'hold of yourself! You can handle this. If she doesn't love you now, then, she will. There was just no other alternative. *Give her time, and don't act like a fool.* He had to use logic to over-rule his emotions.

Helen could hardly wait until Trudy and Cotton had spoken their good-morning greetings, then she projected her thought for his mind only. *Good morning, lover-boy.* Her smile was full of mischief.

Cotton turned away from Trudy, and shook his finger at Helen's big eyes. *Now look, you little eaves-dropper. Stay out of my brain, and mind your own business!* He appeared to be angry, but Helen knew his temperament.

She giggled, then moved closer to Trudy. *You'd better be nice to me, or I'll tell.* Cotton acted as if he were going to choke her.

Trudy was amazed. "My goodness, you two, what's this all about? I feel as if I'm being kept out of a secret. No fair!"

Cotton changed his frown to a smile. "Sorry, Trudy. This little snip needs to be taught some human-type manners. She won't stay out of people's minds. I wish you'd try to teach her not to do that."

"Me? Heavens, Cotton! Is that my job?"

Helen interrupted. Her message was now directed at both of them, and she still smiled. *Yes, Trudy. Everyone else has tried; now it's your turn to teach me how to be a lady.*

"Well, I'll sure try. Your eaves-dropping bothers me, too." She said it in good humor, so not to hurt the little Ezekien's feelings.

We'll see. Helen then skipped off to join one of her human friends.

They watched her while they joined the serving line.

Trudy could not help laughing. "She's such a cute little thing, but I can see that she might be a little pest, too. Can she know what I'm saying now?"

"Don't be surprised if she can, Trudy. I think we've all spoiled her, and she knows that she can do anything she wants to down here."

He explained, during breakfast, that Helen had to attend special education classes during the day, and then outlined the schedule that he had planned for them. Helen ran to them as they were leaving the table.

Why can't I go with you, Cotton? I can help you explain everything. You know I can.

"No way! Sorry, kid, you have classes. I don't make the rules around here."

Trudy bent down for her kiss, and Helen complied. *Okay, I'll be good, just for you, Trudy.* She joined her friends, but not without a parting thought to Cotton, alone. *Bye-bye, lover boy!*

They began with a tour of the centrifuge. The bottom (outer) floor was home for all of the human guests and Helen, but there were also living quarters on the second floor, if ever needed, since the difference in gravity was very little. Besides the cafeteria, there were offices, classrooms, a small emergency clinic, and a one-gee gymnasium. The second floor had additional classrooms, laboratories, and an auditorium.

They entered another smaller gymnasium on the third floor, where Trudy was surprised to see several Ezekien children being guided through physical exercises by an attractive human female instructor wearing very colorfull work-out tights.

Cotton waved, and the pretty instructor waved back. "Hi, sweetheart! Be with you in a moment."

Trudy looked at Cotton, and smiled. He actually blushed, and seemed to be embarrassed, but offered no explanation.

The instructor soon came to them, and offered her hand to Trudy, with an introduction.

"Hello, Trudy, I'm Kathy. Sorry I missed you last evening, but I spend most of my time with these Ezekien children. Aren't they precious? But not *all* of my time. Right, love?" She smiled broadly at Cotton, who looked as if he were choking.

Kathy broke up in laughter. "Never mind, sweetheart. Trudy, I'm not really serious, but I love to see him blush. Isn't he a darling?"

Trudy also laughed. "I guess I hadn't noticed before, but he *is* a darling."

Cotton held up his hands. "All right, girls, have your fun! Kathy, I'm trying to show Trudy around this place. Would you mind being a little more helpful?"

Kathy winked, then hooked her arm into Trudy's, and led her to the Ezekien children. Trudy now felt a bit bouncy while walking, as the gravity on the third floor was considerably lower.

Kathy introduced the children, calling each of them by their human names. One of the male children began to bow, but was corrected by a female classmate. There were ten of them in the group, from ages four through six (Earth age). Trudy stepped forward, and the children gathered around her; all of them looking up with large, adoring eyes. She held out her hands for them to touch.

"They *are* precious. Then, the human facility *isn't* just for humans. These children—and I assume there are a lot more of them—are gradually working their way outward to a one-gee environment. I'm beginning to wonder, now, about the ultimate goal of the Ezekiens. Isn't it really for their *own* benefit? Wasn't this centrifuge *really* intended to accommodate them to our Earth's environment?"

Cotton answered. "We have to acknowledge that, Trudy, but we're here because we want to be here; because we believe that Earth can be a better place to live, with the help of the Ezekiens."

"Yes, I can see that you want to be here, but have you considered that you've grown up, and were educated, to think as they want you to think? Kathy, were you also brought here as a child?"

"Yes, I was—the same as Cotton, but we haven't been required to stay here. We have free minds to do as we wish. Suppose *you* be the judge, Trudy. You weren't raised here as we were, and you have a fresh, open mind about it. I'd be very interested to hear your opinion, later. Cotton, why don't you take her to see Mike."

"Good idea. Thanks, Kathy, we'll see you later."

Trudy also thanked her, and agreed to share her honest opinion after more time. Kathy returned to the children, then called out as Cotton and Trudy were leaving. "See you tonight, sweetheart!"

They found Mike attending the gardens, along with forty or fifty other Ezekiens. The gardens were a large, curving field, of at least twenty acres of waist-high, fern-like plants, growing from jelled chemical beds. Most of them were the plants that bore the distasteful 'cactus doughnuts', now seen clinging in rows to every stem of bright green leaves. The field smelled almost like any green house on Earth, with a high content of fresh oxygen. Trudy could see the sun, directly overhead, shining through large, lightly-screened windows.

Mike was like all other male Ezekiens, except that his color was almost totally brown and lacking the waxy shine of the others that Trudy had seen.

They bowed, as usual, and Mike made her feel his message of welcome. He spent most of the morning showing them around the gardens, and answering Trudy's questions regarding their variety and source of food. She was offered a taste of each different kind, which she still found to be undesirable, until she finally discovered a small, round, grape-like fruit. It had a sweet-sour taste, and smelled likewise.

"I think it's wonderful. Why don't we have it in our cafeteria?"

You will, very soon. This fruit was only recently developed, and it's equally as tasty to us. Perhaps we'll discover other pleasures to share with our human friends.

"Thank you, Mike, for allowing me an opening. You Ezekiens have been very kind and hospitable to humans. May I ask a very direct question about your ultimate objective regarding our Earth? Please, I don't mean to be offensive."

A quest for knowledge is never offensive. Allow me to explain: You must realize that there are millions of habitable planets in our galaxy, and that many of them are much more hospitable to us than your Earth. We've chosen to study your planet because human life-forms are experiencing the same problems that our ancestors learned to overcome long ago. Unfortunately, we can't solve your problems for you because we aren't welcome on Earth; also because we aren't yet accustomed to Earth's gravity. It is our wish that we might help you to find a solution to your own problems. You still have time to do that, you know. In any case, we have the problem of gravity, regardless of which planet we choose. That decision will be made long after I've wilted away.

Now, I've been told that you want to see our source of energy, and that you've been educated to understand it. May I guide you on that tour? Perhaps I may be of some help.

"Thank you, I'd be very pleased if you would."

Good! I believe it's almost time for your lunch. Cotton, can you escort our new friend to the energy facility in about an hour?

"Sure can. Thanks, Mike. We'll be there."

They caught a car to take them back to the centrifuge.

"Cotton, Mike seems to be very old. How old is he?"

"I'm not sure. Probably about three hundred years, more or less."

"Really? What does he do? I mean, do they have certain jobs to do?"

"Sure. Mike is like the president, or mayor of the Colony. They call him 'The Responsible One'."

"Oh, wow! You've named the chief executive of this place 'Mike'? I'd think you'd call him 'Sir', or 'Your Honor', or at least something more respectful than just 'Mike'." She laughed. "Moldy head, you should be ashamed of yourself!"

CHAPTER 19

An hour later, they left a car and pulled themselves along railings into a large, round room, which Cotton explained was at the outer level, and on the axis of the giant colony ship. Trudy could see black space and stars through overhead windows

"Cotton, do you have trouble with 'up' and 'down' here? I feel very disoriented away from the centrifuge; almost to the point of vertigo." She took the little vial from a zippered pocket, and sniffed.

"Not any more, but it was pretty bad when I first came here."

She saw that some of the equipment was on the 'floor', and some was on the 'ceiling'. "Okay, I'll forget floors and ceilings, and try think of them as just walls."

Mike approached them from another corridor, easily skating along one of the many rails, then hopping onto another one to change directions. They bowed, then received Mike's transfer of thought.

Shall we begin? First, I must explain that there are no crystalline metals, as you know them, anywhere in our colony. If you had a metallic filling in one of your teeth, it was removed and replaced during your examination on the shuttle, as was your wrist watch. We do that because the 'heavy' elements change inefficiently from matter to antimatter. Everything here is made from compounds of helium; just as your borazon, an artificially produced crystal with the hardness of a diamond, is a compound of nitrogen and boron. He smiled at Trudy's expression.

You've been taught that helium is an inert gas, or noble gas, because it does not combine with other elements, but we discovered compounds of helium long before our planet was destroyed. As you see, its compounds range from extremely hard to extremely soft. We artificially produce these compounds by restructuring the atoms within their basic elements. I see that you're confused, Trudy.

"Yes, I'm sorry. Are you telling me that you can artificially create new atomic elements, such as hydrogen, or iron, or gold?"

That's correct. As a matter of interest, we have a small laboratory on Earth where our earthside friends create gold to pay for some of their expenses. In essence, that's how we produce the energy to operate this great ship: We rearrange atoms. The secret, of course, is the method by which we rearrange the structure of atoms without losing energy in the form of heat, which is inefficient and destructive. We do that by modifying the binding force that holds atoms together.

If Trudy had been sitting, she would have been on the edge of her seat. Her attention was so intense that she failed to notice the exchange of winks between Cotton and the old Ezekien. Mike's transfer of thought stopped, as if that were the end of the explanation.

Trudy waited for a long moment, then, "Well?".

Mike's expression was blank. *Well, that's what we do, Trudy. We modify the binding force.*

She looked at Mike for another long moment, then at Cotton. "Cotton, have I missed something?"

Cotton smiled, then Trudy began to laugh as she looked back at Mike, who was also laughing.

"Oh, Mike, you're terrible! But I'm glad to see that you have a sense of humor, even at my expense. My father does that to me sometimes, when my expressions become too intense. Can I believe you now?"

The old Ezekien's head nodded as he took her arm. *Come Trudy, let me show you.* He led her, floating along with him, to a guard railing beside a large hole in the 'floor'. Five glowing columns, about ten feet apart in a pentagonal arrangement, projected from the 'ceiling', into the hole, and as far as she could see inside a long tunnel. The columns, also pentagonal, were each about three feet thick, and glowed with a pale blue light. Each of the columns was surrounded, also as far as she could see, by a single, loosely-spaced coil of round, transparent, glowing yellow tubing about three inches in diameter, leading away through conduits to a large cubic box. The yellow coils pulsed rhythmically, changing the pale-blue color of the columns to a pulsing, pale-green.

Cotton spoke. "Listen, Trudy. What do you hear?"

She cocked her head, then smiled. "It sounds like a cat purring."

"Exactly what I thought."

Trudy, these columns are crystals of hydrium, a synthetic element that does not exist anywhere else in our galaxy. It's one of our creations. Hydrium atoms are electrically neutral, but the charge of their sub-particles can be reversed to create either matter or anti-matter, and their energy output is perpetual.

It isn't the same as your idea of transmutation of elements by bombarding an atom's nucleus—that's much too violent. Hydrium atoms do not share their boundary particles, as do normal atoms; therefore, they technically do not exist in a molecular form.

You were taught that an atom's structure contains a positively charged nucleus of sub-particles that you call protons and neutrons, and that the nucleus is surrounded by a cloud of negatively charged electrons. Unfortunately, your human theoretical physicists have stubbornly refused to abandon this illogical concept because they have not yet found an acceptable mathematical alternative. As you are now beginning to understand, the electric charge of such atoms could not possibly be reversed. Our theory suggests that all atoms contain equal numbers and equal mass weights of sub-particles, but the volume of space (anti-mass) is not, necessarily, the same in all atoms. In other words, an atom's electric charge is determined by the volume density of its sub-particles; therefore, we are able to increase or decrease an atom's attractive energy by increasing or decreasing its sub-particle density.

The yellow coils surrounding those columns are superconductive carriers of a form of pulsating static electricity, which excites the hydrium to reinduce attractive or repulsive energy into the coils. It's very similar to your idea of piezoelectricity, which is generated by applying pressure to a quartz crystal. Very good. You do understand.

"Yes, and it's wonderful! But I'm disappointed for Dr. Bonner. His theory is correct, but his experiment will fail. Maybe it's just as well. Our world may not be prepared for it yet."

I'm very pleased with you, Trudy, and I hope you'll come to visit me socially. I want you to meet my family.

Trudy asked more questions, and was shown the complete facility. Cotton also shared in her instruction. She was as much impressed with his knowledge as she was with the old Ezekien. By the end of the day, she was exhausted; not physically, because getting around at zero-gee required very little effort, but she was mentally tired.

They returned to the centrifuge to get ready for dinner. Helen was waiting for them when the elevator door opened. Cotton went off to his quarters as Helen excitedly questioned Trudy on the way to theirs.

You were impressed, weren't you? I can tell. Are you in love with him?

"Good heavens, Helen! What're you talking about?"

Cotton, of course! You're in love with him, aren't you?

They entered the apartment. "Cotton and I are becoming good friends, but you're speaking of love. I couldn't. . . ." She refused to complete the thought. "Anyway, it isn't any of your business, Helen, and you shouldn't pry."

Helen looked hurt. *But it's important to me, Trudy. Why are you angry?*

"Oh, here we go again! Really, Helen, you mustn't be so sensitive. I'm not angry at you, but you're touching on a subject that is very personal. Why is it so important to you?"

Because I want to know everything about you. What is it like to be in love? I know what your thoughts are, but I can't feel your emotions, except for the changes in your expressions. I want to understand human emotions.

"Okay, we'll have a long talk about that tonight. I promise. Cotton has invited us to see one of the latest Earthside movies in the auditorium after dinner. Want to go? I have to get dressed now."

Trudy showered, and decided to wear a nice dress that evening. Helen was fascinated by human clothing, especially the pretty dresses. She watched intently as Trudy fixed her hair and applied her make-up.

Trudy spoke while distorting her lips to apply the lipstick. "You're fortunate that you don't have to do this to be pretty. We humans are very vain about our looks."

Oh, no! I think I'm very unfortunate. You're so beautiful!

"Why, thank you. But that isn't a very healthy attitude for you. I think you're beautiful, too, just as you are."

Trudy commented during dinner that the food was

delicious. "But I really do miss meat. I'm not a very good vegetarian."

Cotton laughed with her. "You got it! When we go back for Christmas, I'm going to ask Leona for a big turkey and dressing dinner, with steak on the side."

Helen appeared to be preoccupied, and did not join the fun, as usual, with her friends. Cotton had to speak twice to get her attention. "What's wrong with you, kid? Are you sick?"

She shook her head, an expression that she and a few other Ezekiens had learned from their human friends. *I'm okay, Cotton. I'm just thinking about something.*

"Fine. Let's go to the movies."

No, I've changed my mind. I'm going to stay in tonight. Do you mind, Trudy?

"Not at all, if that's what you want. Are you sure you're okay? You're not upset with me, are you—about what I said to you?"

Helen smiled, then kissed Trudy on the cheek. *Of course not. I'll never be upset with you.* She asked to be excused, then left the table to return to their apartment, waving to her friends as she passed.

"What do you think, Cotton? Maybe I should go with her."

He waved the issue aside. "Naw, she's all right. Let's go."

They walked back slowly after the movie, Trudy's arm crooked around Cottons. "That was fun, Cotton. So is this. Too bad we don't have a bright moon overhead."

"Hey, I can fix that real easy. You've never seen the moon until you see its backside from here. Want to?"

"Thanks, but I'd better pass tonight. I'm a little concerned about Helen, and I've promised her that we would have a long talk tonight. Rain check?"

"Sure. You look especially beautiful tonight, Trudy.

First time I've seen you in a dress."

She squeezed his arm, and smiled. "Thank you. You look pretty handsome, yourself. First time I've seen you in a tie, too."

They reached her apartment long before Cotton was ready. She released his arm, and turned to face him. "Thanks, Cotton. I really enjoyed tonight."

Despite all of his self-ordered caution, he wanted to enfold and crush her to his chest, but his self-discipline was stronger. He pulled her only close enough, then bent down to brush her lips with his before the prolonged, gentle kiss. He was first, too, to break the bliss as he straightened up and released her.

Her smile was enticing. "I enjoyed that, too. Good night."

"Good night, Trudy. See you at seven." He turned and walked away as she opened the door.

Once inside, she stood for a moment facing the door, then turned toward the bedroom. Helen lay face-up, sprawled on the floor in front of the dressing-room mirror. Her mouth was smeared with lipstick, and she was wearing one of Trudy's dresses.

Trudy raced back outside, and into the main hallway.

"Cotton! Cotton! Come back. Hurry!" She ran back into her room to kneel beside Helen. Thankfully, the little Ezekien was still breathing, but weakly.

Cotton rushed in to kneel beside her, and reacted instinctively when he saw Helen's condition.

"It's the lipstick, Trudy. Hand me some tissues. We can't take it off with your cleanser—that'll make it worse." He worked quickly while Trudy removed the dress, then picked Helen up in his arms.

"Run ahead to the clinic, and push that red button beside the door. Hurry, Trudy!"

She had the door open, and stood aside as Cotton rushed in to lay the sick child on the examination table. He took a bottle from a shelf, and handed it to Trudy.

"This is a special detergent. Squeeze a few drops into that pan, and mix it with water."

He gave the instructions while ripping open a filmy bag. Then he removed a peculiar-looking respirator, which he placed over Helen's upper body. By that time, a nurse arrived to help him hook up the respirator to its source of oxygen. The nurse then took the pan of water, and cleaned away the remaining make-up.

Cotton stood back, to put his arm around Trudy's shoulders.

"Well, that's all we can do, for now. We'll take her up to the Ezekien hospital as soon as she's breathing well."

Trudy wiped tears from her eyes. "Oh, Cotton, I *knew* there was something wrong. I should have stayed with her. I feel so terrible. This is my fault."

He pulled her around to his chest, and folded her into his arms. "Don't even think that way, Trudy. I could take the blame, too, for not listening to your insight, but it wouldn't help her now, would it?"

CHAPTER 20

In mid-December, Georgette Adams was moved to a federal penitentiary in Kentucky. Information regarding the transfer had been delivered to Icy Brooks by an 'inside' informant a few days before the move, which allowed Icy sufficient time to carefully plan Georgette's escape.

On the day of Georgette's arrival, F.B.I. Agent Justeen Miller, accompanied by an average looking, stoutly-built woman, entered the warden's office. The woman beside Agent Miller would not have attracted attention, except for a very evident streak of white running backward over jet-black, shoulder-length wavy hair. Otherwise, her only other distinguishing feature was an over-use of lipstick, intended to disguise her thin lips. Warden Frankston extended his hand in greeting.

"Hello, Miller. Where's your sidekick?" Obviously, the warden was well acquainted with Agent Miller, but accustomed to seeing her together with Agent Drake.

"Good morning, Warden. He's down with the flu, or something. Couldn't make it this time."

In truth, Agent Drake was unaware of Justeen Miller's whereabouts on this day. Unaware, too, that Justeen's visit to the prison actually had nothing to do with F.B.I. business.

"Warden Frankston, this is Dr. Evans." Justeen then explained that Dr. Evans was an expert in the study of guerrilla warfare and interrogation, and a specialist in the regions of southeast Asia where Georgette had been trained.

Dr. Evans switched her bulging briefcase to her left hand, in order to shake the warden's hand, then spoke in an unusually intimidating voice. "Pleasure meeting you, Warden. If you don't mind, I'll get right to the point. Since I've been out of the country for a few months, I didn't know about your new prisoner. They've told me that Georgette Adams has resisted interrogation. Believe me, conventional interrogators don't know how to get a response from her. I do. So, before you send her back to the cells, I'd like to try my own method. We need that information from Eileen Two Bears' files."

The warden stroked his chin, but hesitated only a moment. "Sure, we can handle that. What's so different about your method?"

Dr. Evans' answer indicated a great deal of experience and self-assurance. Her credentials as an expert interrogator [Indeed, she was a well-qualified member of Icy's W.E.B. organization.] were genuine.

"Our records indicate that your prisoner was given injections of hypnotic and anesthetic drugs. That wouldn't work, in her case. You need to understand that Georgette's mind has been well-conditioned to resist that method. Anesthesia means a *loss* of sensation. I intend to *heighten* her sensations, along with hypnotics, even to the point of unconsciousness. But I'll need your complete cooperation, as well as the cooperation of your medical staff. And I'll want her restrained in a straight-jacket after the injection. In this case, I'll also require a padded room. She *will* be unconscious when I've finished."

The timing could not have been better. Shortly after her arrival and check-in, Georgette was brought immediately to the hospital ward. Her hands were cuffed from behind, and her ankles were chained, so that she walked with a stiff shuffle. Her head hung forward, allowing her straight, neck-length blond hair to cover her face.

Dr. Evans' instructions were followed to-the-letter, with no resistance from Georgette, who had been secretly briefed on the procedure by her lawyer, who was also a member of the W.E.B. society. The 'truth serum' turned-out to be a mild saline solution acquired from Dr. Evans' briefcase, but injected by a prison nurse. Georgette's handcuffs and ankle-chains were removed, to be replaced by a straight-jacket. Then, as planned, Dr. Evans led Georgette into the padded room with a final comment to warden Frankston.

"You may hear me do a lot of shouting to the prisoner, but it's an unavoidable part of the interrogation. This may take some time, so you can leave us with a couple of guards outside the door, and get back to your business, if you wish."

The warden nodded his agreement as the two guards laid Georgette on the padded floor, and secured her ankles with a soft leather belt. The guards were then told to leave the room, and close the door. A single, small, wire-reinforced window in the door allowed those outside, only one at a time, to see within the room. Justeen stepped aside to allow the warden to watch. Inside, Dr. Evans helped Georgette to a sitting position, then walked around the small room while talking.

Georgette's first apparent reaction began with a rapid side-to-side motion of her drooping head, which caused her hair to swirl outward. Within the next minute, her body began to tremble, which was followed, a short time later, by violent convulsions. She stiffened, fell back to a prone position, and violently arched her back to give a pitching motion. Dr. Evans quickly knelt to pin Georgette's shoulders to the padded floor. Her shouted command was easily heard by those outside the door.

"Tell me about the W.E.B. society, Georgette! Who gives the orders?"

Georgette's hostile voice was equally as loud.

"Nobody gives orders to me, you traitorous pig! You're wasting your time."

The shouting continued as Georgette broke free of the doctor's hold, then began to roll along the floor until she was out of the warden's view, in a corner of the room nearest the door. The warden stepped back in order to speak, which allowed Justeen an opening to occupy the window position. Her face and hair completely shut-off any view by the warden and guards.

Inside, Dr. Evans moved far enough to see Justeen's face in the window, then snatched-up her briefcase while continuing her shouted commands. Within the next few minutes, Georgette was wearing the doctor's clothes, the white-streaked wig, and the lipstick. By all appearances, the scene within the room again showed Dr. Evans in the role of finally finishing the interrogation. The shouting soon stopped, and only muffled, unintelligible voices could be heard by those outside.

The entire procedure had taken place in less than an hour. At Justeen's request, a guard opened the door to disclose a prone, straight-jacketed figure, again in the center of the room, breathing heavily, but now apparently unconscious. The doctor, also breathing heavily, was seen with her back to the door, and spoke (apparently) while leaning over the prisoner's head.

"I'm . . . exhausted! Justeen, help me . . . get to my feet."

Justeen now assumed command as she helped the doctor up, and took the briefcase. Speaking to the warden, she said, "Maybe I'd better take her to the car. Georgette will be 'out' for a while, so you can just let her sleep it off where she is. I'll call you later to let you know if this worked."

Icy's planning, with a bit of good luck, had again been successful. Georgette was free, at the expense of Dr.

Evans, and with the doctor's wholehearted agreement that the sacrifice was worthwhile. She could not legally be confined for a long period of time. Her only crime was that of assisting a prisoner's escape; far less than the charges against Georgette.

Justeen Miller did not view her own sacrifice as a loss. She could now join Icy at The Tunnel, and assist in the all-important mission ahead. Beside that, she suspected that her long-time partner, Agent Drake, was having suspicions of his own, regarding her loyalty to the F.B.I..

But Georgette had also made plans during her period of confinement. She could not forget, or dismiss, the awesome power of the witch.

CHAPTER 21

Ben listened at his end of the phone conversation with Sheriff Lang. "All right, Sam, thanks for calling." He hung up the receiver, and turned to Leona. "Not good news, Leona. Sam Just told me that Georgette Adams has escaped from prison. They have no idea where she is, or where she's going, but she may be headed this way"

"I'm sorry, Ben, but I don't believe that she wants to harm either of us. If anything, I think she wants to learn more about that levitation experience."

"Maybe. Well, I've been expecting it, and I'll not let her surprise me again. Anyway, Sam thought I should wear my side-arm." He wandered away to go upstairs.

"Ben?" She called him back. "Trudy and Cotton will be here in a few days, for Christmas. Shall I plan for a big gathering?"

"Well, I've been thinking about that, Leona. I'd rather not have a big crowd this year. Let's just plan for our own little group." He again turned to leave.

"Ben? I do have two friends in this area. They don't have families to go to. Do you mind?"

"Friends of the Ezekiens?"

"Yes."

"They're welcome. I'd like to meet them." He smiled. "May I go now?"

The weather outside was threatening snow again.

That area of New Mexico had already received a record snowfall, and the Park Service was concerned about drifts high up on the mountain beyond Ben's home. They were waiting for the weather to clear enough to detonate explosives, and break up the drifts. But it began again before noon, and snowed heavily on the mountain the rest of the day and night.

Ben took his mug of coffee outside the next morning. There was only a foot of snow at the level around his home, and the clouds had lifted to a higher elevation. He was looking up at the mountain when he heard a great, deep, rumbling sound from that direction, knowing at once that it was a large avalanche of snow. A few seconds later, he felt the ground trembling, and saw huge masses of snow sliding and tumbling down the mountain toward him. Leona rushed from the house to stand by his side. The ground shook as the rumbling became nearer and louder; then they watched the avalanche divide as it came to the ridge extending upward beyond Ben's property. He happened to be looking at the big outcropping of sandstone above and beyond his barn, when it suddenly broke away, scattering large fragments of rock almost to the barn.

It was a sight that neither of them would ever forget. Above them, sections of forest in the canyons on both sides of the ridge were buried beneath thousands of tons of snow. Great numbers of trees had been uprooted and carried along, broken and stripped of limbs. Any living creatures in the path of the avalanche could not have survived.

Then it was over, almost before they had a chance to realize that it had happened. The sounds quickly lessened, until all that remained were clouds of powdered snow from the avalanche, and dust from the shattered ledge.

"Great Scott, Leona! Have you ever seen anything like that?"

"No, but it brought back frightful feelings that I had during the London air raids! Ben?" She squinted to see through the settling dust where the outcropping had collapsed.

"Yeah?"

"I think I see something through the dust. Do you think it's safe to go up there now?"

"Well, I guess so. What is it?"

"I'm not sure. Do you mind if I go up?"

"Let's get our boots, and I'll go with you."

He had to wait while Leona changed to warmer clothing, and the dust had settled by the time they worked their way up the ridge. Ben carefully chose their path among the fragments, while Leona followed.

"Smells good," Ben said. "I always did like the smell of freshly-broken rocks. That's weird, isn't it? What're we looking for, Leona?"

"I have a feeling that we're going to find that ancient Ezekien explorer craft. It may be covered with dust and debris."

They separated to look in different directions while Ben warned, "Watch your step. Some of this stuff could slip."

The search continued for almost an hour as they crisscrossed the shattered area, sometimes going back over places they had already searched.

"I don't see how we could've missed anything. If it's here, it must be buried—be careful, Leona!"

She was climbing on her hands and knees among loose rocks and dirty snow that had banked against the wall of the fresh cliff. The rocks suddenly began to slide, and Leona was carried down with them, to land awkwardly in the new pile of rubble. She scrambled to her feet, embarrassed, but laughing.

"I'm okay, Ben!"

Ben hurried to her, almost falling, himself, then began laughing at the sight of her. "Are you sure you're not hurt?"

She wiped dust from her eyes and face, and spat mud from her mouth.

"Not hurt, just foolish. Oh, I must look awful!"

He laughed again. "Well, I guess you could say that." His eyes searched upward at the bank behind her. "What in the world is that?"

Leona scanned around to where he was looking. A dark, glass-like surface appeared through the still-sliding dust.

"Ben! It's the spacecraft!"

They climbed up, and began scraping away debris with their hands, almost overwhelmed by excitement. It soon became evident that there was, indeed, an unnatural object of some size buried in the bank.

Ben stopped digging, and held up his hands. "Wait, Leona. Let's think about this." Leona also stopped, and looked at him. "We can't dig it out with our hands. People are going to be up here soon, probably in aircraft, looking for news coverage of the avalanche. I think we should cover it back up, and wait for a while. We can't let anyone else know about this."

Leona agreed. "You're right, Ben, and we're going to need help. We'll have to wait for Cotton and Trudy."

They scrambled to cover it over again, then Ben piled rocks on top, and none too soon. They heard a helicopter approaching from the canyon below them.

Leona shook dirt from her hair as they retreated through the broken field of rocks. The helicopter came into view through the trees, then hovered and turned when the pilot saw Ben and Leona. Ben waved a signal that all was well. The pilot waved back, then steered the helicopter over the ridge to continue up the other canyon. Leona held her breath as the craft flew over the rock slide, creating a cloud of dust.

"Should we go back to check it, Ben?"

"I covered it pretty well with rocks. We'd better leave it alone until the excitement of the avalanche is over."

Ben turned on the television after showering and changing clothes. All of the local networks were broadcasting news of the avalanche. A park ranger described his view from a snowmobile, then the scene changed to an aerial view from a helicopter. It was a rerun of the scene taped earlier.

Leona entered the room from her quarters, in time to see a panning scene that brought two people into view. It was a distant shot of Ben and Leona on the ridge. The view zoomed, to clearly show Ben waving his signal. It panned again to show the broken-up ledge as the helicopter passed over it, then on to the avalanche ruins again.

Ben laughed. "You ought to be glad they didn't get a better shot of you, Leona."

Leona laughed also. "I am, but I'm more glad that they didn't see the Ezekien spacecraft." She sat down. "Ben, it's a million years old. Can you imagine? And it wasn't even scratched!"

CHAPTER 22

Trudy and Cotton arrived two nights later, on Christmas Eve, to a happy, homecoming welcome. When they finally settled around the kitchen table to talk, Ben wanted to know Trudy's opinion of the Ezekiens and their colony, and her experiences aboard the giant space ship. He listened with eager attention as she described everything.

"Leona, I was almost responsible for Helen's death. I'm so sorry." She explained how it happened.

"Oh, dear. How is the poor child now?"

Cotton interrupted. "She's fine, Leona. And pesky as ever. Trudy, I'm sorry you feel responsible for that. It really wasn't your fault. Anyway, it might turn out to be a fortunate warning to us. Helen certainly knows better now, but others will be following her. Maybe we should consider eliminating things that might harm them."

They discussed it for a while, then Cotton had to tell them about Trudy's somersault accident aboard the shuttle. Even Trudy laughed about it.

"Oh, you big tow-head! I didn't want you to tell anyone about that."

Cotton turned serious when the conversation lulled. "I don't know what this means, but I got a strong signal from the hydrium detector when we came in tonight."

Leona looked at Ben, who grinned widely at Cotton.

"What's up, Ben?"

"We found it, Cotton. You two don't know what's

happened around here lately. Since you came in at night, you couldn't have seen it. We had a big avalanche on the mountain three days ago—it's okay, Trudy, nobody was hurt. But that big ledge up beyond the barn fell apart, and uncovered that old Ezekien spacecraft. It's been there all along, right in our own back yard."

Trudy was excited. "What does it look like? What did you do with it?"

Leona answered. "We couldn't do anything. Reporters and rangers were all over the place, so we covered it back up."

Cotton laughed. "You mean it's still there?"

"We had to wait for you and Trudy to help. Ben thinks we can winch it out with his tractor and chains, and hide it in the barn, but we don't know how big it is."

"Sure we do—at least, I do. I've studied the specs on that little baby. It's exactly the same size as mine, but of course, it's an old clunker. Hey, this is great. Let's get at it!"

Trudy fussed at him. "Cotton, it's almost midnight, and tomorrow is Christmas!"

"Okay, but if we could get the canopy open, I can fly it out of there."

"Fly it? Come on, Cotton! That thing's been buried for thousands of years—a million!"

"Trudy, what did old Mike tell you? It isn't gonna' *rust*, you know."

Ben interrupted. "Now, you youngsters don't get an argument started. I think Cotton may be right, honey. Leona and I didn't even see a scratch on it. Of course, we only saw a little bit of the canopy. Right, Leona?"

"That's right. It looked exactly like the canopy on Cotton's fighter."

Trudy looked around at all of them. "Well, gee, I'm no party-pooper. Let's do it!"

It took them a while to get organized, and into warm clothing, then Ben and Leona led the way with flashlights. Trudy hung onto Cotton's arm. The weather had now cleared, allowing moonlight to reflect dimly from the surrounding snow. Ben cautioned Leona again to watch her steps, and delighted in telling the young couple about her awkward slide down the bank.

They had to crawl on hands and knees up the loose slide, then all pitched in to clear away the rubble. A short time later, they had the canopy uncovered. Cotton brushed away dirt and small rocks with his hands, explaining that he was searching for a hatch that covered the canopy switch.

"Like I said, this is an old clunker. Everything's manual, not mind-controlled, like my little fighter."

Ben responded, "Sounds like *my* kind of flying."

"Now that's a thought! Why not, Ben? Wait . . . here it is." He blew away the dust, then carefully lifted the hatch. "Everybody stand back, okay?"

They complied, and moved away as Trudy said, "I can't believe this!"

Cotton shined the light inside the hatch, and found a small lever. He tripped it, then waited. They heard a series of clicking sounds, then a light came on inside the switch compartment, and a small button glowed with green light. He pressed it with his finger, and the canopy snapped open, scattering dust and gravel around. He shined his light inside.

"Smells funny, but it's okay. Come have a look, everybody."

Ben and Leona stepped forward eagerly, but Trudy hung back. "No. I'm afraid to look. What's in there, Cotton? The Ezekiens?"

Cotton shined the light all around. "Nope, nothing." He cleaned debris away from the canopy seal, stepped inside, then lowered himself into the seat.

"Come on, Trudy."

"No way, Cotton! What're you going to do?"

"Okay, you and Leona get back out of the way. Hop in, Ben. We're gonna' unstick this baby."

Leona took Trudy's hand, and carefully slid down the bank, while Ben climbed inside.

"Well, I'll be. . . ." Ben said. "it's dual-controlled."

Cotton found the inside canopy switch and tripped it. The canopy closed, the cockpit and panel lights came on, and they felt a movement of stale air, which quickly freshened.

"It's been a while since I studied the specs, Ben. Won't take but a minute or two for a cockpit check."

"Sure, take your time." Ben looked outside to see Trudy and Leona silhouetted behind their flashlight beam, picking their way safely beyond the rock field.

Cotton reached forward, pulled a control yoke from the panel, then locked it in place before him. It was a round disk, about ten inches in diameter, with vertical grips projecting from each side. An array of lighted, push-button switches around the edge of the disk were within easy reach of his thumbs.

"Ben, can you believe this baby hasn't been touched in a million years?" His smile seemed to reach from ear to ear. "Ready?"

Ben had not felt such exuberance since his youthful time as a fighter pilot. His eyes followed Cotton's every movement. "Let 'er rip!"

Cotton touched a lighted switch with his right thumb, then pulled the yoke slightly toward him. They heard crunching sounds from the outside, and felt the craft move very slowly upward, with no apparent effort.

Trudy and Leona stood outside the slide area, far enough to be safe from falling rocks, yet close enough to hear every crunch and scraping noise as the little craft arose from its ancient grave. The moon, now full, was just beyond the zenith, providing enough light to add a sinister feeling to the event. Trudy moved close to Leona and squeezed her arm. The sounds were enough to make her skin crawl, but the sight of the craft rising out of the earth caused a chill to creep over her.

"Leona, this is scary. Don't you feel it, too — that Cotton is awakening something from death?"

"Yes, dear, I do. And I think your father feels the same way."

"But Cotton doesn't, does he? I know he's having fun. He's the most amazing man I've ever seen, Leona. Sometimes I think he has freon, instead of blood, in his veins, but other times I see warmth and sensitivity. Did the Ezekiens make him that way? Oh . . . here they come!"

Her question was not answered. The shadow-like craft eased down beside them, to hover slightly above the ground. Its canopy snapped open to reveal two smiling faces.

Ben spoke. "Can you girls make it down to the barn okay? We're going to lock it up for the night."

"Go ahead, Pop. We'll be right behind you."

The canopy closed again, and the little spacecraft rose, then disappeared beyond the trees with absolutely no sound. Trudy and Leona retraced their path through the snow.

"Trudy, I often still think of Cotton as the little boy that I helped to raise, but he grew up to his own will. If I, or the Ezekiens, had any influence in the shaping of his life, it was only guidance. Cotton is his own man, but if you're asking for a testimonial, I'd have to tell you that I believe a finer man does not exist." She laughed. "But my opinion might be a bit biased."

Trudy returned a giggle. "Goodness, Leona, where did I ever get the crazy idea that you liked him?"

Ben and Cotton heard the two women's distant laughter as Ben climbed out to open the barn doors.

Cotton chuckled. "Sounds like something funny

going on back there." He eased the craft inside, and parked in front of his own little fighter. Ben closed the doors, and turned on the lights as Cotton climbed out. They walked around, looking and feeling for any signs of damage.

Ben's voice was reverent. "I don't believe what I'm seeing. How could they make something like this, that never seems to age? There isn't even a blemish after scraping through all those rocks."

Cotton gave a brief explanation of the compounds of helium before the two women arrived.

"I know that isn't enough, Ben, but you can have the whole course later, if you want it."

They heard Trudy and Leona crunching through the snow, while Cotton held the door open for them.

The women walked around the craft, inspecting it as the men had done, then Trudy leaned over to look inside.

"I still don't believe this. What happened to the Ezekien pilots?"

"No one knows," Cotton answered. "Their history on the subject isn't clear, but it's assumed that they left the craft to do some exploring, and just never returned. They may have perished due to an inability to cope with the earth's gravity, or they might have lost or damaged their life-support equipment. Most likely, they were killed by some force of nature, probably lightning. It must have been sudden death; otherwise, they would have communicated the problem."

They were silent for a moment, then Trudy again asked a question. "Pop, do you really think you could fly it?"

"I know I can. I'd need a lot of cockpit time, and I'd need an interpretation of those symbols, but it looks easier than any aircraft I've ever flown."

Cotton spoke. "Sure he could, Trudy. It's a dead-cinch for an old fighter pilot like Ben, but so could you or Leona. The thing that blows my mind is so little change in technology for the past million years. The only improvement that I see is from manual-control to mind-control."

Ben was equally amazed. "I've been wondering about that too, Cotton, but I was born at the tail-end of 'horse and buggy' days. We had automobiles back then, and airplanes, but I didn't see an airplane until I was six years old. The Wright brothers made their first flight in 1903, and look how far we've come since then.

"I flew the best fighter in the world, back in Korea, but I had to fly straight down from high altitude to exceed the speed of sound. Now we have fighters that can easily beat that, flying straight up. And we've seen television pictures of men walking and driving around on the moon! All this improvement, from the Wright brothers until now, was only in about eighty years.

"The point I'm making is this: The Ezekiens are a million years ahead of us, so they've had plenty of time to develop the perfect flying machine. No sir, I shouldn't be surprised that they haven't changed much in only a million years."

Trudy covered her mouth, and yawned. "Excuse me, Pop. Hey, Merry Christmas, everybody!"

CHAPTER 23

Leona's friends were Clarence and Evelyn Hartley, a senior citizen artist couple from Red River who added pleasant variety to the holiday conversation. They were both dressed in brightly colored, Indian-styled clothing and jewelry. Trudy noticed that they also wore the Ezekien gold bands (their's were disguised by Indian silver), which complimented their style of dressing. Trudy and Ben learned from Evelyn that friends of the Ezekiens, worldwide, already knew of Trudy's recent acceptance into their group.

"Evelyn," Trudy commented, "this gold band is a wondrous thing. I had a conversation with Helen last night—well, I have no idea how far away she is—but that was from me to an Ezekien. How do you converse telepathically with other humans?"

"We can't, with one exception, unless we relay our thoughts through an Ezekien, who transmits the message to another one of us. But we can all talk to Leona, and she doesn't need the band, unless she has to communicate with the Ezekiens." Evelyn patted Leona's hand. "This is a very special lady, Trudy."

"Oh, I know . . . or, at least, I'm beginning to see it more all the time. Aren't you, though, putting a great deal of trust in the Ezekiens? It seems that they must know every move you make."

Clarence asked if he might answer her question.

"For us, it isn't a question of whether or not we can trust them; we *know* that we can trust them. Rather, it seems, should they trust *us*? After all, regardless of what your lawyer might say, we don't own this planet, we only inhabit it; although, I must say, our presence here is no kindness to Earth.

"Consider this: We estimate that intelligent human life has existed on this planet for less than forty thousand years, and in that short period of time we've wasted, polluted, and destroyed so much of our natural environment that we're seriously endangering our own species. This is a very big place where we live; yet, we're running out of room.

"On the other hand, the Ezekiens have managed to survive, quite nicely, in their small synthetic world for more than a million years. You must answer this question for yourself: who's better qualified to assure our continued existence? We, or the Ezekiens?"

"But that isn't the question," Trudy said. "Of course, the Ezekiens seem to be better qualified, but isn't the real question: who will inhabit this Earth in *another* forty thousand years? Humans, or Ezekiens?"

"Very well put, Trudy—an excellent question. But why not both? I realize that it wouldn't work now; our prejudices are much too strong to accept them. However, isn't that why *we're* here? Isn't that why the Ezekiens have educated us?"

Ben interrupted. "That's the question I've been wanting to ask." He turned to Leona. "Leona, it seems that you're pretty special to these people, and to the Ezekiens. But why are you my housekeeper, and why do you need my daughter? You told me before that 'we're here to save our planet from ourselves'—that isn't what I want to know. I want to know *how* you can save this world, and what role each of you plays in that mission."

"I'm sorry, Ben. I didn't realize that I hadn't told

you." She settled into a more relaxed position. "I suppose we'll always have evil, greedy people among us — that's part of our nature — but they shouldn't have control over the rest of us. Unfortunately, they do have control in many parts of the world now, but it's because we've allowed them to do so. Our objective, then, is to select the good people among us — those capable and qualified to be in charge — and promote them into the positions of leadership. In order to do that, the good people must be educated and trained for that purpose. It can't be done overnight, of course, but it can be done if we have the patience to wait for it.

"With that in mind, the Ezekiens have selected gifted children, whom they believe are inherently good, and trained them to perform specific tasks on Earth that will eventually bring about the desired change in human behavior. Remember, too, that each of us selected were children who had no families, or were not wanted by our families. This requirement narrows the field considerably, as you might guess.

"Clarence and Evelyn have done a wonderful job. They were the original 'flower children'. Some called their followers 'hippies', or other names for people who advocate love, beauty, and peace. Granted, some of them were unconventional in every sense of the word, but they've attracted attention to our problems, which is their goal. We're all very proud of Clarence and Evelyn. Their movement is beginning to purify itself, and is spreading world-wide.

"We're trying to promote the virtues of good living, but, at the same time, we realize that evil must sometimes be overpowered by strength, so we also have people trained for that purpose. Cotton is one of them. He's a giant of gentle strength, and my darling of them all." Cotton blushed, while Trudy giggled. "He's also the only human fighter pilot, so far, in our group. But we have professional military people, too, as well as lawyers, judges, politicians, and scientists around the world. And spies. But we need good teachers more than anything else, for it's our children who will eventually achieve our goal."

Ben again interrupted. "And what about you, Leona, and my daughter?"

Leona stood, and walked to the fireplace, turning around to warm her back.

"I suppose you could call me a scout, and there are several of us. Our job is to help the Ezekiens discover qualified people; mine, specifically, is now to recruit adults, like Trudy. But Trudy was an accidental discovery, much to our great fortune. Her task, when she's properly trained, will be to continue my work. She's overly-qualified to do so, but I think it's where she'll do the most good."

Trudy was startled. "But I'm a scientist, Leona. I don't have the talents for your job. It isn't that I'm not grateful, and I'd be honored to follow you, but. . . . "

"As I said, dear, you may be overqualified, but you're free to choose your own endeavor. It's something you can be thinking about."

Leona then directed her attention back to Ben. "Ben, I had a motive in becoming your housekeeper. Cotton's primary mission was to find the ancient Ezekien explorer craft, and it was an impossible coincidence that the little ship happened to be in your back yard. It's one of those wonderful, rare incidences when the right people—you and Trudy—were in the right place at the right time. Our mission has since been changed. Trudy became our first priority because she needed our help. Our mission is now to ask for *your* help; to recruit *you* into the service of the Ezekiens."

Ben was totally unprepared for Leona's statement. He could only stare at her for a moment, while fighting to control his composure. Then he stood, and spoke with a mildly exasperated voice, "Leona, this is not a good time to bring that out—in front of our guests." He opened his hands toward Clarence and Evelyn. "Why?"

Leona covered her smile with her hands as she remembered his outrageous behavior in the hospital. She backed away, and wagged her finger at him.

"Because I knew that you might blow-up, and that I might need their help."

Ben forced himself to speak with an exaggerated gentleness. "No, Leona, I mean why do you need *me?* I just retired. If you want to make a fighter out of that little ship we dug up, I'd give my right arm to fly it, but I'm too old to be a fighter pilot again."

"You may use the little ship as your own, Ben. In fact, you may need it very much before your mission is accomplished on this earth. But that isn't why we want you. Please sit down again; you've made me nervous." She waited while he complied, then took her own seat beside Evelyn. "We've grown to the point where we now need an expert, another human, to direct us. Ben, we want you to be our leader, on Earth. Cotton has much more exciting assignments than serving as my escort. You and I can work in consort, if you'd like, but we need your abilities."

Ben half-stood, and directed his attention to Clarence:

"Clarence? Evelyn?"

Clarence stood. "She's right, Ben; we need your help."

Cotton also stood. "That goes for me, too, Ben. Leona and Clarence have done a good job, but now we need a professional with your leadership experience."

Ben sat back down, and all remained quiet for a while, giving him time to think. Finally he spoke, this time fully composed.

"What about the Ezekiens? Were they in on this plan of yours?"

"Yes, Ben," Leona said. "This wasn't a spur-of-the-moment decision by any of us."

Ben stood again, and walked to the fireplace. "Folks, I don't know what to say. Trudy?"

"Don't look at me, Pop! Remember what you told me? 'It isn't my decision, Trudy.' Well, the same to you."

He grinned at his daughter. "I should have known that would come back to me. Well, let me think about it. I'll give my answer tomorrow." The party broke up with friendly promises to get together again soon.

Ben had been alone on the patio for some time before Trudy joined him. The sun would soon be out of sight beyond the mountain, shutting off the dynamic display from the red cliff. She put her arm around his waist.

"I know what you're thinking about, Pop. She's been on my mind all day, too."

He hugged her closer. "I wasn't looking forward to this day, honey. This is the first time since I came back from Korea that your mother and I haven't been together on Christmas." He expelled a deep breath. "What do you suppose she'd think about all this business with the Ezekiens?"

"Oh, I *know* what she'd think, Pop. She'd be as excited about it as we are. I've imagined her so many times, by my side, as I experienced all those exciting things. What do *you* think?"

"I think she'd want me to join with you in this Ezekien mission. Honey, why do you think they picked me? I don't know anything about the Ezekiens, or their objectives. It seems to me they'd want someone they'd trained since childhood."

"But it does make sense, Pop. If we're really doing this for our own kind, and not for the Ezekiens, then it makes sense that we should have an open-minded leader; especially someone *not* trained by them. I know that I feel better about it. Besides, who could do a better job than my Pop? And look at the side benefits: you'll have your very own little space ship!"

"By George, you're right!" He brightened up. "I've gotta' get Cotton to give me a check-ride in that thing!"

He gave his daughter a hug, and they went inside.

CHAPTER 24

It was a perfect night for flying: unlimited visibility, cold, and dry. The snow-covered terrain was easily visible, reflecting a dim whiteness from the moon's light.

Ben now sat in the left seat as pilot, with Cotton in the right as instructor. Cotton had thoughtfully attached descriptive labels to all important instruments and controls.

"We'll get a translator band for you as soon as possible, Ben, but for now, I've made up this check-list, which you can memorize later. Are you ready?"

"Let's get at it, Cotton. I'm rarin' to go!"

Cotton called out the simple preflight cockpit checks, which he demonstrated, then again as Ben went through them. They were soon in the air, and Cotton demonstrated the extreme simplicity of the little craft's controllability.

"This is like child's play, Ben. In some ways, I like this one better than my own because you *feel* what's happening in this baby. Don't let the manual controls fool you though; we aren't actually in control of the craft, the computer is, but what we're doing reprograms the computer to respond to our command.

"Look at it this way: I'm on a true-north heading, at fifty thousand feet. I want to continue that course, but I also want to make an attitude change. Let's say I want to turn around and fly it facing backward, so I punch this yellow button with my left thumb, which tells the computer that I want to maintain this course, regardless, then I rotate the yoke until we're facing backward."

He demonstrated the maneuver, to Ben's delight. "Now, watch this." He rotated the hand grips to cause the craft to roll, head-over-tail, in a tumbling maneuver.

"We're still following our course precisely, but tumbling at the same time."

Ben was absolutely amazed.

Cotton returned to normal, forward flight. "You try it. Got it?"

"Got it!" Ben took over control, and cautiously performed all of the maneuvers that Cotton called out.

"Okay, now park it about two feet above that mountain peak."

Ben followed the instruction, a bit nervously, and held the craft hovering above the highest jagged rock.

"Fine! Now, punch the green button with your left thumb, then take your hands away, and relax a minute. The green button tells the computer to continue your present program."

Ben complied, and the craft held its hovering position automatically.

"Beats anything I ever saw, Cotton. If I'd had guns on this baby back in Korea, I could've wiped out every MiG in the sky—single-handedly. That was about thirty-five years ago, which seems to be a long time; yet, even back then, this little spacecraft was somewhere around a million years old. What a machine!"

Cotton looked overhead to see a flashing strobe-light traveling high above them. "Let's have a little fun, Ben. I've got it." A few seconds later, he held them in a close formation 'slot' position behind and below the high-flying aircraft.

"It's one of our B-52 bombers. We can't be 'seen' by their radar, so those guys don't even know we're here. You take it, Ben, and move up into their jet-wash if you want to. You won't feel it." Ben again followed instructions, and flew directly behind the tail of the bomber, a maneuver that he had been trained never to do. The little craft never wavered, even in the extremely turbulent wing vortices and exhaust gases from the bomber's jet engines.

"Beats everything," he chuckled. "I did this accidentally once, behind a B-36, if you can imagine that, and it almost knocked me out of the sky! What happens if I punch the green button now?"

"Try it."

Ben pressed the green button, then released the control yoke. The little craft held its precise position behind the bomber's tail.

"Let's take her into space, Ben. I've got it." He veered away from the bomber, pulled the nose upward, and shoved the throttle forward to its three-gee acceleration position. "Always try to keep the gee force toward your back; that way you won't black out." He throttled back in less than a minute, and they were in a weightless Earth orbit. "It takes a little time to get used to zero-gee; that's why I want to be with you for a while." He then pointed to a small dot on the navigation display. "We have a 'bogey' ahead, want to check it out?"

"You bet."

Cotton explained how to 'lock-on' to the target. "You can turn it over to George (the auto-pilot), or fly it yourself. Do it yourself this time, and we'll let George take the next one."

"Okay, I've got it."

The target turned out to be a discarded third-stage rocket from an old NASA mission. "It's space junk, Ben. Most of the stuff we've thrown up here is now junk; that's the price we pay for progress, and it can't be helped. It's like the litter on our highways. I try to clean it up when I don't have anything else to do."

He maneuvered into position, bringing the discarded rocket into contact with the bottom of the spacecraft. They heard a mild 'clunk' when Cotton pressed a switch.

"That couldn't be a magnet," Ben said. "Those things aren't made of magnetic metal."

Cotton smiled. "You're right. Don't be surprised about anything the Ezekiens do, Ben. It isn't a magnet, it's more like concentrated gravity. This baby could pick up your house if you wanted to. What do you think we should do with the junk?"

Ben thought for a moment. "Well, we could put it on the moon, or take it back to Earth where it would have a lot of people scratching their heads, but it would still be litter. If it's possible, I'd send it to the sun."

"Correct! That's what I've been doing. Hold onto your hat." He showed Ben how to select the proper trajectory to the sun, then shoved the throttle up to three gees again, and pushed the green button. When they reached a velocity of thirty thousand miles per hour, he released the discarded rocket, and veered away to begin deceleration. They were soon back in orbit at eighteen thousand miles per hour. "How're you feeling, Ben?"

"Fine . . . maybe a little queasy in the stomach." He took the little vial from Cotton, and inhaled it as instructed.

"I think you've had enough for tonight. It's time to go home. Where are we, Ben?"

Ben looked around outside, then at the navigation display. "Darned if I know, Cotton. We're on the dark side of Earth, and it's almost midnight, our time, so I'd say somewhere around North America. I can't make out those symbols."

"That's better than I thought you'd do. You didn't know this, but I hid a little 'homing' transmitter in your barn."

"Okay, let me figure this out. You've labeled this switch 'home', so I punch it, then the George button. Right?"

"Right-on! I'm proud of you, Ben. We've asked

the right man to be our boss. You've got it. Take us home."

Meanwhile, Trudy and Leona were having a conversation about telepathic communication.

"Have you deliberately tried it before, Trudy?"

"Only with Helen, but that's with the band. It's as though I were talking on the phone. How do you do it, Leona, and how do you know that I have the gift?"

"It isn't easy to explain, dear. I believe that our subconscious minds are somehow interconnected with every mental activity in our universe. Every thought of our conscious mind is transferred to the subconscious, but it's only a one-way transfer. Except in extremely rare cases, the transfer cannot be reversed. My mind is one of the exceptions: I can reverse the transference, and receive thought from the subconscious. The Ezekiens mastered reverse-transference many thousands of years ago. I believe, also, that some 'lower' forms of life on Earth have that ability. The Ezekiens can teach you to access the natural brain power that you were born with. You're 'one in a billion', Trudy — one of the very few people who are born with this gift of telepathy.

"However, I knew when we first met that you possess the gift because I could see it." Leona smiled. "Although it's visible only to the Ezekiens and me, I can see an aura surrounding your head."

"Great heavens, Leona! Are you serious?"

"I've never been more serious in my life, Trudy, and when I teach you how, you'll be able to see the aura about mine. Are you prepared for it?"

"Whoa! I don't know. . . ." She literally shook the thought from her head. "Okay, Trudy, it's time to get your feet wet. Yes, Leona. I may not be 'prepared', but I'm ready to give it a try. Tell me what to do."

"Very well, I want you to think about your vision

when Kitty was hurt. You received the vision because her mind was distressed. Did you hear her call your name?"

Trudy concentrated to recall the vision. "I . . . yes, she called my name. She said, 'Trudy. Oh, Trudy, you've got to hear me.'. But it wasn't exactly in words, Leona. And it wasn't like my conversations with the Ezekiens, either. I saw her crawling on the floor, and I knew that she wanted to warn me of something. I think I just read her mind, as if she were thinking *for* me."

"That's a very good way to describe it, Trudy. You felt her message, but you didn't speak to her?"

"No, I didn't know that I could."

"It's all right, dear. I was only trying to establish the fact that your minds were connected. Now, I want you to close your eyes and clear your mind. Just relax, and let me know when you're ready."

Almost a minute later, Trudy nodded her head, and spoke.

"I think I'm ready, Leona. My mind is relaxed."

"I'm going to speak to you with my mind only." *Do you hear me now, Trudy?*

"Yes, very clearly."

Tell me your middle name, but don't use your voice.

Trudy smiled. *It's Eileen—after my mother.*

Good! Your middle name is Eileen. Now, I want you to open your eyes, and describe the aura surrounding my head.

Trudy opened her eyes, and smiled. "It's beautiful . . . very dimly glowing . . . white and blue. Leona! It's wonderful. And it's true. I read your mind!"

Leona beamed her delight. "Yes, and your mind wasn't in a state of alarm. Marvelous, Trudy!" She stood, as Trudy jumped to embrace her. Both of them were excited.

Trudy's expression changed. Tears welled up, then drained down her cheeks. "Leona, all of a sudden, I'm afraid of this. It isn't natural. I feel freakish, and I don't want to do it anymore. Look at the goose-bumps on my arms!"

"I'm sorry, Trudy." She took Trudy's hands. "Latent telepathy must be very frightening, and I don't know how to advise you. Do you feel tired, or drained?"

Trudy wiped her eyes. "No, I feel fine, physically, but it's as if I'm meeting another me, whom I've never seen before." She covered her face, and began to cry openly. Leona moved close to hold her as she started to tremble. "Suppose I'm a *spirit medium!* Oh, Leona, don't let me do that!"

Leona stroked Trudy's hair, and patted her shoulder. "Don't think about it, dear. I've never done that, and I don't believe in it. Try to think of it as a special gift; something good and positive. Your gift can be a great service to humanity, and I know that you'll never use it for anything that isn't good. Relax, dear."

Trudy felt a wave of calmness sweep over and relax her. She exhaled a deep breath.

"You did that, didn't you? Thanks, Leona. Could I do that—relax someone?"

"Of course. You can do anything that I can do—maybe more. I'll teach you everything I know, but we must go slowly; otherwise, it might be too much of a mental strain. Don't you agree?"

"Whew, absolutely! But I do have a question that's been puzzling me for a long time: Remember what you did to Georgette Adams? How'd you do that?"

"Oh, dear! I knew I'd have to explain that to you some day, and I haven't been able to give your father a satisfactory explanation, either." She got up to refill their coffee cups. "Trudy, I don't know. That was only the third time that I have ever levitated someone. All three were during some type of emergency. It must have been the state of my mind at that time—extreme anxiety from the fear that your father might have been mortally wounded. Oh, it was such a dreadful feeling—that I might have been too late. Technically, it's called 'telekinesis', and it's a very rare occurrence. Maybe you can do it. Would you like to try?"

"Whoa, not me!" But it was an enticing idea, and Trudy reconsidered. "Well . . . maybe later. It might come in handy sometime."

Ben gave them his decision the next morning, when they found him sipping the last of a pot of coffee.

"Well, folks, I've been sitting here trying to think of a good reason why I shouldn't join you, but retirement isn't the answer for me. They don't make rocking chairs in my size, so I guess you'll just have to put up with me. I'll do the best I can for you."

"Darn, Pop! We forgot all about that!" Then Trudy grabbed him in a strong hug as Leona and Cotton also expressed their welcome.

"Honey, I've been thinking about little Kitty. . . ."

"Oh, so have I! Are you thinking what I think you're thinking?"

"Well, I'm afraid that she won't be safe anywhere on this earth for a long time. That W.E.B. bunch is probably after her head, you know, and she can't have police protection forever. Leona, this is your business. Do you think the Ezekiens could use her?"

"I hope so, Ben, but I'll have to talk with her. Can you bring her here for a while? She might not be interested, you know."

Trudy's enthusiasm was obvious. "I'd like her to come for a visit anyway, Leona. May I ask her?"

"Of course. Why don't you try your new-found telepathy."

Ben's interest changed to another subject. "Leona, I suppose you'll want me to go to the Colony; I've been wanting to see that place, anyway. When do you think I should go?"

"Anytime you're ready. The Ezekiens are eager to meet you."

He rubbed his hands together. "Good! I'm ready to get this show on the road. We'll go soon. Cotton, I need some more cockpit time; want to help me?"

CHAPTER 25

Georgette quickly crouched in the dark night shadows when she heard Ben and Cotton crunching over the snow-packed trail.

"Most fun I've had in over thirty years, Cotton. That little spacecraft makes an F-86 look like a toy!"

She waited as they stamped and scraped wet snow from their shoes before entering the house. It was past midnight, four days after Christmas, and the men were returning from Ben's third check-flight.

Spacecraft? Georgette did not understand Ben's meaning of the word, but she was definitely interested in its implication. She retraced their clear trail through the snow, to find that it led to a large rock building. A person who survived in her way of life was one who never rushed into something unknown. She approached the barn cautiously, knowing that a spacecraft must surely be protected by an alarm system. Ben Two Bears was an electronics engineer; therefore, his alarm would be something elaborate, probably a silent system connected to his home; also, probably an infrared system. There were wild animals in the area that would be large enough to activate an infrared detector, so the system would probably not be set to detect the presence of anything outside.

The building was far enough from Ben's home to make an ordinary radio alarm transmitter unreliable; therefore, there must be wires coming somewhere through the rock wall. She used a small penlight to search overhead. Electric transmission lines and a telephone line; it must be the telephone line. She searched the rock walls, but could find no other wires.

Almost an hour later, she cut the bundle of smaller wires with an intricate, multi-purpose tool from her pack, then worked her way back down the pole that she had leaned against the wall. The lock was easily picked, and she was soon inside the barn. She scanned the large room to see that there were no windows, then closed the doors, and turned on the lights.

Georgette was seldom impressed to the point of excitement, but the sight of the two space ships brought her heart to a rapid beat. Her mind raced with thoughts of the power that she could have with such a machine. The explorer craft was in position before the doors, so it was the logical choice. It never occurred to Georgette that she knew nothing of the craft; therefore, she should leave it alone. It was something that must be done in order to arrive at a goal. It also had not occurred to Cotton that the little ship might be stolen, and as a convenience to Ben, he had thoughtfully attached descriptive labels and instructions wherever they might be needed. A check-list and simple manual were all that Ben needed, and it was all that Georgette would need.

Georgette read the hatch label, opened the canopy, and stepped inside. She was amazed at the craft's simplicity, compared to the helicopters that she had flown. She read Cotton's hand-written check-list, and Ben's manual, then identified the switches and controls as they were indicated.

Such stupidity, she thought. *The fools have made it easy for me.*

Before attempting to fly it, however, she decided that a bit more caution and patience might be worthwhile. She removed a miniature voice-activated recorder from her bag, and placed it in the craft where she knew that it would not likely be found by Cotton or Ben. Then she stepped out of the craft, closed the canopy, and left the barn. After repairing the wires that she had cut, and brushing her footprints from the snow, she retreated into the pine grove, and prepared to wait for Cotton and Ben to give her more instructions.

After Ben's next check-flight, Georgette again disabled the alarm system, and entered the barn, as before. By combining the information from her recorder with Cotton's written instructions, she decided that she now had sufficient knowledge to attempt the theft.

Any normal human being would have been nervous, and inclined to rush through the check-out, and escape. Not Georgette. She took her time, carefully and cautiously following the written procedure. She memorized the instructions after reading through them three times; then, only after she felt confident, she stepped out to turn the lights off, and open the barn doors. Twilight was beginning to show when the little craft eased through the doors, and lifted slowly above the trees.

The power of the witch could wait. It had been Georgette's plan to somehow discover Leona's power of the mind, but now the spacecraft had been miraculously placed in her hands. She believed strongly in divine intervention, as evidenced in her own life. How many times had the course of her life been suddenly changed? How else could she have survived the physical abuse in her youth? The only explanation was by divine intervention; she thought that she was guided and protected by God, Himself.

And now the course had changed again. She must find a safe place to hide out until the spacecraft could be mastered. She maneuvered into a wide, sweeping turn, with the rising sun to her left, and headed south toward Mexico.

Ben and Cotton walked toward the barn for

additional instruction in the little spacecraft. Ben was in his glory, and feeling quite young again. Each flight with the spacecraft was a new experience, and he followed Cotton's instructions with great interest and enthusiasm. For the first time since Eileen's death, Ben was having fun, and was eager to continue his learning.

Neither of them were prepared for what they saw: both barn doors were wide open.

"Hold it, Cotton! We didn't leave those doors unlocked. The alarm system!"

Cotton was the first inside, and Ben felt sick at his stomach when he saw the younger man's expression.

"Your little ship! It's gone, Ben!"

Cotton ran back toward the house to tell Leona, but stopped with the receipt of her mental message. *I know, Cotton! You and Ben hurry; you might be able to find it.*

She was joined outside a moment later by Trudy, and they rushed to the barn in time to see the little fighter float out and upward. Cotton seldom flew during the hours of daylight, not wanting to disclose the spacecraft's existence.

The telephone line lay on the ground, obviously intentionally cut, and a pole leaned against the barn wall. Leona studied the foot prints, still plainly impressed in the snow around the pole and barn walls. She returned to Trudy, who stood silently and bewildered, watching the expressions of Leona's face. It had not occurred to Trudy that she could have read the other woman's thoughts.

"Trudy, we have a very serious problem. I'm almost certain of who did this. Georgette Adams escaped from prison a few days before you and Cotton came back from the Colony. I think it was Georgette who stole the spacecraft. The problem is, Georgette has somehow blocked her mind from me. Such brilliance! If only she'd been guided to goodness. But I suppose the Ezekiens can't find all of them, or perhaps she was inherently bad from the beginning." Her sigh was deep and saddened. They closed the barn door, and returned to the house.

"Leona, what you said about Georgette: you know, goodness and evil. I've thought a lot about that. Can people be born inherently bad? And are all Ezekiens good?"

"I don't know, dear, about people. The Ezekiens have told me of their history. They weren't always good, just as they weren't always small. In fact, they were very warlike when they lived on their planet. Even after migrating to the Colony, there were power struggles, assassinations, and all sorts of violent crimes. They had emotional and behavioral problems, just as we have now, and it took them a while to realize that their very survival depended on harmonious cooperation among themselves. Then they discovered that virtuous living led to love, happiness, and contentment."

Trudy was thoughtful. "I wonder if they could be corrupted by association with us. I'm thinking specifically of Helen. She's good, I know, but she can be a little snip, at times. I wonder if she acts that way among her own kind?"

Leona laughed. "I think we all agree with you on that. She does become a bit saucy at times, but they all enjoy fun and frolic. I like that quality about them."

"Oh, so do I! And I'm not criticizing her, I'm trying to be philosophical. Here's what I mean: Helen cheats when she plays games with her friends, by reading their thoughts. Does she do it only in fun? Suppose they were playing for stakes. Would she cheat to gain a reward? In that case, she'd have a very unfair advantage; so, wouldn't that be considered bad?"

"I see what you mean," Leona replied. "Oh, dear, I don't think I want to get into that subject now."

"Okay," Trudy laughed. "Maybe I don't, either." She looked at the kitchen clock. "I wonder how the men are doing."

Ben and Cotton returned before noon, with the bad news that they had found no evidence of the little explorer craft.

Ben seemed to be depressed about it. "I'm afraid it's gone, Leona. It could be on the other side of the world by now, or on the moon, for that matter. Who'd take a chance like that? I'll tell you, that took a lot of guts!"

"I think I know, Ben," Leona said. "I think it was Georgette Adams."

Ben's eyes showed the hatred that he still held inside, and it came out with the tone of his voice. "Well, if it were only me, I'd turn over every rock until I found her." He lost himself in thought for a moment, while the others waited. "Leona, if you still want me to lead this mission, you need to understand that leadership, in my opinion, is mostly a matter of making correct decisions. But I don't issue major orders without the approval of my staff. That little spacecraft is going to nip at our heels later, but we can't cry about it now. We need to bring Kitty down here for a few days. You can arrange that, Trudy, and it might be best for her to fly down by a commercial airline, in case she doesn't like our idea. Then, we all need to go to the Colony to make plans with the Ezekiens. Do you agree, Leona?"

"Yes. And I want to say, Ben, that I'm very proud to have you as my leader." She offered her hand to him.

He took it, then offered her his smile. "Two heads are better than one, Leona. In the meantime, Cotton and I can be looking for the stolen spacecraft at night, it's too risky in the day-time. Cotton, what's the range of your hydrium detector?"

"I can only scan about a hundred miles in diameter, at an optimum altitude of, say, twenty miles. It won't be easy to find, Ben, but I agree that we should search before Georgette becomes very familiar with its operation. I'm sorry about that check-list. I made it easy for her."

"Don't be too hard on yourself, Cotton. I'll take my own share of the blame for underestimating that W.E.B. bunch."

CHAPTER 26

Kitty arrived two days later, accompanied by a police guard. Trudy and Ben met her at the airport, along with Sheriff Lang, who accepted the responsibility for her protection. He then passed a badge to Ben, with the instruction, "Consider yer'self deputized again, Ben. Strap on yer' side-arm." Trudy cried when she saw her friend's bandaged head.

"Hey, you should've seen me three weeks ago. I was some sight! But, really, it's much better now, except for occasional severe headaches."

Cotton was waiting for them when Ben drove up to the house.

Kitty exclaimed. "Wow! Who's the big guy, Trudy? You don't waste any time, do you?"

Trudy laughed. "Well, you just keep your gorgeous sloe-eyes to yourself."

Ben smiled as he parked the car and switched off the ignition. "Welcome back to the mad-house, Kitty."

They visited as a group for a while, until Trudy suggested that Kitty might need rest. Cotton carried the luggage to Trudy's bedroom, then left the two women alone.

"Trudy, I've been crazy to get you alone. You have a lot of explaining to do, you know."

"I know, and so do you!"

"You first. Tell me about this telepathy stuff. I

thought I was losing my mind when you broke into my thoughts. Is it for real, or have I been dreaming?"

"It's for real, and it scares me, too. Kitty, there's so much I want to tell you, but I have to hold back on some of it. You'll understand why, later. I'm sorry. You wouldn't believe it, anyway. I think, though, that Leona wouldn't mind if you knew that she has the gift, too. Actually, she's the one who brought it out in me." Trudy laughed at Kitty's expression. "Don't look so stunned. You haven't heard *anything* yet!

"Kitty, I've also had mental visions. I saw everything when Pop was hurt by Georgette Adams, but I couldn't tell you about it because I couldn't believe it myself. Then, I saw you after you'd been shot, while you crawled to open that door." She covered her face. "It was horrible! You had blood all over you!"

Kitty's face was a mixture of disbelief, belief, and compassion for her friend. "You. . . . Trudy, you're asking me to believe some weird things, aren't you?"

"You *have* to believe me—it's true. Kitty, my life for the past few months has been like a ridiculous fantasy. I'm asking you to condition your mind to believe anything that you're told while you're here. Can you do that?"

Kitty hunched her shoulders, and spread her hands. "Okay, I'll believe anything you say, but only because you've never lied to me before. Now?"

"No. Leona will tell you when she's ready. I want you to trust her, Kitty."

"Thanks, Trudy! You've carried me up this far, now you're dropping me. That isn't fair!"

"I know. I'm treating my best friend terribly, but you'll have to trust me. Now it's your turn. What's been happening to you?"

"Well, you're a tough act to follow." She began by telling of her confession to Trudy's mother, exposing the secret W.E.B. society. The reference to Eileen was tempered with sympathy for the sake of her friend.

"I've agonized for months, Trudy—the feeling that I might have been responsible for your mother's death. This is the first time I've spoken of it, but Icy found out. That's why she shot me. Will you please forgive me?" She wiped tears from her eyes.

"Forgive you? Kitty, you didn't do anything wrong. I just wish that you'd told me about it months ago. Why didn't you?"

"Because your mother asked me not to tell you. I thought it would be, like, disrespectful to her memory."

Trudy hugged her. "Bless your heart. You couldn't do anything bad if you tried to. I think you need to rest, Kitty. Why don't you nap for a while, then come down when you feel better. Okay?"

Kitty smiled, and nodded. "I do feel pretty weak. Trudy, thanks for inviting me. I was going crazy with those guards around all the time, and now I feel safe, here with you." Trudy left the room, crying silently to herself.

Kitty came down for dinner, then visited for an hour until she asked to be excused because of a painful headache. It had happened for the past several days, she said, when she felt tired.

On the second morning after her arrival, Kitty seemed to be in good spirits. Ben asked for a meeting after breakfast, and they all remained gathered around the kitchen table. He directed his attention to their new guest.

"Kitty, we want you to feel comfortable with Leona and Cotton—I assure you, they can be trusted—and we're all concerned about your injury. If you'd rather not talk about it now, just speak up. We'll understand."

Kitty glanced quickly at the others, then shrugged her shoulders for Ben.

"I feel fine, Ben. But something tells me that I'm not here for just a visit. What's this all about?"

Ben grinned. "Sorry to put you in the spotlight. I didn't intend for this to look like an interrogation. Kitty, this W.E.B bunch has been pretty rough with my little family, including you. Maybe you can tell us something about them, and how you became involved. We're all in this together now."

She began with an apology to Ben, in the same manner as with Trudy on the afternoon of her arrival. After a brief hesitation, she stood, while grabbing her head in both hands.

Leona was walking around the table, even before Kitty had stopped talking.

"I hope you don't mind, Kitty, but I've been listening to your thoughts. Your head. . . ."

"It's splitting!"

"Please be seated, dear."

Kitty obeyed, while Leona placed her hands on the bandaged head. The results were almost immediate. Kitty relaxed, and the deep furrows between her brows disappeared.

"Oooh . . . that feels *so* much better. What did you do, Leona? Am I hypnotized, or something?"

Leona gently patted the bandage. "It *is* a form of hypnosis, I suppose. I've only commanded your mind to relax. Maybe you should lie down for a while."

"No, please, I want to finish. I need to get this guilt out of my mind." She now turned to face Trudy. "Trudy, do you remember how we used to argue with your mother about women's rights and female repression?" Trudy nodded, and Kitty returned her attention to Ben. "But Trudy wasn't as serious about it as I was. Frankly, I was a bit resentful that she took my side of the argument. I felt that Trudy hadn't earned the right to understand prejudice as I had. On the contrary, I knew that Icy *did* understand.

"I first met Icy Brooks when she enrolled in one of my martial arts classes, and we became friends. That was long before Trudy moved to D.C.. Of course, I didn't know then that Icy had planned our meeting. I was a push-over, Ben, because Icy told me what I wanted to hear: that women *deserved* vengeance.

"I worked and studied very hard, in order to earn a promotion to the second tier. I served as Icy's body-guard on several occasions, just to earn her recognition. You see, the learning tier was very idealistic. It made a lot of sense to me, so I was impatient to become an active member. Trudy, I could hardly wait to get you involved.

"My first doubts were awakened when Icy told me about the abortion clinic bombings. It was a horrible act of terrorism; although, at that time, it didn't seem to be so wrong. As Icy stated, 'The end result justified the means.'. Later, thank God, my conscience returned, and I began to think reasonably again.

"By the time Trudy arrived, I understood my errors, but I didn't know how to get away from Icy. She's very perceptive, Ben, so I had to be careful. The *last* thing I wanted then was to involve Trudy; yet, I couldn't tell her of my own involvement. I felt so ashamed." At that point, Kitty's throat constricted, and she fought to control her emotions. She reached to squeeze Trudy's hand, but shook her head when Trudy tried to speak. After a long pause, she again turned to Ben.

"On one of her visits with us, more than a year after Trudy moved in with me, I had an opportunity to talk to Eileen alone. Trudy went to work early that morning, and I called-in an excuse to be late. Eileen had already heard rumors of the W.E.B. society, so I had no problem getting her attention. I didn't want to tell her of my involvement, but I couldn't keep it inside, either—it all came tumbling out. Before I knew it, I was in her arms, and crying my heart out.

"After that, I felt clean again, until she was murdered. I knew then that I could *never* escape from Icy.

Ben, I'm so sorry. I'll do anything to. . . ."

Ben interrupted with a soft command: "Please don't do that to yourself, Kitty." He reached across the table to pat her hands. "We've all agreed that your confession to Eileen was the right thing to do, and we're thankful to have you back with us. Now, that has nothing to do with the reason we've brought you here. Our only concern now is for your health and safety, and that's where Leona and Cotton come in; they can help you. But you'll have to be patient with us for a while longer. Meanwhile, just try to be comfortable, get plenty of rest, and enjoy your visit."

The rest of the meeting was occupied by Kitty's endless questions about mental telepathy and Leona's awesome ability to soothe her painful headache. At later times, when they were alone together, Kitty persistently pried Trudy for the real reason of her visit; only to be told again to "please be patient".

Ben and Cotton continued to search for the missing spacecraft for at least four hours every night, each night returning more discouraged than the last. Meanwhile, with Leona's occasional aid, Kitty's health appeared to improve, if only psychosomatically.

On the fifth morning of Kitty's visit, Leona announced to Ben and Cotton, before the young women came down to breakfast, that she heartily approved of Kitty as a candidate for membership in their group. "Do you agree, Ben?"

"Of course. I could've given you my agreement before she got here."

"Cotton?"

"Fine with me, Leona. I've checked her head wound a couple of times, and I'm a little concerned about it. If she accepts your offer, I think we should get her on the shuttle within a day or two, to get that wound healed."

After breakfast, Leona informed Trudy of their

decision.

"Would you like to speak to her, or shall I?"

"Please, I'd like to break-the-ice if you don't mind, then I'll bring her to you. Thanks, Leona. I knew you'd accept her."

Kitty was talking to Cotton when Trudy sat beside him, waiting for a break in the conversation.

"Cotton, do you mind if I show Kitty what's in the barn?"

He smiled, guessing what Trudy had in mind. "Good idea—go ahead. Call me when you're ready, and I'll pop the lid."

Trudy returned the smile, then leaned over to briefly kiss him on the lips. "Thanks. Kitty, want to come with me? I've got a surprise."

"Sure. You know how I like surprises, but you're doing this to get me away from your guy, aren't you?"

"Of course." She winked at Cotton, then led Kitty to get their coats and the key to the barn door lock. Once outside, Trudy took her friend's arm, and guided her up the path.

"Trudy, you're being awfully mysterious. What's up?"

Trudy squeezed Kitty's arm. "I could hardly wait for this. Now I'm getting nervous. This is it, Kitty. You've passed Leona's tests, so now I can tell you everything."

Kitty stopped. "Wait, Trudy. What do you mean, I've passed Leona's tests?"

"Oh, I shouldn't have said it that way. It sounded as if you were being inspected. Well, that's what it was, I guess. Kitty, it's only for your benefit. Please be patient. I'm being clumsy, but I'm trying to ease you into this. Okay?"

She again took Kitty's arm, and led her to the barn.

Inside was dark, after the doors were closed. Trudy

felt her way, and switched the lights on.

"Look, Kitty." She pointed to Cotton's fighter craft. "Can you guess what that is?"

Kitty walked around it, feeling and inspecting. "It's beautiful. Is this the airplane your dad is building?"

"Nope. That's Pop's plane over there, and he hasn't touched it in weeks. This is a space ship." She waited for the words to sink in. "It's Cotton's space fighter."

Kitty looked at her friend, but said nothing for several seconds. "Okay, I promised to believe you, but this is a joke, right?"

"It isn't a joke. Look, stand over here with me. I'm going to call Cotton." She spoke on the intercom system. "Hi, Cotton. We're in the barn now. Will you please open the canopy." A moment later, the canopy snapped open.

Kitty jumped a step backward, put her hands over her mouth, and looked at Trudy.

Cotton's voice came back. "Are you standing clear, Trudy?"

"Yes, Cotton, we're clear."

The little fighter rose a foot higher above the floor, and Kitty jumped another step backward.

"I'm sorry, Kitty. We didn't mean to scare you, but now do you believe me?"

Kitty said nothing, but approached the fighter to look inside, then up through the clear canopy. She bent down to look beneath it before returning to Trudy.

"Could I go for a ride in it sometime?"

Trudy burst out in laughter. "Kitty, you're amazing! I expected you to faint, or something. Aren't you even excited?"

"Of course! I love this! Have you flown in it?"

"Sure. Okay, let's see how this grabs you: I've been to the moon in it; to another space ship much larger than this one, and then to a giant space colony ship, far on the other side of the moon, that's inhabited by little green people."

She again had to wait for a reply.

Kitty looked skeptical, and smiled, then laughed aloud. "You're really telling me the truth, aren't you? This is for real! Trudy, you never knew how often I've dreamed of this stuff! I fantasize about traveling from planet-to-planet in space." She clapped her hands together. "Trudy, don't you *dare* tell me this is a joke now."

Trudy laughed happily. "And here I was, worrying about you! Cotton, you can close her up now. We're coming back."

Kitty, now definitely excited, pressed Trudy for answers all the way back to the house.

"What does it feel like in space? How'd you fall into this? Who are Leona and Cotton, really? Are they aliens? What about the little green people? Trudy, tell me!"

Trudy laughed at her friend. "Heavens, Kitty, can't you wait for just a minute? If you don't simmer down, you're going to get another headache!"

The others were seated around the kitchen table when the young women entered. Trudy was all smiles. "Hey, I'm beginning to think I have a tiger by the tail. Help me, someone!"

They spent the rest of the morning answering Kitty's inexhaustible questions, and explaining the Ezekien mission.

Trudy and Cotton went for a walk after lunch, leaving Kitty's education to Ben and Leona. Trudy snuggled close, her arm around his waist, with his over her shoulders.

"Cotton, are you and Pop going out again tonight to look for the missing spacecraft?"

"Probably not. I think we should get Kitty aboard the shuttle as soon as possible. She needs to get that head-wound healed."

"Oh, I forgot about that. Mo can do it, can't he?"

"Sure, no problem for Mo. Why'd you ask? Got something in mind?"

She stopped walking, and stepped around to smile up at him. "Yes, would you mind taking me back to our mountain peak? Just for a little while, before the shuttle comes?"

Her smile was enticing and bewitching at the same time.

He pulled her close, and smiled down at her upturned face.

"Hey, are you reading my mind? Don't do that, Trudy."

"No way!" She tried to look hurt, but it didn't work; her smile returned. "Well, if you don't want to. . . ."

He bent down, folded his arms around her waist, then straightened up to bring her head to his height. She wrapped her arms around his neck, her feet dangling above the ground.

"Who says I don't want to?"

Their lips came together by mutual desire, for a prolonged, delicate kiss. Cotton struggled, inside himself, to contain his long pent-up feelings. He broke the kiss, and drew his head back.

"You don't know what you're doing to me, girl."

Her head moved forward again. "Maybe I do, Cotton. Maybe the feeling's mutual."

"Trudy. . . ."

Not now, Trudy told herself. *This isn't the right time, or the right place.* She drew back, and put her fingers over his mouth before he completed the sentence.

"Wait, Cotton. Tell me tonight." She removed her hand from his mouth, and blew him a kiss.

"Girl. . . ." He stopped himself, then lowered her back to the ground. They held closely to each other without speaking for another few minutes before returning to the house.

The issue with Kitty was settled by that time.

"Pinch me, Trudy, so I'll know I'm not dreaming! Can you believe this? Listen, they want us all to go to the Colony *tonight!* Will you please help me think? I'll have to quit my job, store my things—everything this afternoon. Help, Trudy! It's impossible!"

Nevertheless, everything was arranged before nightfall. Cotton made excuses for himself and Trudy to be absent for a while, before the shuttle arrived.

They left at sundown, and settled onto their ledge atop the mountain in time to watch the sun set again. It was a beautiful scene, and a perfectly romantic setting; yet, both of them felt uneasy, and a bit awkward as they watched the colorful display fade into twilight. This time, the cockpit lights were dimmed. Both of them tried to speak at the same time, then their laughter broke away the tension.

Trudy crawled across the console, and Cotton lifted her onto his lap. "This is much better," Trudy commented, as she snuggled into a comfortable position with her head against his chest. "I love this place, Cotton. No one else has ever been here before." She lifted her head to smile up at him.

He stroked her hair, then gently pulled her head back to his chest.

"Trudy, I've been back a dozen times since the day I first brought you here. It's always the same: I sit here and remember every detail, every expression of your face, every word you spoke. You were a grown-up woman and a child; scared out of your wits, but the bravest woman I've ever known. Don't say anything. Just let me get this out."

Trudy could feel his heart pounding against her cheek. She closed her eyes, and pressed closer to him.

After a moment, he continued. "You showed me every feeling and every emotion of your soul that day. I fell in love with you, Trudy, and every day it's gotten stronger and more difficult to hold inside."

She knew that he was through talking when she felt his deep sigh. Her head remained at his chest while she replied.

"I think I loved you, even before we met, but I fell in love with you that day, too. Cotton, I'm so happy. I don't want this feeling to end, ever."

"It doesn't have to. Trudy, will you marry me?"

She leaned back, to put her arms around his neck, then answered in the teasing, coquettish mood that he loved.

"Yes, moldy-head. But you can't ever take me away from this mountain."

He responded with a happy chuckle: "Do I have to ask Ben for your hand?"

"Of course you do! He might say 'no', and spare me a life of misery."

"What if he says 'yes'?"

"Then I'll have to obey, won't I?"

"You'd better; otherwise, *I'll* have a life of misery."

She put her fingers over his mouth, her smile faded, then she met his kiss as he pulled her forward. They whispered, and laughed, and shared their intimate thoughts and dreams for almost an hour, when Trudy pulled away, and arranged her hair.

"We have to go, Cotton. What time is it?"

He looked at the panel clock. "Almost seven." Then his attention was suddenly drawn to the hydrium detector display. Its dim, flashing signal, too weak to indicate direction, was just then fading out.

His abrupt reaction startled Trudy. "What's wrong, Cotton?"

"I wish I hadn't looked . . . sorry, Trudy. He picked her up, and helped her back across the console. "It's the hydrium detector, Trudy. Ben's little ship just passed within detection range, and it's gone now. Strap in, we'll take a quick look." Hurriedly, he fastened his own safety harness, and put the band on his head.

He guided the little fighter outward and upward into a wide spiral, holding their speed and gee-force within a tolerable range for Trudy. They searched for three complete rounds before he spoke.

"It's no use, Trudy, she's gone. Let's go home." He fixed the course, then reached across the console to take her hand.

"I shouldn't have hurried off that way, Trudy. You mean more to me than any spacecraft."

She gripped his hand in both of hers. "I wouldn't have had it any other way, Cotton. I wanted to find it as much as you did." She blew him a kiss.

They waited in a small open area in front of the barn. Ben, Trudy, and Kitty, who wanted to experience levitation by the mysterious blue light, would go first; to be followed by Cotton and Leona, who would dock the little fighter.

Cotton gave last-minute instructions. "Remember, no metal objects. They'll replace your tooth fillings, Ben. No more headaches, Kitty. They'll heal your head-wound, and you'll both be issued everything you need when we get to the Colony. Ben, you have a good strong heart, but try not to let this excite you too much."

Leona spoke from the fighter's cockpit. "It's time, Cotton."

"Okay. See you all inside."

Ben and the two young women walked to the center of the small clearing, and joined hands.

"Girls, I hope I'm not too old for this. You two hang onto me real tight. I don't want to lose you." He looked upward in time to see a large, dark, disk-like shape settle in place, about two hundred feet above them. It seemed almost as though the craft had instantly materialized in its present position. Had he not been told what to expect,

Ben would not have believed that such a large mass could so defy the presently known laws of physics. A moment later, the craft descended lower, while their entire area, for about a hundred yards in diameter, was flood-lighted by a circular array of domed, or dish-shaped, white lights that completely encircled the bottom periphery of the craft. It seemed to be about the same brightness as a lighted football field; yet, Ben could clearly distinguish the other features of the craft's bottom without an uncomfortable glare from the bright lights.

He could see another less-bright circular array of lights, a soft yellowish color, about four or five feet inside the white lights, and about three feet apart. Several feet inside the yellow lights was a clearly defined, thin, solid circular light, which Ben thought was similar to a very large circular fluorescent lamp with approximately the same brightness. Still further inside were a circular array of five large, flat-black, joined elliptical shapes, which reminded him of the appearance of a sand dollar. The size of the craft appeared to be about one hundred and sixty feet in diameter. The color of its surface was a glossy dark-gray.

Ben's mental description required only a few seconds of time before the array of lights blinked out, leaving only a shadow of the craft's shape against the background of stars. Then, without any warning, they were suddenly enveloped by a beam of bright blue light. Ben felt a slight warmth from the beam, and could see its glow surrounding them, but there was no spot of blue light on the ground, and no shadows on their bodies. Everything that he had been told before had no effect on him now. His heart pounded, and his breath rushed out as he felt himself being drawn upward, completely weightless, with Kitty and his daughter. He felt their hands squeezing his, and saw that they experienced the same sensation, but none of them could speak.

CHAPTER 27

Things were not going well for Icy Brooks. Nadezhda, the Russian physicist, had turned out to be overbearing and uncooperative, and Icy was certain that it had something to do with skin color. She scorned anyone with Nadezda's attitude, yet was unable to accept that she, herself, was strongly bigoted.

Nevertheless, she had worked hard to get along with Nadezhda, trying to encourage expedient development of the anti-matter bomb. Trudy's journal had been no help at all. Nadezhda had studied its contents, then rejected it as wholly absurd.

Icy was finally forced to make the decision that her ingenious plan to take control of the U. S. Government must be delayed for another year. Arrangements had been made, and Nadezhda was now on her way back to Russia. The W.E.B. society staff was worn out from working long hours overtime in preparation for the plan. Then, when the decision was made to retreat, Icy had sent them all home for a much needed rest. They had shown extreme regret and disappointment, especially for Icy's sake, as she had been an excellent leader.

It was now mid-January. Icy was alone, standing outside the western entrance to The Tunnel as darkness began to settle over the hills. She shivered from the cold, but decided to stay outside a while longer before going back into the cavern that was now her home. The vast openness of the cavern, echoing every sound, made her feel depressed and lonely.

Something, only a contrasting movement, caused her to take a second look at the dim outline of the next hill to the west. Now it was gone; maybe only a bird. Then she thought of the light from the open doorway behind her, and admonished herself for the carelessness. As she turned to go inside, a startling black shape, coming from nowhere, it seemed, hovered above the concrete loading dock, then lowered to the surface. The unexpected presence terrified her, and she threw out her hands and screamed. Icy Brooks, the unshakeable, now stood frozen with fear before the open doorway.

The canopy snapped open, and Georgette stood up in the cockpit. "Icy! It's me, Georgette!"

Icy continued to scream at the top of her voice. Georgette jumped out, and ran to the terrified woman. She slapped the horror-struck face, then brought her own face into the light, so that Icy could recognize and identify her. The screaming stopped, and Icy's face began to relax.

"Georgette?" Recognition finally came, then Icy threw her arms around the other woman, desperately trying to regain her composure.

"I don't know why that happened, Georgette. I've been alone here for almost a week. The loneliness is maddening." She tensed again, and drew away to point at the spacecraft. "What *is* that?"

"It's a spacecraft. Are you sure you're all right now?"

Icy was, indeed, almost recovered by then. She was a remarkable woman, and she spoke as if nothing had happened.

"Yes, thanks. Georgette, what are you doing with a spacecraft? Where did you get it?"

"It's a long story, Icy. Help me get it inside. Can you open the service door?" She was speaking of a large, camouflaged door, opened only when necessary for large-sized loads.

Icy complied as Georgette stepped back into the spacecraft, then eased inside when the door was fully open. The door closed behind her.

Georgette climbed out, to find that Icy was still standing beside the door switch, obviously in deep thought.

"Icy?"

The sound of her name brought Icy back to awareness. She rejoined her lieutenant, but her mind still worked on another thought. As if by habit, she said, "You must be hungry."

"Starving! I've been living on wild game and roots for two weeks. Where is everyone?"

"Huh? Oh, I'll explain in a minute. Georgette, tell me about that spacecraft."

They went to the kitchen, and Georgette explained, while preparing her own meal, how she had stolen the craft from Ben Two Bears' barn.

Icy laughed. "So the Two Bears are still in our lives, huh?"

Georgette nodded as she began to eat. "They have another one, too."

"Another what?"

"Another spacecraft."

Icy's attention heightened. "Very interesting! What's going on there?"

Georgette chewed another bite, and swallowed. "No idea." She took the last bite, then got up for a second helping of food.

"I think the witch may have something to do with it."

Icy appeared to be impatient, but controlled the tone of her voice. "And who might *that* be, Georgette?"

"I told you, it's a long story. She lives with Ben Two Bears, and I think she may be from another planet."

"What?" The idea was ridiculous; yet, where else could such a spacecraft—two spacecraft—be from?

Georgette was, by no means, dim-witted, and she had been a reliable source of information many times in the past. Icy had never rejected an idea merely because it sounded illogical.

"Finish your meal, Georgette. I want to think about that for a minute."

Georgette finished eating, then automatically cleaned up afterward, and sat down to wait for Icy to continue.

Finally, Icy spoke. "How well can you fly it?"

"Flying it isn't the problem. I'm pretty good at that now. It's the instruments; they have no meaning to me. They're in some kind of code that I can't figure out, so I have no radio communication, and I can fly only by sight. I would've been here sooner, but I couldn't recognize this place from the air. When I saw your light from the door, I just took a chance."

"Lucky for us that you did. Is it armed for combat?"

"I don't think so, but I've found a way to carry bombs."

"Good! What about fuel? What kind of range does it have?"

"I don't know, Icy. It seems not to need fuel, but I haven't yet found a way to check its power source."

Icy's thoughts raced to a decision. "Georgette, if I had more women like you, we could conquer the world tomorrow. You've just brought me the means to go ahead with my plan."

CHAPTER 28

The congressional recess had been no help at all for Mary Armstrong. She had not slept well since Icy's disappearance, and she had stayed at home constantly, waiting for a message or phone call from her beloved foster child. Kitty Yamada's testimony had shaken Mary's very roots; she had personally visited the young woman at her hospital bedside in order to obtain first-hand knowledge of the accusation. She was convinced that Kitty had spoken truthfully; yet, somehow, the evidence of Icy's evil nature only strengthened Mary's determination not to give up. Icy must have psychiatric treatment. The direction of her life could still be turned around, if only she would call.

It was Saturday afternoon, approaching the last week of January. Mary sat behind her desk at home, trying to concentrate on the business to be resumed when Congress began its legislative session the following week.

The telephone rang. Her hope rose, as it had done with every call.

"Hello."

There was a pause, then, "Aunt Mary?" It was Icy's personal pet name for her foster mother, used only when they were alone together.

"Oh, yes, darling! I've been waiting desperately for you to call! Are you all right?"

"I'm fine. But I miss you very much. Have you

been well?

"Yes, sweetheart. Where are you? No, don't tell me. Is there anything I can do for you?"

"There's nothing you can do, but I want to see you. Can you meet me somewhere?"

"Of course, my sweet, but you can't come here. I don't see how. . . ."

"Aunt Mary, do you remember our game?"

Mary became excited. She remembered very well the game that they often played while Icy was growing up. "Yes, yes . . . I'll be waiting, my precious." She listened for the disconnection, then hung up the receiver.

The game! How well she remembered! It was the only way that she and Icy had been able to have fun as ordinary people. Mary's life as an easily recognizable public figure would have otherwise made it impossible.

Sunday morning church service was as routine for Mary as it was for many other governmental officials. Some were there only to be seen, but for Mary, it was honest worship. Except for this Sunday. This day she would be deceptive, and the purse she carried was larger than usual. Inside was the costume that she had not worn in many years.

She was early, and went directly to Father Roy's private quarters, and knocked on the door. Father Roy's face brightened when he recognized his guest.

"Mary! Come in, please. This reminds me of old times!"

"Good morning, Father. Are you alone?" She was smiling.

"It so happens that I am. Don't tell me you're up to your old game again." He meant it as a teasing statement, but then saw that her smile changed to a serious expression. "How may I serve you, Mary?"

"I don't have much time, Father. You've heard, of course, that my India is now a fugitive?"

His face showed the honest gravity of his sympathy. "I'm sorry. You've made arrangements to see her?"

"Yes. Needless to say, I trust your discretion, as usual. May I change here in your quarters?"

"By all means! I'll only be a moment, then you'll be alone." He left the room, but returned in a short time to give her his blessing, then left.

Thirty minutes later, Mary examined herself in the full-length mirror. *Great ghosts! It's as if I went back twenty years in time!* The reflection showed a plain-looking, middle-aged black woman; so far removed from Mary's present status that it would be almost impossible for anyone to guess her identity. This was the disguise that had enabled her to go freely, anywhere that had made Icy's childhood a happy occasion. They had gone to the zoo, the parks, movie theaters, ball games, amusement parks, and carnivals. But Icy's favorite was the Lincoln Memorial, which they always visited after church. Their most enjoyable times together were always associated with Mary's disguise; when she could abandon her guard, to play the game, and to become the character that Icy so enjoyed.

Mary was forced to stifle the tears, so not to ruin her make-up. She wrapped her other clothing into a bundle, then left the church at a rear entrance. Once on the street again, she hailed a taxi, instructing the driver to take her to the Lincoln Memorial.

Icy was almost startled when she immediately recognized the character who, given more time, might have changed her destiny. She walked casually in front of, then past Mary, testing her own disguise, but she had underestimated her foster mother's memory. Her choice of perfume gave her away. She felt the hand touch her arm, then the whispered voice.

"My darling!"

Icy smiled, then turned with outstretched arms to receive Mary's embrace.

"You look wonderful, Aunt Mary. If only. . . ." She was unable to finish the statement. This woman brought back the memory of a lie. It was senseless to believe in fairy tales.

"I love you, my precious, but we have so much to discuss. May we speak of this dreadful mess?"

"Yes. . . ." She had almost said 'Aunt Mary' again, but, in a final resolve, she put the past out of her mind. "Yes, Mary." She took Mary by the arm and guided her from the building while speaking in a subdued voice. "We do have a lot to discuss, but not here. Are you free to spend some time with me?"

"Of course, my dear, as much as we need." Mary knew that was not the case; the affairs of government were waiting, but she also had an affair of the heart that called for her attention.

A car waited outside the bounds of the memorial; its driver was a loyal member of the W.E.B. society. Icy introduced the two women as she stepped in to take the rear seat. "Mary, you remember F.B.I. Agent Justeen Miller, don't you?" Icy did not attempt to hide the sarcastic tone of her remark.

Justeen extended her hand, but withdrew it when she noted the obvious contempt in Mary's expression. Mary refused to recognize the introduction, and took the seat next to Icy.

"Feel free to say whatever you wish, Mary." Her next statement, as she examined the appearance of her foster mother, was intended to remove any remaining affection from her own mind. "Oh, my! We'll have to get rid of that awful disguise."

Mary felt the sting of the remark, but refused to accept its implication.

"My dear, I've been forced to acknowledge some

very painful evidence; yet, I cannot believe that it's too late to help you."

"Not now, Mary, please." Icy had to admit that she still held a very deep respect for the senator.

Mary remained silent for a long while before speaking again. "India, is this an abduction? I'm not frightened."

"No, it isn't. I didn't intend it as an abduction, or to frighten you. I'm counting very heavily on your complete cooperation. I'm sorry if I've been too harsh with you. You must try to understand the strain. . . ."

"It's all right, sweetheart, my feelings are unimportant. Do you mind telling me where we're going?"

"We're going to . . . where I've been living."

"Am I to assume that I'll be away overnight? Perhaps longer?"

"Yes."

Mary resigned herself to the fact, then appeared to relax. "Very well. This will be difficult to explain, my dear." She was thinking of the commotion that would arise when her disappearance was soon to be discovered.

They arrived at The Tunnel after nightfall. Mary was surprised that Icy had allowed her to keep mental track of their route, although such knowledge seemed insignificant at the moment. She was introduced to Georgette, then the four of them, including Justeen, went directly to the dining area. Mary again took mental notes of everything in sight. The dark spacecraft had no meaning to her at that time, only as a curiosity.

The Tunnel appeared to have been, at one time, a single, large cavity surrounded by a ceiling and walls of solid rock. Its floor was now level sections of thick concrete with numerous steel support columns reaching to the ceiling. Various rooms had been added along the walls; otherwise, the cavity was mostly empty space, allowing their footsteps to echo back from all directions.

None of them spoke during the meal, as Icy appeared to be in a bad mood. Mary was disappointed when Icy finally did speak.

"I know you must want answers, Mary, but tomorrow will be a very busy day, and I have a lot to think about. May I have your word that you'll not try to escape tonight?"

"I'll do as you say, for now."

CHAPTER 29

It was early Monday morning aboard the colony ship. The cafeteria was not yet open for breakfast, but the usual noises and smells of preparation were evident. Ben sat alone at one of the tables, having his second cup of coffee. He had been thinking of Eileen, knowing from deep within his soul that she was always present, and helping him through difficult times, as always. But now he was accustomed to living without her physical presence, and he had even given up the thought of avenging her death. He had found a new mission that would have been unthinkable, even in his wildest dreams, only a few months ago.

He knew that Trudy was now completely content with her life. She was very much in love with Cotton, and extremely excited about her involvement in the Ezekien mission. She had wisely put the depressing events of her recent life behind her, and now eagerly looked forward to a lifetime of new goals.

Kitty had also blossomed, seeming to be an entirely new person. Her guilt-ridden memory of the W.E.B. society had been replaced by a serious, inexhaustible dedication to the Ezekien mission. To everyone's surprise, she had asked immediately if she might serve as a member of the shuttle's crew. Mo had endorsed her request, and a decision was now in the hands of the Mission Council.

Ben was well aware that the recent uplift of their spirits was directly attributable to Leona and Cotton, and ultimately, to the Ezekiens. Could there be some dark, hidden motive responsible for the evident kindness of the Ezekiens? He was absolutely confident that Leona and Cotton were good-hearted, well-adjusted, responsible people, which offered enough proof that the Ezekiens were sincere, and entirely selfless in their mission to help save the human species. He and Trudy had spoken of the subject several times; concluding, each time, that they could find no fault with the Ezekiens, or with the manner that they had conducted their mission. Furthermore, Ben could not think of a better way to prove their kindness than by rescuing and redirecting the lives of destitute, orphaned, or unwanted children.

Only recently, the Mission Council, which included human as well as Ezekien membership, had decided that it was time to begin recruiting more adult humans, and that Ben, himself, had been targeted to serve as their leader on Earth. The question 'Why?' had been replaced by 'Why not?'. How could he refuse to serve such a worthwhile endeavor, especially since his own daughter had already accepted their offer?

At noon, Ben's little group met for lunch. They discussed some of the morning's events, then Ben voiced his enthusiasm about the Colony.

"More fun than fishin'!"

"Too bad, Pop. Maybe you'll learn to like it better." Trudy's comment drew a round of laughter.

Cotton asked, "How was the meeting, Ben?"

"Couldn't have been better! Old Mike has a *head* on his shoulders. Cotton, I'm convinced more every day that we can greatly improve our social conditions on Earth, with the Ezekiens' help. Don't you think it went well, Leona?"

"Absolutely! Trudy, you would've been proud of your father. He presented some excellent ideas that we've been neglecting: most importantly, that we should concentrate more training in communication and politics. Tell them about it, Ben."

"Well, I don't think I should push too soon for changes. People tend to resent that sort of thing from a newcomer. My job is to lead our mission on Earth, but I had two suggestions in mind: We need to convince people everywhere on our planet to be more involved in their governments. We've grown to be apathetic because we think there's nothing we can do to stop governmental oppression. Well, that isn't true, and it's a dangerous assumption.

"Let's use our own country as an example: The United States is viewed as a model nation by ordinary people in most parts of the world. Our government is a representative, or republican, form of democracy, in which the citizens elect representatives to speak for them. Democracy, by definition, means *primary control by a majority of the common people*, but, as we now realize, such control becomes improbable when the elected representatives of the common people tend to favor their own special interests. Greed for money and power are now almost casually accepted as commonplace and unavoidable.

"Another, more favorable form of democracy, is known as *pure*, or *direct democracy*, in which every adult citizen is a direct participant in government. The ancient Athenians of Greece governed themselves by a pure democracy, and as Mike described it, the Ezekiens are also governed by a pure democracy, known to them as The Service.

"The Service consists of a president, his administrative staff, and a Judicial Council. Every Ezekien is required to present himself for election to The Service on his three-hundredth birthday. To serve is considered a privilege and an honor, and the reward for service is an honorable retirement as a ward of the government.

"Their judicial system is based on ethical, rather than

legal law. Judgment is decided by the Judicial Council, and any citizen judged to be guilty of a crime must receive punishment that is determined by the individual circumstances of the crime. The severity of the punishment is determined, in part, by the defendant's previous record, which is fully disclosed to the Council.

"I'm extremely impressed by the Ezekiens and their government. All major issues are voted on by all adult citizens in a popular referendum, and the majority rules. Pure democracy works for the Ezekiens because of their personal interest, and their telepathic communication. Everyone is well informed, and major issues are carefully explained and discussed. Folks, there isn't any reason, with modern communication technology, why we shouldn't have direct involvement in our own government. The technology is working right now for commercial pollsters in our country. But our problems, as Mike pointed out, are worldwide.

"Changes in government should come from the people, although it's almost impossible for suppressed people to make great changes in their own government. Leona and Clarence have started out right. The movement to promote virtuous living has been in effect for many years now, but it can go only so far until it meets resistance from the power-grabbers.

"Our next step, it seems to me, is to start training people now; to work up the political ladder to the highest positions of governments everywhere—it's the quickest way to get the job done. Now that might require some devious working, in some cases, but it can always be accomplished without violence and terrorism. You seem to be eager to say something, Kitty. Please feel free to speak up."

"Oh, I agree with you, Ben, but that's exactly the strategy that Icy Brooks plans for her W.E.B. society. I hope you don't mind my saying that she might be far ahead of us, already. And it seems to me that it's easier for her to recruit bad people than it is for us to recruit good people."

"You may be right about that. Do you know what her plan is?"

"No. I was only in the second tier, but I was being educated to believe exactly what you just said, except for a different objective, and *with* the use of violence and terrorism, if it was thought to be necessary."

"Well, we're lucky to have you with us—her loss, and our gain. How's your head?"

"It's well! Mo cured it in a minute. I still have to pinch myself occasionally, to make sure that I'm not dreaming."

"Me, too, young lady. And while you're the center of our attention, I have an announcement to make: The Council has allowed me to inform you that your request is granted. Effective immediately, you are assigned as a crew member of the shuttle craft. Please report to Mo for further instructions."

Kitty jumped up, while punching the air with her fists, and shrieked her pleasure as the group rose to congratulate her.

Their discussion continued for some time, when Cotton noticed that Trudy seemed unusually withdrawn and preoccupied in thought.

"What's the matter, Trudy? Something bothering you?"

"I don't know, Cotton, something. . . . It's more like intuition than anything else, I guess. I don't know." She smiled, and rejoined the conversation.

Ben looked at the wall clock. "Got to get back to work, folks. Leona and I have another session with the Council."

By two o'clock, Trudy's strange feeling became intense. "Cotton, something's wrong. I can't get Senator

Mary out of my mind, and it has something to do with Icy Brooks. I can't concentrate enough to see what it is, but I don't want to call her and reveal the telepathy. Can we go to Earth in your fighter without moving the shuttle?"

"Sure, I do it all the time. If you feel strongly enough about it, we'd better go. I'll call Ben and let him know what's going on."

CHAPTER 30

Mary remained voluntarily confined in her small bedroom prison until noon. She had not slept well, and it bothered her now to think that Icy was up to something evil. What could it be? The first-hand knowledge that she had gleaned from Kitty Yamada, plus additional information from the F.B.I., had told her a good deal of the W.E.B. society's eventual goal, but Icy's present behavior indicated that something big was now in process. Mary's own goal of complete equality for women seemed paltry when compared to the impossible goal of the W.E.B. society. But was it really impossible? And could Icy's goal really be so wrong? What about the old adage, 'An eye for an eye, and a tooth for a tooth.'? Mary had often thought of the victims of violent crimes; was revenge not morally justified in some cases? If that was so, then why should violence not be countered with violence?

Mary paced the floor. All arguments had two sides. Icy must surely feel that her course of action was justified. Accepting that, was her ultimate goal acceptable? Throughout history, men have been the masters of women. Would it be more wrong, then, for women to be the masters of men? The adage that 'Two wrongs never made a right' was an idealist's sentiment; it was not a practical thought because moral purity can never be achieved. Supposing, then, that the society's goal is acceptable, is violence an acceptable means of achieving that goal? Mary thought of the murders that had been committed. Eileen Two Bears had been an opponent, even of Mary's own movement, but her opposition had been conducted with dignity, and in a respectable manner. Mary had even considered Eileen as a friend. Georgette Adams, who was obviously a close associate of Icy's, had been charged with the murder, but had Icy not actually been responsible?

As a horrible precedent to excuse her crimes, Icy had stated, 'War is war, and murder, however despicable, is considered acceptable—even encouraged—in acts of war.'. No doubt, Icy saw her revolution as a justifiable act of war; therefore, the killing of human beings, in this case, was apparently justifiable. The end result justified the means.

These thoughts troubled Mary's mind when she heard a knock on the door, then Icy entered the room.

"I'm sorry you had to wait, Mary. My time is now yours. Before we get started, are you hungry?"

"Yes, I haven't had breakfast, you know."

"No, I didn't know. You could've helped yourself. However, I'm again sorry for having neglected you. We can talk while we eat."

Justeen had lunch waiting for them. She and Georgette had just finished eating. Mary served her plate from food on the large cook stove, then sat on a bench at the kitchen table.

"Do you mind if we talk alone, India?"

Icy nodded to the other women, who left the room.

"Do you prefer to start with questions, Mary, or shall I begin the conversation?"

"If you please, I have many questions, but I'd prefer to hear your story first. Please be thorough and honest with me."

"Very well. You've no doubt heard, by now, a lot more of the W.E.B. society. I'll begin by giving you an accurate definition, and an explanation of our organization."

She started out calmly, then her voice became

sometimes passionate, sometimes vengeful, and sometimes reverent, but she left no room for doubt regarding her wholehearted commitment to the cause. The explanation required a full half-hour as Mary sat quietly, and fully absorbed in Icy's talk. It ended with the grave statement, "We intend to make men our submissive servants, just as they've done to us."

Mary broke her own silence. "Oh, my darling, why are you so bitter?"

"Yes. I am bitter! I'm bitter because I've never received a true kindness from any man. My own father abused me, and then left me in the hands of a devil, who ruined my life."

"But your life wasn't ruined. Can't you remember kindness after your tragedy?"

"No. It was too late, by then. The only kindness I received was from you. But enough of that; the past has passed. What other questions do you have?"

"My dear, would you please explain the death of Eileen Two Bears. Why was she murdered?"

Icy did not hesitate. "Because she had written evidence of the society's existence, and of my involvement. I wasn't ready, at that time, for our movement to be publicized; also, I didn't want my name associated with it. You'll remember that she stopped short of actually accusing me in your meeting. I couldn't take the chance of that happening again. And I wasn't sure of how much you knew at that time, either, until you defended me. You didn't know, did you?"

"No. But I had suspicions. Perhaps I didn't want to know. Love does strange things to our rationality, darling. You wouldn't know about that, would you?"

"About love?" Icy laughed. "Don't be absurd, Mary. Love is a ridiculous myth; it's only a confusion of the mind that causes people to act, as you say, irrationally."

Again, Mary recognized the futility of that

discussion. "Very well, tell me how Eileen was drugged. Was it in the coffee?"

"Of course not. You served the coffee yourself, remember? It was in the cream. I knew that Mrs. Two Bears was the only one who used cream."

Mary closed her eyes, and sighed deeply. "And what about Marcella Silman? Why was she spared? You must have known that Eileen would have shared the information with her associate."

"Yes, I took a chance on that, but it was the written evidence I needed. Marcella was a stupid fool; I know her kind well. She tried to show courage, but I knew that she was really a coward, and that her organization would deteriorate with her as its leader.

"But I needed Trudy, and I was willing to risk the chance that she would eventually discover the truth of her mother's death. We've been very lucky in some ways, too. I still don't understand why Kitty never told Trudy about me, now that I know that Kitty was Mrs. Two Bears' informant. But that's all irrelevant now, isn't it?"

"I suppose it is. India, why did you bring me here? Surely you don't intend to harm me."

"Ah, now we're getting to the real issue." Icy assumed a very smug expression. "My compliments to you, Mary; you've shown a great deal of courage and self-control. Later, you'll receive my hearty congratulations; you'll be a wonderful President."

Mary gasped, and covered her mouth. Realization of the dreadful truth began to dawn, and her worst fear was about to become reality.

Icy smiled. "Don't be so shocked, Mary. Surely you've had thoughts of being the leader of our great nation. Now you'll have your wish."

Then Mary knew, and the horror of such knowledge showed plainly on her face. She must now do anything, even at the expense of her own life, to stop Icy before it was too late. But she had to know the plan. She tried desperately to gain control of herself.

"India, I . . . you'll have to explain what you mean. I want to be sure."

"It's very simple, Mary. All we have to do is eliminate the President, along with his successors to the job, and it's yours. And they're so steeped in tradition that the fools have set it up for us. The President will deliver his State of the Union address tonight. Everyone will be there: the President and his Cabinet, members of Congress, the Supreme Court, military Chiefs of Staff—everyone but you. And you'll be returned after it's over." Unbelievably, Icy was smiling.

"Dear God! After *what* is over?" Mary had to hear it.

"It all depended on Nadezhda and the anti-matter bomb, but Nadezhda failed, and I gave up the plan. Then, Georgette brought me the perfect solution: we're going to drop a bomb right into the President's lap in the House of Representatives." Icy laughed, and rubbed her hands together with excitement.

"Oh, my precious, you don't know what you're saying. It can't be done! Don't you realize that no one can penetrate the protective net surrounding that building tonight. Please, I beg you. It isn't too late yet to change your mind. Won't you let me take you to a doctor? You need professional care, my darling."

Icy suddenly stopped laughing. "Do you actually think I'm crazy?" She stood up, then walked around the table, and roughly seized Mary's arm. "Come with me, Mary. I'll show you something."

She jerked Mary from the bench, and led her into the open cavern to the little dark spacecraft. Justeen was assisting, while Georgette lay on her back making adjustments to a very large conventional bomb attached to the bottom of the craft.

"This little machine is a spacecraft, Mary. Yes, you heard me correctly. It's perfectly capable of dropping that bomb, and it can't be detected by radar. It'll be night-time, so it won't be seen. Georgette is its pilot. I assure you that Georgette knows what she's doing. Do you still say it can't be done?"

Mary's distressed mind saw everything very clearly: Icy's reasoning was distorted, but her intelligence was sharp and rational. The plan *could* work, and Mary had no misconceptions of Georgette's ability.

Georgette's attention had been momentarily distracted by the two women, then she returned to her task of arming the bomb. The little spacecraft hovered silently in its fixed position above the floor.

Icy led Mary back to her bedroom. "As I told you before, Mary, I'm counting on your complete cooperation."

"And if I refuse?"

"You have no choice. I *will* succeed in this, and I'd much prefer to have you on my side. I'm well aware of your loyalty to your government—that's to your credit—but my mission is far too important to let you stop me. All I ask, for now, is that you think about it." Icy looked at her watch. "You have two hours. We drop the bomb at precisely 8:30." She left the room, and closed the door. Mary heard the lock click.

CHAPTER 31

The moon was an hour's travel ahead as Trudy noted the Earth time displayed on the panel. It was 3:30 p.m.

"We should make it in about four hours, right?" The navigation display indicated exact time to the moon, but she wanted Cotton to know that she was estimating travel time to Earth.

"Not bad, but you forgot that we had to allow for deceleration to the shuttle, before. Now we're going direct, so you can subtract an hour. Watch the NAVDIS." He mentally caused the navigation display to switch over to DESTINATION: EARTH. It now indicated an ETA (*exact time of arrival*) at 6:39 p.m., MST.

Trudy smiled. "Okay, three hours and nine minutes, tow-head." She leaned back, and tried to relax, but Senator Mary kept coming back into her mind.

The moon passed beneath them an hour later, when Trudy became very excited. "Cotton, I see it now! Senator Mary and Icy are in a room—a bedroom. Senator Mary is very distressed. She...." Trudy stopped talking in order to concentrate. Her hand signal to Cotton told him not to interrupt. A moment later, she spoke again.

"Oh! Hurry, Cotton!" She was now extremely upset.

He took her hand. "Calm down, Trudy. Tell me what's happening."

His touch was reassuring, and she was able to calm

herself to a reasonable state of mind.

"They're going to bomb the House of Representatives tonight! The President's State of the Union address . . . Georgette has a bomb on the other spacecraft . . . 8:30. Oh! She's forcing Senator Mary to be president. What time is it now?"

"4:36." Cotton relaxed. "We still have plenty of time. Where are they?"

Trudy closed her eyes. "In a cavern. But I don't know where."

"All right, take it easy. We'll. . . ." He looked at the NAVDIS, then slapped himself on the forehead. "Trudy, I programmed our destination for 'HOME'. That's in New Mexico—*mountain time!* Washington, D.C. is eastern time, two hours later!" He quickly changed the destination to DCA (National Airport). The NAVDIS then indicated an ETA at 8:48 p.m., EST. Earth-time at DCA was then 6:37 p.m., EST.

Trudy spoke, barely above a whisper. "We can't get there in time, Cotton!"

"Don't bet on that, girl!" Cotton mentally increased their velocity by one gee of acceleration. "We can't enter the atmosphere too fast—couldn't take the heat—but I'll push it. Tell me what's happening down there, Trudy."

Mary sat on the edge of the bed, looking around the room for some means of escape. It seemed impossible. There were no windows, or other opening of any kind, only the door. But what could she accomplish by escaping? If only she could reach a telephone. The Tunnel was completely isolated; much too far away for telephone service. But they must have radio communication. She looked at her watch. 8:12. Something caused her movements to freeze, leaving an expression of doubt on her face. She cocked her head, then it came again.

Senator Mary, this is Trudy Two Bears. Do you

hear me?

Mary jumped from her seat to look around the room. "Trudy? Are you here?"

I'm not there, Senator Mary. My voice is in your mind. I know it's hard to believe, but you must trust me. I'm communicating with you by telepathy. Do you understand?

"No, I most definitely do *not* understand!" Her eyes looked around wildly, and she pressed her hands to her cheeks.

Regardless of how you feel, please don't scream or raise your voice. Icy might hear you. You have to trust me. You're in someone's bedroom inside a large cavern. You've been forced there against your will, and Icy is planning to murder a lot of people. Does that help you to believe me?

Mary sat back down on the bed very slowly as Trudy read her thoughts.

No, I'm very much alive, Senator Mary, and we're coming to rescue you. Don't speak to me with your voice. Just think, in your mind, what you want me to understand.

Oh, Trudy, do you hear me?

Yes. We don't have much time, but we're going to try to stop Georgette. Just pray that we aren't too late.

Oh, I shall, my dear! Where are you?

I'll explain later, Senator Mary. I don't know yet where you are, but we'll come for you as soon as possible.

Icy stood beside the spacecraft. "We'll be waiting for you when you return. Good luck, Georgette." She gave the thumbs-up signal, which Georgette returned from the cockpit, and the canopy closed. Icy nodded to Justeen, who was standing beside the door switch. The little craft lifted slightly as the door opened fully, then floated out, looking ungainly with the huge bomb attached to its belly. Justeen stepped outside to watch while it floated out of sight.

Icy went to her own quarters feeling extremely

confident of success. The goal that she had so long planned for was now almost within reach. In a matter of minutes the entire governing body of the most powerful nation on Earth would be wiped out. Her own hand-picked staff of women were now standing by to move in and take charge. It was a brilliant, well-organized coup d' etat. Only one obstacle remained: she must convince Mary.

Trudy felt their plunge into Earth's atmosphere as a slight increase of pressure at her back. The long period of deceleration had been uncomfortable; now she found it hard to breath.

"Hang in there, girl. This might be a little rough." Cotton's calm voice was a welcome reassurance. With a determined effort, because of the increasing gee-force, she reached across the console to take his hand.

They entered at an angle, cutting through the atmosphere in a gradual arc that brought them downward, from west to east over the United States. The little craft's unearthly computer measured and analyzed, then controlled the craft toward its programmed destination, also within the physical limits of its frail human crew. When sufficiently decelerated, the fighter again rotated to allow forward view. The lighted city of Washington, D.C. lay ahead, and ten miles below.

Cotton explained what he had in mind: "We're going into a circular holding pattern around the city, Trudy. If Georgette comes within range of the hydrium detector, we've got her."

Trudy looked at the panel clock. 8:22 p.m., EST. The fighter was banked to the right in its holding pattern, giving her a good view of the lighted city.

The anxiety and suspense were almost overwhelming for Trudy. "I don't see any fires, or anything unusual. We can't be too late, can we? Maybe I was wrong."

"You have to trust your talent, Trudy. I don't think

you're wrong. Buck up, girl. We're not too late."

"But what're you going to do? How can we stop her?"

Cotton waited a moment before answering. "I hate to say this, Trudy, but I don't know what else we can do. I'm afraid I'll have to destroy Ben's little ship, and Georgette. I'm sorry."

"Oh, Cotton." She squeezed his hand, and brought it up to her lips. "That must be a terrible decision for you to have to make. I love you so much." She held his hand to her cheek.

"This is what I was trained for, Trudy. I'm just sorry that you have to see it." He removed his hand to stroke her hair.

At 8:30, there was still no signal from the hydrium detector. Trudy felt the suspense building. Then, at 8:32, she saw a faint flashing of the hydrium warning light.

Cotton made a quick decision, and touched Trudy's shoulder. "It's behind us, Trudy. I'll have to make a hard turn, so you may black-out. Squeeze your gut, and fight it the best you can." The turn had already started.

Her body was pressed downward into the seat. The first sign of black-out came with a dullness of vision. She held her breath, and tightened her stomach muscles as Cotton had taught her to do, but the blackness continued. Strangely, she had awareness for a moment, even though her sight was gone; then her breath rushed out, her lips became slack, and her head dropped as she slumped forward into the harness. She was unconscious.

Cotton also lost partial vision for a moment, but he was well experienced, managing to prevent the over-loss of blood to his brain. When the detector instrument indicated dead-ahead and low, he stopped the turn, and rolled into a downward arc that enabled him to pinpoint, and lock onto, the target. It was now turned over to the computer.

Georgette was then seventy eight miles ahead, and closing extremely fast.

Trudy's blood returned to her brain, bringing her back to consciousness. She had no memory for a moment, but she lifted her head, then turned to look at Cotton. His expression was stern, showing a menacing fierceness that Trudy would never forget. Memory finally returned, causing her to quickly straighten up, and direct her attention to the instrument panel. The NAVDIS, which had once delighted her with a three-dimensional display of her own image, now displayed a magnified clear image of the stolen Ezekien explorer craft with a large bomb attached to its bottom. Trudy had no doubts regarding its present mission, or the identity of its pilot. She knew, too, that Georgette was totally unaware of her impending doom; that her fate had already been determined, and was now being translated by a gold band worn by Cotton O'Brien.

Positive visual identification was confirmed. The explorer craft's image zoomed outward and smaller, to suddenly be encircled by an orange-colored ring of light, which momentarily wavered, as if to pin-point the target's exact center of gravity, then quickly constricted to become a bright orange cross.

Trudy looked outside and ahead, in time to see an instant, narrow beam of intense white light, then a tremendous, silent explosion that brightened the surrounding sky. Georgette and the little space ship were instantly disintegrated. Trudy closed her eyes, and covered her face as the fighter evaded the explosion, and maneuvered back upward.

Cotton unbuckled Trudy's harness, then lifted her over the console to his lap, enveloping her in his arms.

"I'm sorry, Trudy. What else could I have done?"

She clung tightly to him for a moment, shivered, then slowly relaxed.

"I'm okay now, Cotton. You must feel ashamed of

me." Her head remained firmly against his chest.

"Not ashamed, proud." He stroked her arm. "The first time is almost unbearable, Trudy. I hope it always stays that way for you."

"Oh, Cotton, I'll never forget your face . . . but I love you more for it. You did what you had to do, and we'll never be able to change that. Hold me just a little longer."

After a minute, he lifted her chin to look into her eyes. "We aren't finished yet, Trudy."

"I know." She patted his chest. "I'll be brave now, I promise." Then, after a quick kiss, she crawled back to her seat, and buckled herself in. "Where are we?"

"We're stationary, about twenty miles above National Airport.

"Okay, give me a couple of minutes to relax." She took a deep breath, then slowly pushed it out. After a quick search outside, she closed her eyes to begin the concentration.

CHAPTER 32

We've done it, Senator Mary. Trudy's thoughts were distinct in Mary's mind. *The President and everyone else are safe.* Georgette's name was intentionally not mentioned.

"Thank God!" Mary whispered the words, then remembered not to speak aloud.

My dear, you've been of great service to our nation. I'll see that you're well rewarded.

No, please. You mustn't mention this to anyone . . . especially to Icy! Where is she?

I don't know, dear. Mary looked at her watch. *But I expect her to be here soon.*

Do you know where you are?

I'm in the mountains, but I have no idea where. The last highway sign that I remember was Interstate 81, somewhere in western Virginia, but we traveled west on winding roads, long after leaving the interstate.

It's okay, Senator Mary. Try to concentrate on the things that you remember, and we'll find you. Having said that in her mind, Trudy felt guilty. She actually had no idea of how to find the senator, but she repeated the information to Cotton.

"I don't know what to do, Cotton. How did you find me at Chesapeake Bay?"

"Leona guided me, but I couldn't tell you how. Look, I'll drop us down, and head southwest. Just concentrate, and see what you can do."

A minute later, Trudy closed her eyes, and held out her hands.

"Cotton, this way!" She waved her right hand in a direction to their right.

Mary thought of her present situation, deciding to act as though she knew nothing of Icy's thwarted plan. At that point, she was uncertain of her own safety. Then, remembering Trudy's instruction, she settled down to concentrate on what she could recall of their route.

A short time later, she heard the lock of her door being opened, but it was Justeen who entered. "Icy wants to see you, ma'am."

She led to a large branch-opening farther inside the cavern. It appeared, at first, to be dark, but then Mary discovered that another dimly-lit room opened to her right. Glistening, moist stalactites hung everywhere from the ceiling, and two large glistening mounds of stalagmites grew upward along the rear wall, leaving a spotlighted space between, where Icy stood, arms folded, feet apart. But she was a person that Mary had never known. She wore a lustrous black leotard, complete with black, high-heeled boots and a long cape, black on the outside, and bright, scarlet-red on the inside. A dueling sword hung from her hip, and on her abdomen was a large, scarlet-red hourglass figure. Mary saw her as the epitome of a black widow spider, exactly as Icy had intended.

Icy smiled as Mary was led forward. "What, no expression? I thought you'd be surprised, Mary."

"Shocked, maybe, but not surprised. Am I to receive an explanation?"

"Of course. This is the costume we wear for ceremonial occasions. Don't you agree that tonight qualifies as a ceremony?"

"Perhaps." Mary felt suddenly tired; drained of the

love that she once held for the woman standing before her. "Your appearance is disgusting, India."

The smile faded as Icy pointed and spoke to Justeen.

"Go back and wait for Georgette. Escort her to me when she returns." Then her attention returned to Mary. "I assume that you've made your decision. Was that remark meant to imply your answer?"

"My statement implied nothing. You'll receive my answer in due time."

"Then, I suggest that you choose your words more carefully". Icy looked at her watch. "Georgette should be back in a few minutes. You have until then to make up your mind."

Mary stood in place as Icy paced the floor. Icy's hand touched the hilt of her sword, as if she had finalized her own decision.

Cotton watched Trudy's hand signals, maneuvering the fighter in her indicated directions until he saw light shining from a doorway ahead.

"I think you've found it, Trudy. Look ahead."

She opened her eyes. "I can't believe this. Just wait until I tell Leona!" They drew nearer, then she exclaimed, "Cotton, there's someone waving to us!"

Cotton's surprised expression changed to a smile. "You know what, girl, I'll bet they think we're Georgette. Guess who's gonna' be surprised."

They hovered before the lighted doorway as a long line of light appeared below and to their right, indicating that a large overhead door was opening. They moved over as it opened fully, and Trudy whistled softly.

"Oh, wow! This is crazy!"

They moved inside. The door closed behind them, then Justeen walked before them and motioned. Trudy was excited.

"She wants us to follow her. Wait . . . I know that

woman! She's the F.B.I. agent who. . . . Cotton, what're we going to do?"

He grinned. "We're gonna' follow her."

Trudy looked around at the huge cavern. "Spooky!" Then she directed her mind to the senator.

We're inside the cavern, Senator Mary, and we're being escorted by Justeen Miller. She thinks we're Georgette. Are you all right?

The answer came back calmly. *I'm unharmed, Trudy.*

A new thought came to Trudy. *Are there any armed women in here?*

There's only India and Justeen. India is wearing a dueling sword.

Trudy explained the information to Cotton as they came to the intersecting opening. Justeen stopped, indicating that they had arrived. She smiled and waved, then approached the fighter, but Cotton continued to maneuver on into the opening, then into the other room. He stopped when he saw Icy and the senator.

"For Pete's sake, Trudy! What the heck is that?"

Trudy covered her mouth, then whispered, "It's Icy! That's Senator Mary behind her. Now what?"

"Time for the showdown, I guess."

Icy smiled broadly, and threw out her arms as she walked toward the little fighter. Never in her life had she been more relieved to see someone.

"Georgette! You're wonderful!"

The canopy snapped open to reveal, not Georgette, but two people: a white-haired man and a woman—Trudy Two Bears! It was an instant of intense emotional disturbance, and Icy's brain was not prepared for the sudden shock. Her expression changed from a look of elation to a look of extreme horror. She clawed at her face, and emitted a blood-chilling, drawn-out scream, then collapsed heavily to the floor.

Mary rushed to her side as Trudy, now driven to action, jumped from the cockpit, and ran forward. Justeen fled from the scene, while Cotton, thinking that she was running to escape, hopped out to join Trudy, and offer what medical attention he could.

Icy's breathing had stopped completely, and her heartbeat was weak and erratic. Cotton stretched her out on the damp floor, beginning immediate CPR treatment. Between breaths, he asked for his stethoscope from a compartment in the fighter's rear deck.

Trudy jumped up and turned, in time to see Justeen run into view from the main cavern. Justeen stopped, then began to raise a small automatic weapon into firing position as Trudy yelled, and instinctively thrust-out her hands. Justeen plunged backward, hitting the cave wall behind her. The weapon spun from her hands before she slumped to the floor.

"Oh!" Trudy gasped. "Cotton, I've killed her! Her head's split wide-open!"

But it was not a time for weakness. Trudy quickly retrieved the stethoscope, and brought it to Cotton. Her hands shook violently, but she clenched them hard to force herself in control.

Mary left her stricken foster child to attend Trudy, embracing and soothing her until the tremors ceased.

"Oh, you dear child. I saw it, but I can't believe it. You saved our lives, Trudy. God bless you!"

Cotton stopped the CPR to examine Icy. "She's breathing now, and her heart's stronger."

Trudy released herself to kneel by Cotton's side, while Mary sat on the floor, and cradled Icy's head on her lap. Icy moved, then turned on her side, and drew her knees into a fetal position. Her eyes opened to a blank stare. She raised her free hand, then began sucking her thumb.

Cotton gently placed his hand on Mary's shoulder. "I'm sorry, ma'am. I'm afraid she's lost her mind."

CHAPTER 33

Three days later, Mary welcomed Trudy and Cotton into her home, and served them coffee at her kitchen table.

"I just returned from the hospital," she said. "India's physical health is stable, but she'll probably have to spend the rest of her life in a mental institution. Poor child."

Mary's voice was saddened, but she was in remarkably good condition, otherwise.

"Now, my dears, it's time for you to receive my wholehearted thanks, on behalf of our nation, for your heroic deeds. I understand your reluctance, under the circumstances, to accept an official award, but don't you think that I, at least, deserve some explanations." She was now smiling.

"You do, Senator Mary," Trudy replied. "But I just don't know where to begin."

"Oh, nonsense, my sweet. Don't you know by now that you can trust me? And you must drop that silly formality. Call me Mary."

Trudy smiled, and looked at Cotton, who returned the smile with an affirmative nod.

"Well, you've already seen the space ships, and my gift of telepathy, and . . . oh, I wish I could forget that awful experience of telekinesis. But there's much, much more that you might not believe."

Mary laughed. "Trudy, after what I've seen, you may rest assured that I can believe almost anything.

However, haven't you forgotten something? You call your handsome friend 'Cotton', but I'd welcome a better introduction."

Trudy was embarrassed by her thoughtlessness, and slapped her own forehead. "Oh, I'm so sorry. Cotton, this is Senator Mary Armstrong. I've already told you about her. Mary, I'm very pleased to have you meet my handsome, tow-headed friend, Mr. Cotton O'Brien. But he's more than just a friend: Cotton and I are engaged to be married soon." She giggled. "The first time I met you, Mary—only a few months ago—I was engaged to someone else. Cotton knows all about Darrin."

Cotton stood for the introduction; now he bowed. "My pleasure, ma'am."

"I'm most delighted to meet you, Cotton. My goodness! You must have swept Trudy off her feet. You have my sincere congratulations. Where are you from, Cotton?"

He sat back down. "Originally from Tennessee."

"And where now?"

Cotton winked at Trudy. "My home is a synthetic world in outer space."

Mary smiled. "As I suspected . . . now, you see, Trudy, I didn't faint, did I?"

Trudy was surprised. "You're amazing, Mary. I can't believe you've accepted it that easily."

"I suppose I'm not being exactly honest with you, my dear. UFO's, and such, are not really new to me. I once chaired a special investigating committee that dealt with the subject. Our evidence was overwhelmingly in favor of factual existence of UFO's. It may surprise you to learn, too, that, not only am I a believer, but I've continued the investigation on my own, since the committee was adjourned. This subject is terribly exciting to me."

"I had no idea! What evidence did your committee have?"

"Only photographs, and testimony of reliable witnesses, but they were conclusive enough. Now, I'd very much like to hear your story, if you please. I give you my word that what you tell me will go no farther."

Cotton began by telling his own story, just as he had told it to Trudy. Then Trudy explained how she had met Cotton, and told of her experiences aboard the Colony. She also described the Ezekiens, and explained her relationship with Helen, but neither of them mentioned Ben, Leona, or Kitty.

Mary was held spellbound during the lengthy stories, and spoke only when they had finished.

"My dears, I feel almost speechless for the first time in my life. It's absolutely marvelous! Why did the Ezekiens come here?"

Cotton answered. "That's the truly amazing part, Mary. Their mission is to help us to make Earth a better place to live."

"I understand, and I totally agree with the need. I'm so impressed. If only. . . ." For a moment, Mary was lost in thought. "Trudy, if they only enlist children, how did you become one of their group?"

"But they don't enlist only children."

Mary was again thoughtful, then she looked from one to the other of the young couple.

"My dears, do you suppose . . . ?" She left the question dangling.

Trudy smiled at Cotton, who nodded, then at the senator. "Mary, we have a very dear friend — someone I'd like you to meet. Her name is Leona."

EPILOGUE

Mary Armstrong was eagerly and quickly accepted as a member of the Ezekien mission. Her political career teetered for a while, and she was mildly censured by her congressional associates (particularly by the opposition party), because of her relationship with Icy. An outraged general public, stirred by the news media, refused to recognize the difference between the W.E.B. society and the innocent Women's Liberation Movement. As a result, the women's movement suffered a temporary set-back, and Mary was forced to renounce her further involvement with the group. When it boiled down to a matter of most importance, the Ezekien mission came first. As always, people forgave and forgot, and Mary regained her popularity. She devoted the rest of her long political life contributing greatly to the Ezekien mission.

The W.E.B. society eventually crumbled as a result of internal power struggles to take over Icy's monarchy. The world was shocked, for some time afterward, when it was occasionally discovered that some prominent woman turned up with a red hourglass tattoo on her abdomen. Many women tried to evade guilt by having the tattoos removed by surgery, but rumors always seemed to escape via some member of the medical or mortician group.

Icy, herself, never recovered from the mental breakdown, and unknowingly suffered abuse many times during her confinement in several mental institutions. It was extreme misfortune that a brilliant person's life was ruined by such base treatment.

Ben and Leona remained together as respectable companions, managing the Ezekien enterprise from Ben's ridge-top home. He was provided a new, mechanically-controlled spacecraft, this time a fighter, designed to his own specifications. Nothing on Earth could compare with the combat capability of the Ezekien fighters, and when the Mission Council found it necessary, on several occasions, Ben and Cotton turned major wars into short battles. It was literally a case of 'They never knew what hit them'.

It turned out that Kitty possessed an exceptional aptitude for space flying, and she wanted to pilot the shuttle. She saw the need, and convinced the Mission Council that the shuttle was not used to its fullest potential because of the Ezekien crew's low tolerance for gravity. Seven years later, she was given full command of the ship, eventually with an all-human crew.

No one was surprised, however, when Kitty and Johnny J. Jones announced their engagement to be married. Johnny was transformed by Kitty's love, seeming to become a different person: confident, outgoing, and aggressive. He was later promoted to purser when Mo retired to the Colony.

Trudy and Cotton were married twice; the first time in a traditional wedding at Springwater; the second, a short time later, by Mike, in a charming Ezekien wedding aboard the colony ship. Their happy life together was blessed with two children: Casey O'Brien, Jr. and Leona Eileen O'Brien.

After her children were enrolled in school, Trudy succeeded Leona as scout for the Ezekiens. Her gift of telepathy proved to be a tremendous advantage in her part of the Ezekien mission.

Today, friends of the Ezekiens are steadily increasing their numbers world-wide. The next-door neighbor, the police officer living in the next block, the local news analyst, and many other impressive people are beginning to make a difference. As a result of their effort, ordinary citizens have begun to openly express their discontent with greed, selfishness, and politics-as-usual.

The idea of pure democracy is becoming increasingly more attractive as friends of the Ezekiens spread the news of corruption and waste in government. Politicians are finally getting the message: reform or pay the penalty—the taxpayers demand changes.

Young, eager, and impressive, Helen is now impatient to be introduced as the first Ezekien emissary to visit Earth. Will she be welcomed, or rejected as a freakish alien? Will the Ezekiens continue their mission to help make Earth a better place to live, or will they search for a more hospitable planet?

If you enjoyed reading this book,

please recommend it to your friends

and

your local bookstore.

QUANTITY SALES

RIE books are available at special discounts when purchased in bulk quantities.

INDIVIDUAL SALES

Any of our books can be ordered directly from RIE. For individual requests, include the book's title and author, along with a check, bank draft, or money order (payable to RIE) for the full retail price, which includes shipping, handling, and Texas sales tax. U.S. orders are delivered in 10-15 days using book-rate postage. All non-U.S. orders are delivered using Global Priority Mail in order to avoid long delays by ship or truck.

For all inquiries, including a list of books and tapes offered, contact:

RIE
1700-A R.R. 12, Suite 325
San Marcos, Texas 78666

and visit our web site at
www.4rie.com

or contact RIE on the Internet at
gr@4rie.com